Amira & Hamza

The Quest for the Ring of Power

ALSO BY SAMIRA AHMED

AMIRA & HAMZA

Amira & Hamza: The War to Save the Worlds

YOUNG ADULT

Hollow Fires

Internment

Mad, Bad & Dangerous to Know

Love, Hate & Other Filters

Amira & Hamza

The Quest for the Ring of Power

SAMIRA AHMED

LITTLE, BROWN AND COMPANY
New York Boston

This book is a work of fiction. Names, characters, places, and incidents are the product of the author's imagination or are used fictitiously. Any resemblance to actual events, locales, or persons, living or dead, is coincidental.

Little, Brown and Company
Hachette Book Group
1290 Avenue of the Americas, New York, NY 10104
Visit us at LBYR.com

First Edition: September 2022

Little, Brown and Company is a division of Hachette Book Group, Inc. The Little, Brown name and logo are trademarks of Hachette Book Group, Inc.

The publisher is not responsible for websites (or their content) that are not owned by the publisher.

Library of Congress Cataloging-in-Publication Data
Names: Ahmed, Samira (Fiction writer), author.
Title: Amira & Hamza : the quest for the ring of power / Samira Ahmed.
Other titles: Amira and Hamza
Description: First edition. | New York : Little, Brown and Company, 2022. | Series: Amira & Hamza | Audience: Ages 8–12 | Summary: "Amira and Hamza must race against time to stop an ancient evil from obtaining a ring of power." —Provided by publisher.
Identifiers: LCCN 2021048390 | ISBN 9780316318617 (hardcover) | ISBN 9780316318815 (ebook)
Subjects: CYAC: Fantasy. | Brothers and sisters—Fiction. | Muslims—United States—Fiction. | Supernatural—Fiction. | Good and evil—Fiction. | LCGFT: Fantasy fiction. | Novels.
Classification: LCC PZ7.1.A345 Ah 2022 | DDC [Fic]—dc23
LC record available at https://lccn.loc.gov/2021048390

ISBNs: 978-0-316-31861-7 (hardcover), 978-0-316-31881-5 (ebook)

Printed in the United States of America

LSC-C

Printing 1, 2022

For Lena & Noah,
the brightest stars in the universe,
the magic in my life.

(And no, you can't stay up late
"just this one time.")

Contents

ORIENTAL INSTITUTE
CHICAGO
JACKSON PARK
NEW MEXICO
STAR AXIS
IFTAH YA SIMSIM!

DESIGN! YOUR! DESTINY!
BRITISH MUSEUM
LONDON
PARIS
LOUVRE
ARABIAN DESERT
EMPTY QUARTER
UBAR

CHAPTER 1

Pick Your Poison

Amira

"ZOMBIE BOWCASTER OR THWIPPING?!" MY LITTLE BROTHER, Hamza, shouts as he runs around me, chasing imaginary villains. "Pick your poison, fool!" I'm lying in our backyard reading a book about ancient astronomy, and all I want is to be left alone. Fat chance if you're related to my brother, though.

I shake my head at Hamza as he shoots some red Silly String out of his Spidey web-slinger glove at the unsuspecting pine tree in our yard. "You know you can't really thwip, right? You don't have any actual powers. You don't even have Spidey sense. Or really any sense most days. I mean, your villain is a tree."

"Hahaha. I'm entertaining myself, just like you asked me to." Hamza harrumphs at me as he draws his slinger glove back. "Besides, sometimes a tree is more than just a tree, or do you not remember the jinn trees that tried to eat us?"

"That's not how I remember it," I say, sitting up from my perfect reading spot under the shade of our weeping willow. "Besides, the trees in the kingdom of Qaf—"

"Not to mention the land of sneeze!" Hamza giggles. I scowl at him, which makes him laugh harder.

His laugh is so high-pitched and annoyingly infectious, I literally pinch myself so I don't join in. "Ugh. Let that joke go already. It's so old and boooor-ing." I fake a snore.

"It's a classic. Classics never go out of style. Dad told me so himself," Hamza says.

"All old people say that," I smirk.

"I am telling Dad you called him old when he gets back from work."

I shake my head. *Whatever.* I ignore his threat. "Is *pick your poison* your new motto or something?"

"Nah. It's the title of the *Design! Your! Destiny!* book I'm reading—the last in the series. But it's not a bad idea; every superhero needs a cool activation phrase. Maybe I'll start using it when I'm facing the enemy in battle."

"There's no such thing as superheroes, bro."

"We rode through a dragon's mouth, defeated Ifrit, who was way more muscular than both of us, by the way, and, oh, we also saved the entire universe! If we're not superheroes, what would you call us then?"

"I actually have lots of names I call you," I deadpan.

"I'm so telling Mom."

I shake my head as I stand up, brushing some bits of grass and leaves off me. I head toward our deck. The sky is dark blue and clear, and if I'm lucky, I might be able to spot Mercury from my telescope. It's supposed to be visible today.

Hamza tags along. Of course. "What are you doing now? Do you want to sword fight?" Out of the corner of my eye, I see him swooshing through the air with an imaginary blade, his Spidey glove still on.

"Fake-sword fight, you mean."

"Duh. But I wouldn't mind if we had the real thing."

"Yeah, Ummi and Papa would really go for that."

Hamza rolls his eyes. "We wouldn't ask permission, obviously. I mean, it's not like we haven't been keeping the giant-est secret from them the whole summer. C'mon, sis."

I pause. Hamza's right. We have been hiding the truth from our parents. I mean, how exactly would we tell them we were the Chosen Ones, well, sort of anyway, who were whisked away by a jinn army to Qaf, a land of fantastical creatures, to help them end a giant civil war that almost broke apart the moon? I stare at my little brother and sigh. "Sorry. Hard pass, Hamz. I'm going to the roof to try to find Mercury."

"You do know it's daytime, right?" My brother gestures at the sky.

I ignore his snark. "Some planets are actually

visible during the day. But you have to be careful not to look at the sun through the scope."

"I know that. Otherwise, your eyeballs melt."

"Uhhh. Something like that. But if you want to check out Mercury, you can." I actually hope he says no, but before my mom left for work, she told me to be nice to Hamza because we've been fighting a lot and she said I need to *make more of an effort*. I'm the big sister. So, of course, I'm the one who gets the talking-to.

Hamza scrunches his nose at me.

I sigh. "Did you know that medieval Islamic astrologers used to say that Mercury ruled over logic, memory, and lies, and is also the domain of little brothers. So it's basically your planet."

"I thought studying the planets was astronomy, not astrology."

"It is. But I was doing some historical research for fun to learn about—"

"Research for fun? I'd rather get my tonsils taken out. *Again.* At least there would be Popsicles after."

"Oh my God. You can't—you know what, never

mind. Have fun with your fake-sword katas in the backyard."

Hamza shrugs and walks onto the grass to grab his plastic sword. He's made up an entire series of moves with it, pretending he's doing my karate katas but with a sword. I climb the winding metal stairs from the back of our deck up to our little roof terrace. I hear Hamza's grunts and attack sounds with each clink of the steps as I head up.

The sky is so amazingly clear, and as I position my telescope so that it's directed toward the deepest, darkest blue, I feel my eyes get almost lost in it. Like I'm staring into a black hole of sky, but it's blue and surrounding me. I read once about scuba divers who dive into water so pure blue they sometimes can't tell what is above and what is below. It's dangerous because they might think they are rising to the surface but they're really going deeper and deeper into the ocean. I spy a barely visible whiff of grayish-black smoke—exhaust from a factory, maybe? No. It's moving too fast for that. Maybe a dense flock of birds? I quickly adjust my telescope in the direction of the chalky trail of cloud, but it disappears before I can see what it is.

My mind pops back to a moment earlier this summer, after we'd gotten back from defeating Ifrit in Qaf and we were all safe and the moon was whole again. There was a second when I thought I saw a shadow, a dark mist, slink into the alley. And those creepy yellow eyes. I shiver. Goose bumps pop up all over my arms. It was nothing, though. Just like this time. Or all the other times this summer when it seemed eyes were on us, watching, but it always ended up being nothing. I've been having nightmares, too, ones where we lose and the moon breaks apart. Maybe that's normal? But I wish my normal was like Hamza's. *He* seems to have no trouble sleeping. We might've saved the day, but we're not exactly Avengers-in-training, even if Hamza wants to pretend we are.

I readjust my telescope and open the notebook I forgot up here last night to record interesting observations. So far this summer I've seen Venus rise and set, which required getting up at four AM but was so worth it. I've also glimpsed Mars—I spotted it without my telescope at first—a teeny-tiny, glowing orange speck above the tree line across the street from our house. During astronomy camp at the Adler Planetarium, I got to check out Betelgeuse from one of their super-powerful telescopes—it was so bright, sitting there on Orion's right shoulder. I've also been keeping an eye on the moon. It's kind of my job now. It's still wild to check out the Amir Hamza Sea and know that Hamza and I are the only humans on Earth right now who can remember there was a time it didn't exist. But I haven't detected a single crack, crevice, weird discoloration, or anything on the moon since we've returned. The jinn Emperor of Qaf did a good job gluing it back together. Every time I spy it through my scope, it's a relief. Normal is good. I love uneventful, do-nothing days.

"Sis!" I hear Hamza call up from the backyard. I walk to the edge of the roof terrace and look down at him as he puts his plastic silver sword back into its gray sheath attached to a belt around his waist. *I just jinxed myself by talking about how much I love normal, didn't I?*

"What is it, dude? I told you I'm trying to spot Mercury."

"I'm bored! Let's figure out an adventure."

I groan. "Hamza, you'd be bored if a herd of elephants were running at us."

"Uhh, yeah. Totally bored. By their tusks!" Hamza bends over laughing and drops to the grass, dramatically clutching his stomach and making splooshing sounds like blood is oozing out of his belly.

After a second, he glances up at my not-laughing-at-all face. "What? Don't you get it? Bored? As in they'd drive a hole through me?"

"Don't give me any ideas." I smirk.

"Ha! I'm telling Mom you threatened me with violence," Hamza says, rising from the grass.

"Go for it."

"Seriously, Amira. Let's ride over to Jackson Park. I want to check out Palmer Castle—it's only a little past the lagoons."

"No way. That thing is falling apart and supposed to be haunted."

"Uhhh...haunted is exactly the reason we *should*

check it out. Totally up for battling a ghost!" Hamza shouts as he punches at the air with terrible form. I have zero desire to meet a ghost—I mean, I've met enough terrifying creatures already; I don't want ghosts to be real, too. But this is exactly the kind of thing that Hamza thinks of as fun.

"Hamz. No. We're not allowed to go there. That's why all those orange construction cones block the path. It's off-limits."

"We busted our way through an oobleck wall and you're worried about stepping around plastic cones? Non-killer, non-shape-shifting cones? C'mon, it's the last Friday of the summer. Let's do something fun."

"Mom and Dad would not be ok—"

"We could bike there and back before they get home from work. Stop acting like a cranky desi auntie who got a cold cup of chai. You're twelve, not fifty!"

"I'm in charge because I make responsible decisions that *don't* end up with our being whisked away to a jinn universe where an evil monster and his army are trying to kill us."

"You're not the boss of me!"

"Actually, Ummi says I am."

"That's so not what she said!" Hamza runs into the house. I think about climbing down from the roof to follow him, but I don't. I cannot wait for school to start. Just have to make it through the weekend without my brain exploding. Hamza has been in his most-annoying-little-brother mode since we got back from Qaf. And I cannot deal anymore.

I go back to my telescope, but I can't concentrate. I should be able to find Mercury without a problem. I checked all the astronomy daily observation charts, but nothing seems to be lining up right. It's like the whole sky is tilted wrong and I can't get anything in focus with my lens. I give up, for now. I grab my notebook, climb down the stairs, and head to my room.

I flop onto my bed after grabbing my tablet. Not *the* tablet—the jade tablet from Qaf, which is sitting on my desk collecting dust. But my *tablet* tablet, the one that gets Wi-Fi and actually works. I've been bingeing episodes of *The Bridge*, a new animated series about these two kids, Zayn and Jinan, who get sucked into a book, but when they return to their world, a strange creature comes back with them and havoc ensues. It's pretty fun actually, and I can totally relate. And, bonus, they're both desi! My windows are open and a little breeze rustles my curtains. I prop myself up on my belly in a slant of late-morning light that's crossing my bed.

Through my open windows, I hear the motorized whir of the garage door being raised. Ugh. What is Hamza up to *now*? Neither of us are supposed to be alone outside. It's one of the fifty rules our parents gave us when I begged not to have a babysitter for the summer. They were pretty much okay with it and switched off working from home when they could and came home for lunch and stuff. But this week they've both been extra busy, so Ummi wanted to get someone to hang with us, but I said, *No way, I can watch Hamz.* I mean, who needs a babysitter after you've saved the world? Our parents didn't know that, of course, but if we could survive being kidnapped and stranded on the Island of Confusion and defeat Ifrit by ourselves, staying at home alone, together, obviously should be a piece of cake.

Wow. Was I wrong. I'd rather be battling Ifrit on a crumbling balcony.

I move to the window and crane my neck to see Hamza pull his blue metallic bike out of the garage. "Dude! What do you think you're doing?"

"If you don't want to go to the old castle ruins, then I'll go by myself!"

I start to panic. I'm going to be in so much trouble if Hamza takes off and my parents find out. "No way. You know we're not allowed off the block. I'm so going to call Ummi and tell her."

"Go ahead," Hamza eggs me on.

"Seriously, Hamz. It's not safe. And it's not even a real castle. Just an old, crumbling stone house that some rich dude built to *look* like a castle. Not that there's a dungeon or an actual buried treasure."

"You're scared of the ghost!" Hamza makes *wooo wooo* ghost sounds because he's the most mature ten-year-old in the world.

"Nah-uh. I am scared of…the wrath of Ummi and Papa when they find out and ground us until we're in college!"

"Fine! I said I'll just go by myself. It's not fair that I can't do what I want to because you're boring and afraid of everything."

I grit my teeth. "I am not..." I don't finish the sentence. What's the point? I can't stop him. Even though my parents will say I should have.

Hamza begins to bike down the driveway. He glances up at me as he passes under my window. "Last chance!" he yells. "If I find treasure, it's all mine!"

I shake my head and draw the curtains.

This is so Hamza. I grab my phone to call my mom. I can imagine how the conversation will go: *Well, why didn't you stop him? You promised to look out for him. You're the older sister.*

I put the phone down. I'll wait half an hour. He might get there, figure out there's nothing to see, and be back. So there's no point calling Ummi now and getting a lecture that would ruin the last weekend of summer because, with my luck, Hamza and I would both get grounded.

I lie back on my bed. A bunch of images from

our time in Qaf flash in my mind like one of those movie scenes with characters remembering happy times when they're really down. It's Hamza and me dumping that hairy-footed dev who kidnapped us overboard from his flying pot and into the ocean. It's the two of us swinging across the broken balcony on that weird, stretchy cummerbund thingy. It's Hamza being trapped by that evil jinn tree. It's Hamza letting himself be bait for the minty-green ghul. It's Hamza making me laugh at his really dumb jokes.

Darn it. I sit up on the edge of my bed and take a breath. My dad always says that making bad decisions is part of being human but that the important thing is how we try to fix them. And even if Hamza sometimes (lately, all the time!) annoys me, he's still my family, my only brother.

I hear a buzz from my desk and walk over to grab my phone, but the screen is blank—no missed calls or texts. While I'm holding it in my hand, I hear another buzz.

I glance down at the jade tablet. The one that

gave us weird messages that turned out to be clues while we were in Qaf but has been dead since we left.

Oh no.

A swirl of mist appears on its surface, and lit-up words appear: *Danger, Amira & Hamza. Danger.*

CHAPTER 2

Design! Your! Destiny!

Hamza

AS YOU SLOW TO A STOP AT THE ABANDONED INTERSECTION, you come face-to-face with a literal crossroads. To your right, the hard-dirt path, orange cones blocking the way, yellow caution tape tangled on the ground in front of you. The path leads to the abandoned relic of Chicago's only sorta castle. You can circle back home and likely sneak a mango ice-cream bar out of the freezer before your big sister busts you. To the left: sweet, frozen deliciousness and a sister who will probably yell at you. To the right: danger, uncertainty, possible ghosts. So is it right or left? Design! Your! Destiny!

Okay, fine. That's not exactly how the *Design! Your! Destiny!* books go, but only because ice cream is never the other choice. Neither is getting yelled at by an older sister. Unless you're me and have a sister who is twelve but acts ancient because she's drunk with the power given to her by our parents, who really only told her to "supervise" me when I microwave mac 'n' cheese. Give me a break. So I *tried* to explode a few Peeps in there once. Or five times. Technically, it wasn't even an explosion, because they just got super puffy and blobby and oozed off the plate. Not even sure what the big deal was. I've made way bigger messes than that.

And it's not my fault she would rather be all boring and stay at home. I mean, it's the last weekend of summer. And, okay, all right, we did already have a major adventure earlier this summer. And by adventure I mean the ultimate, epic-level, save-the-world, kill-the-monster quest, with flying thrones and deadly face-mutating fairies and jeweled daggers. But we can't even tell a single person about it. I get that superheroes are supposed to have secret identities, but, hello, WE SAVED THE WORLD!

Anyway, it's been two months, and everything since then has been normal. Too normal. Boring. Weird is awesome! And if weirdness doesn't come my way, I'm going out of my way to find it! Hopefully this time without ghuls who want to suck my blood and pick their teeth with my bones. I don't want that much evil-y weirdness, only enough to be interesting. I mean, we've already nearly died a bunch of times. Pretty sure destiny or whatever is on my side. Besides, when the Emperor of Qaf sealed the hole between our world and his with the moon again, he kept the super-bad guys on his side. And I guess it's all going fine since we haven't heard a single thing from anyone all summer long. I know the jinnternet was glitchy while we were there, but you'd think Aasman Peri would find a way to FaceTime or Zoom with the other fairies and jinn to say hi, considering we saved their butts!

I take a gulp from my water bottle and wipe my mouth with the back of my hand. This is it. My moment. Maybe the rumors are true—that the old man who lived in the castle actually did hide treasure in there. There're so many stories about it. Papa says they're all urban legends meant to keep people away. But away from what? How does that explain all the tales—about firelight coming from inside and eerie noises? Some people say that on Halloween, gray mist spreads around the whole outside of the house. Or is it New Year's Eve? I dunno. One of those. One thing I learned in Qaf is that things are not what they seem and your own eyes can play tricks on you. Even if you're the Chosen One. I mean, uh, Ones.

I unbuckle my helmet and run my hand through my hair. It's already sweaty. I've been letting my bangs grow long and floppy, and even if Amira says I'm only doing it because our friend Inara thinks it's cute, I swear that's not the reason. Not the only reason, anyway.

My phone buzzes. I swing around my backpack and unzip it. A bunch of texts from Amira. *I was so right!* I read the first one and then shove the phone back into my bag. She's such a know-it-all, bossy worry-wart. I check to make sure I have my Swiss Army knife. It may not be a bejeweled dagger or sword made of celestial steel—we had to leave those in Qaf—but it fits in my pocket and has tiny scissors, a bottle opener, and some kind of twisty screw thingy. Pretty handy. It's not technically mine. I borrowed it from my dad. Without permission. But I'm going to return it as soon as I get home. I swear.

I put my helmet back on and take a deep breath. When school starts on Monday, I'll finally have an awesome story I *can* actually tell. *What did I do over the summer? Oh, not much, found a lost treasure and explored a haunted house that everyone else in Chicago was too scared to go in. You know, the usual.*

I smile. This is going to be epic.

I walk my bike around the cones, my wheels rolling over the caution tape. Then I jump onto the seat and kick off, pedaling super fast down the dirt path; dust puffs up around me. No one is here to see, but I'm pretty sure I'm setting some kind of world speed record for biking *toward* a possibly haunted house.

The farther I pedal into Jackson Park, the quieter it gets until I can't even hear cars from Lake Shore Drive. This out-of-bounds part of the park is wild and overgrown. Some of the trees are so tall they stop the light from hitting the ground. Even though it's super sunny and warm out, I shiver. But only because it's cooler in the shade. One hundred percent not because I'm scared or anything. And, FYI, goose bumps can mean a lot of things besides being afraid. I pant a little; pedaling so hard is making me feel winded. Also, the air feels thicker in here. Maybe because of the plants? Do plants make a place more humid or less? Amira would probably know. Maybe I should text her and ask.

A curve in the path is coming up, so I slow down, trying to decide if I should call Amira. Or maybe go back and get her; she probably would think all these overgrown weeds are interesting. She'd probably want to do a science report on tall prairie grass. She'll definitely be mad if I don't tell her about these, uh, strange plants.

I coast to a stop and pull my backpack around to grab my phone. If I call her, she might think I'm scared. Which I am 100 percent totally not. I'll just text her. I never call anyone except Ummi and Papa when they make me check in when I'm at a friend's house. If I call her, she'll freak out and think something is wrong. Which I'm totally sure it isn't, even though the temperature seems to be dropping and the sky is a lot darker than what it was a few minutes ago and goose bumps are popping up all over my skin. This could all be normal—I mean, sudden summer storms exist.

I scroll through my favorites, but when I hit Call, nothing happens. The call doesn't go through. I have one bar, so I should get service. I mean, I'm not in the boonies or even the real woods or anything. It's the city. Lake Shore Drive is a few minutes away. Maybe my phone is busted. Maybe I should turn back so Amira doesn't worry. That's what a good brother would do—think about his sister. But if I turn back now, I'll have zero exciting summer stories to share....

I'm gonna bike a little farther. I'm almost at the castle. It'll be fine.

I bike around the next curve and there it is.

Dirty yellow stone. A fading red door. Broken windows and a totally busted roof. There're two turrets, but chunks are missing from each one. And there's a tree growing inside the house. I slow down. Then I hop off my bike and walk it forward a little.

Did a giant dark cloud just move over this exact spot? Because it seems pretty dark. If my life were a *Design! Your! Destiny!* book, then the destiny decisions at the bottom of the page might be something like: If you open the red door, turn to page *x*. If you scream and run because maybe your sister was right all along, turn to page *y*.

Ashy-colored smoke starts slipping out of the bottom of the door.

Leave. *Now.*

Definitely the best option. Get back on the bike, pedal hard and fast toward home. Toward people. The smoke is creeping down the broken stone steps. And there's a lot of it, large, rising clouds full of it. Move, legs.

My legs refuse to move. Okay, okay, leave the bike. *Run.*

Didn't I tell myself to run? Why are my feet not listening to me? This is a terrible time for my legs to get a mind of their own!

I grab my right thigh with both hands to try to move it a step, but it's frozen. I'm frozen. My legs can't move. Have I stepped in some kind of poison? Did I get hit by a paralyzing dart? Are these the last words I'll ever think? Will my brain be frozen forever? My neck feels stiff. My eyes dart around, watching as the dark mist pools around my feet. I am screaming at myself, but no words are coming out. What is happening? Someone help me!

The wind kicks up, throwing bits of gravel and dirt in the air. I blink. At least my eyeballs still work! A funnel of smoke swirls around me and I can't even see the ground anymore. I'm in the middle of a tornado!

"Prepare to meet your destiny, child of Adam."

What the...? That's not my voice. I don't think. Unless my voice is now really super old and gravelly and if I suddenly have kind of a weird, definitely not American accent.

My feet lift off the ground. "Oh no. Oh no. I am going to puke. I didn't take my motion-sickness meds!" Something grabs me by my belt. "Oh my God. I'm going to die with a huge wedgie! I will not die with a wedgie!"

Amira was right. (Don't tell her I said that.)

"Silence!"

"Put me down, storm! I'm going to puke into your eye!" Wait, are tornadoes the storms with eyes or are those hurricanes? I really wish Amira were here to give me a lecture about weather. And...why does this tornado have an accent? WHY IS THIS TORNADO TALKING?!

"How dare you insult me, human! I am no mere storm. I am a nightmare cast down upon the earth."

I shut my mouth. I gag a little. The storm is whirling too fast. I can't see the ground, but I can tell we're high up. I hate heights! I open my mouth and spew all the M&Ms I scarfed down earlier into the twister. Then everything goes dark.

CHAPTER 3

Under the Weather

Amira

I PEDAL AS HARD AS I CAN. I DON'T KNOW WHAT DANGER the jade tablet is talking about. Ghosts? The haunted castle collapsing on Hamza? Whatever it is, it has to be major for the tablet to come back to life when it's been dead all summer and it didn't come with some magical charger. (Note to self: Is there electricity in Qaf? How did the lights work?) I hope I'm not too late to save Hamza. I'm always saving him, but in Qaf, especially when it counted the most, I have to admit he saved me, too. (Don't tell him I said that.)

My backpack buzzes. I don't stop. It's probably the jade tablet telling me to pedal my butt off and, *hello,* I'm trying! Sweat beads up on my upper lip, and strands of my hair stick to my clammy cheek. Gross. I speed down the path, maneuvering around the orange construction cones meant to keep people out. Obviously, anyone can walk or bike around them, but I think the creepy tales about Palmer Castle are the real roadblocks that keep anyone from venturing here. Anyone normal, anyway.

There's a story about a high school kid going to the house on a dare and never coming back. My mom says it's not true, but even thinking about it sends goose bumps up my arms. As I go deeper into the woods, the air gets soupier and the sky darkens above me; a giant storm cloud seems to be following me. I gulp a giant breath of air and bend low over my handlebars to gain speed, but as I turn the corner, I screech to a halt, clumps of dirt and stones kicking up around me.

A soot-colored tornado is swirling in front of me. Directly ahead of me on the path. It's not one of those wide-as-a-block twisters—it's about the size of a big SUV—but still big enough to suck me into it. I freeze. I don't think I'm breathing anymore. This can't be real. How is it real? My mind is screaming at me, but nothing makes sense as I try to remember what we learned during tornado drills. Duck and cover? Find a ditch? Move to the lowest ground far away from things that could fall on you, such as every tree surrounding me right now? The real thing is way different from the videos they make us watch in school!

The entire world around me stops—everything except this swirling spiral of dirt and leaves. My heart pounds in my ears. My bike lurches forward. I'm not pedaling. I'm standing over the crossbar with my feet planted on the ground, but the twister is pulling me toward it. I dig in my heels. I feel heat from the friction as I get dragged forward, inch by inch. I grit my teeth and force the handlebars to turn a little to the left; it takes every ounce of muscle I have. (Note to self: Take up Sensei Seijo's suggestion of using soup cans to weight-lift at home.) I scream and fight against the tornado's pull.

Then it's like when the bow went slack when Maqbool was teaching me to string arrows in Qaf but I wasn't pulling hard enough. Oh God, I wish Maqbool were still alive and here right now to help me. I'm released from the pull and tumble back, my heart thumping against my rib cage. The tornado lifts off the ground. My eyes sweep the path up toward the haunted castle, searching for Hamza, hoping he didn't get pulled into this impossible tornado on what was a blue-sky day only a minute ago. I can't see him anywhere, but dust and twigs are being thrown at me, so I can barely keep my eyes open. "Hamza!" I scream, but my voice disappears into the whirlwind.

Then I hear something. "I'm going to puke into your eye!" It's Hamza's voice. And it's coming from *inside* the tornado.

"Hamza!" I scream again, louder, more frantic. The tornado lifts up into the sky and heads out of the park toward the neighborhood, like it's being steered in that direction.

Hamza's backpack comes twisting and twirling down from the sky and plunks down in front of me.

I suck in my breath.

I have to follow that tornado! That weirdly moving, now-on-its-side tornado? That makes no meteorological sense. I wipe my face with the sleeve of my white T-shirt. It comes away streaked with dust. Ugh. I hope this comes out in the wash; it's my favorite *You Are Here* galaxy tee. What am I saying? This is not the time to think about laundry!

The dark cloud has already started moving out of the park. How am I supposed to chase a storm? On a bicycle? It's not even a ten-speed! Still, I don't have any other choice. I hop on my bike and swing it around the path.

"No way you're going to catch up with him on that slow contraption." Aasman Peri stands in front of me. The literal fairy princess wears her signature crooked smile that makes her look like she's judging me. Her arms are crossed over her fancily embroidered green kurta pajamas, and her dandelion-colored wings are fully unfurled.

"What? How did—"

"No time to explain and no time to waste, silly

human!" Aasman Peri flies over to me, seats herself on the small cargo rack I have on the back of my bike, and starts flapping her wings wildly. "You still have to pedal and steer. I can't do everything from back here."

I crane my neck to look over my shoulder. "What are you talking ab—ahhhhhhhhhhh!" I yell as my bike starts moving forward and begins to lift off the ground.

"Pedal and steer!" she shouts. I do as I'm told even though questions are making my brain spin faster than that tornado. My bike lifts into the air like in that movie about the wrinkly alien with a light-up finger. But my bike is powered by a fairy's wings. I hope no one is looking, because there is no way I can explain this if someone records us and it goes viral, which, obviously, it would. Except without Aasman Peri on back, because only people anointed with this magic eyelid gunk that Hamz and I have can see the creatures of Qaf.

We rise higher and higher and I'm pedaling, but we are heading straight for a treetop. I close my eyes. Worst rescue ever! I'm going to eat it on an oak!

"Pull up!" Aasman Peri screams. With my eyes closed, I shift my weight and pull back on my handlebars. Sure, tons of kids pop wheelies, but I'm not one of them! Too high a chance of totally wiping out. And did I mention I'M IN MIDAIR! This is 100 percent not normal in any way! Normal is totally underrated. Normal is nice and comfy and two wheels on the smooth pavement. But here I am feeling the front end of my bike tilt up. I open my eyes in time to get whacked in the cheek by a branch. At least I'm not dead, which I could very easily be since there is no seat belt on this thing. Probably because BIKES ARE NOT SUPPOSED TO FLY!

"I told you to steer," Aasman Peri says.

"Oh, excuse me, Your Highness. Sorry I don't have a flying-bicycle license."

"Humans have flying-bicycle licenses? How odd. Considering these are such archaic modes of transport."

"Yeah, you're right. As opposed to the totally high-tech flying pots you have in Qaf." I turn to give Aasman Peri *a look.*

She snorts. "It's truly a wonder to me your species hasn't gone extinct yet or been murdered by rabbits."

I roll my eyes. "That doesn't make any—tell me what's happening! Why did a tornado suck up Hamza and where is it going?"

"Did you not read the tablet? Abdul Rahman assured me the tablet would give you some kind of message."

"Oh, I'm sorry. I guess I was too busy being almost dragged into a tornado to consult my jade tablet that usually only speaks in Magic 8 Ball messages or poetry and that hasn't worked at all for the last two months!"

"Stop being so dramatic. It's not an Earth tornado." (Note to self: Remember to ask if there are tornadoes in Qaf, potential science fair project on weather patterns in the multiverse.)

My heart jumps into my throat. Oh no. If it's not a storm…could it be…no. No way. It's impossible. But I've witnessed so many impossible things. Heck, I've done impossible things. So I know the impossible isn't always, uh, impossible. Oh my God. It is…it has to be? *Ifrit.* We didn't technically see his body, only puffs of smoke from the rubble. We did see the City of Gold crumble and get swallowed into some kind of air pocket. But what if he made it out somehow? My stomach twists. I absolutely cannot deal with fighting Ifrit again. And now, if he's here, in Chicago?

I gulp and turn my head so Aasman Peri can hear my voice, which feels like a scratch against the wind as it rushes by us, "Is it... is it Ifrit?"

"That's ridiculous! Ifrit is gone. You turned him into dust and banished him to the Realm of Nothingness, remember?"

"Duh. I was there. I saw Ifrit get, uh, smoked," I say, annoyed. But I still breathe a sigh of relief. Okay, if it's only an odd weather pattern, that means it will eventually drop Hamza somewhere. Hopefully in one piece and hopefully still wearing his helmet.

"It's not Ifrit. It's his father."

"WHAT?! The dad Suleiman trapped in a brass lamp and buried in the moon? The one that Ifrit was trying to release? The one even more powerful than his son? H-h-how?"

"We think Suleiman's prison for Ahriman was dislodged when the moon began to break apart. And crushed when the pieces of the moon crashed back together into a whole. Then, when the emperor used starshine fire as glue—"

"What? Stars can make glue? How do you use a star's fire as glue? And didn't anyone think—"

I have a million more questions, because of course, but I stop short of asking them. We are flying through a puffy white cloud, and the trail of dark gray smoke that swallowed Hamza seems farther and farther away. But that's not what shuts me up. It's the lightning-fast dark blue swarm that's heading directly toward us.

"Aasman Peri, do you—"

"Steer right! Riiiiiiiight!" Aasman Peri says as she flaps her wings so fast they're a blur when I grab a quick glance over my shoulder.

My sweaty palms almost slip from my handlebars, but I do what she says. We bank right and she flies us higher, the ground falling away so fast, too fast.

I'm not scared of heights like Hamza, but I close my eyes.

Don't look down.

Don't look down.

Crud. I looked down.

I snap my eyes shut again.

My stomach somersaults. There is no invisible barrier around my bicycle keeping me from falling like the golden throne had, and I'm guessing there is only a fifty-fifty chance Aasman Peri would fly after me if I started plummeting toward Earth, and my probably-certain-pancaking when I crashed into the concrete.

I want to pretend none of this is happening. *Again.* I want to believe that I'm asleep and that this is all a nightmare and that we're not the Chosen Ones. I want to believe I'm a regular twelve-year-old with a normal, boring life. But I know better. I wish I didn't.

"Amira!" Aasman Peri butts the back of my helmet with her head.

My eyes fly open in time to see a flock of mean-looking jays flying right at us, mirroring our every move.

"Jinn jay strike! Brace for impact!"

I pull my hands off the handlebars to shield my face as my bike nose-dives toward the ground, barely missing the direct bird hit, except now we're on a collision course with the glass egg-shaped dome of Mansueto Library. The wind rushes by my face so fast it stings my cheeks and I can't keep my eyes open. I grab the handlebars again to try to do...well, anything. But when I do, they jerk to the right and we start spiraling, twisting, a flash of chrome, the purple iridescent paint of my bike, and bright-yellow wings trying to fight against gravity.

My heart pounds. The other sounds quiet all around me and all I can hear are our screams.

CHAPTER 4

My, What Big Teeth You Have

Hamza

I WAKE UP ON A COLD MARBLE FLOOR. THAT STORM must've knocked me out! But how the heck did I get inside a building? Where's my helmet? I'm going to be in so much trouble if I lost it (again). Also, that was the weirdest storm ever!

"Ow!" I stand up, rubbing my backside, shaking twigs and leaves out of my hair. Ugh. My mom is going to make me wash it (again). If you ask me, one shampoo a week is enough. My parents strongly disagree. I look around as I wonder how the heck any of this could have happened. I'm in the Oriental Institute, only a few blocks from my house. We come here on a field trip every year—it's a museum with a lot of professors and archaeologists on staff who dig up ancient tombs and get weirdly excited about broken vases. Maybe the tornado dropped me here because it wanted me to learn stuff? Which... is that a thing? Thinking tornadoes who want you to do homework during summer? I bet Aasman Peri sent this storm to play a joke on me. This has peri-trick written all over it.

I step forward but stop because I seriously think I'm gonna hurl. I grab my stomach. Ugh. I don't want to puke! *Again!* I'm glad the tornado sucked up all the sick instead of blowing it back on me. I shake my head. I feel out of it. Not only puke-y but all out of balance like I just rode on a Tilt-A-Whirl. Maybe because I was whirling around in a talking tornado. *Wait.* The tornado talked. TALKED! And it definitely wasn't Aasman Peri's voice—it sounded like an old guy with a cold.

Oh no. Holy goose eggs!

I must've hit my head. I have a concession! No, a concussion. One of those two. I bonked my skull and now I can't remember words. Am I dying? Am I dead? I hope not, because I do not want heaven to be a museum, especially a creepy one with mummies. Maybe I'm dreaming. No. No. There's scaffolding in here. And I remember the Institute is closed right now for repairs and to set up for a new exhibit on ancient telescopes or something that Amira was super excited about. *Nerd.* Besides, I would never dream about dusty, old museums. That's a total waste of a good dream.

I see a water fountain and head over to get a sip. That talking tornado made me really thirsty. Also, it was telling me to shut up. Which is rude considering it basically kidnapped me.

Oh no.

My bike. Crud. Is it still by the haunted castle? Amira was right. It was a dumb idea to go; now I have to walk all the way back to Jackson Park and hope that it's still there. Or else wait till my parents get home and tell them what I did. Which I definitely do not want to do, because they will ground me for the entire weekend. Goodbye last days of summer vacation. So much for one last adventure and a cool story to tell everyone at school. I walk toward the exit but am stopped in my tracks when a loud voice booms behind me.

"Step away from the door. You cannot escape me. I have sealed the way out."

I freeze. My body goes cold, but my hands are all sweaty like I need a blanket *and* to crank up the air-conditioning. The last time a strange, loud voice ordered me to do something, I ended up having to save a lot of supernatural butts in Qaf. This is so not what I need right now. I whip around, "Who do you think—"

Whoa.

It's a jinn? No, a dev. Cuz of the stripes? I think? He's red. Evil red. Darth Maul red. Red Skull red but with gold stripes on his ginormous biceps. He's also kind of...short for a creature of fire, barely taller than Amira. But that makes his very sharp, pointy, vampire-y teeth look extra huge. *Please don't suck my blood. Please. Please. Please.*

My voice catches in my throat and I make a sound like I'm gargling with salt water, which my mom makes me do when I have a sore throat. Ghh-ghhhhghhhhhghhhh. Yuck! Now I'm all phlegmy. My sister always says I'm so suggestible! I clear my throat. Fake it till you make it worked in Qaf, sort of. Might as well try it now. "Did the emperor send you? Answer me!" While I try to ignore the one million butterflies in my stomach, I notice that even though this dude's skin is bright red, his clothes are dull and tattered: a long, loose shirt over pants, kurta pajama–style. Also, a cape-y cloak type of thing. But his whole outfit is shades of gray like the color was erased from it.

The creature in front of me roars. With laughter. A scary smile spreads across his Darth Maul red face. At the edge of his grin, I notice he has double ears. Two ears on each side of his head, one behind the other. And orange hash marks along his neck.

"You are as irreverent as all humans. Perhaps

even more a fool. Do you not recognize me? Me? The most feared of all devs? Did the emperor not warn you of the fate that might await you? Speak!"

"Let me guess...you're all ears? Get it? 'Cause you have four..." The dev scrunches his bushy eyebrows. "Never mind. Why would I recognize you? Are you supposed to be famous or something? Are there jinn and dev celebrities? I didn't get a chance to watch any TV in Qaf." I shrug. "We had a job to do—destroy Ifrit—and we did it. We crushed him and—"

"Ifrit...was my son." The little red dev glares at me, then thunders: "And you will pay the price for what you have done."

Oops. Did he say...oh no. No. No. Stop the world. I want to get off. Because whatever is going to happen next can't be good. The Darth Maul-y dev inches closer to me, points a long, bony finger right in my face. I guess now is probably not a good time to tell this dude that he needs a serious nail trim and that he smells like upchucked M&Ms. I slide back, my sneakers squeaking against the marble floor. But I don't have anywhere to go. The door behind me is magically sealed and I don't think I can run by this dev to the other exit.

"H-h-h-owww are you even here? Weren't you literally stuck in the moon?" I look up at him as I try to stall, a fiery glow behind his violet eyes. I know he could kill me in a second. Probably wants to, also. My only sort-of weapon was my dad's Swiss Army knife, which is handy for fixing my bike and for when my dad wants to pretend he's outdoorsy and whittle a stick, but it was in my backpack and I'm pretty sure all my stuff is spread across the neighborhood. My phone is probably busted into a million pieces. *Great.* Amira isn't here. Abdul Rahman and the Khawla ki Supahi do not have my back. And I'm using a lot of energy trying not to pee my pants. But I refuse to let him scare me to death.

"Ifrit was going to destroy Qaf and Earth and also kill my sister. Maybe if your son hadn't been Qaf's number one jerk face, then he wouldn't have ended up buried in fake gold rubble." I clench every muscle in my body. I really, really don't want to pee myself, but now all I can think about is pee. I screw my eyelids shut. *Don't think about pee. Don't think about pee.*

"Pee!" I blurt out.

Oops.

This dude is probably going to kill me, and even if I talk the tough talk, I do not want to look death in the face. First of all, it's kind of ugly. Second, I'm ten. I'm not supposed to die. Third...hold up. Can he... shape-shift into a tornado? Because...whoa. I didn't know that was a thing. Holy devnado power!

"I will not stand this insolence. I am Ahriman. Most ancient and mighty among creatures of fire. Known to grind the bones of my enemies into tooth powder."

Tooth powder? I think that's old-timey toothpaste. My nana told me he used to use charcoal powder to clean his teeth when he was a kid, but this is a whole other level. "Gross! Why would you use bone dust for that when there's aisles full of minty, fruity toothpastes?" Grinding your enemies' bones is very villain-y and terrifying, and one thing I know from experience is that when you're scared out of your brain, the best plan is to just keep on talking so you can distract yourself from the horror show.

"I have returned to Earth, broken free from my brass prison, to seek the Ring of Power. You, Chosen One, will help me find it."

"Whoa. Whoa. Hold up now. Suleiman's ring? The one that controls every fire spirit? Nuh-uh. Why would I help you?"

"Because I can destroy everything you love with a mere snap of my fingers?"

I snort. "Dude, cliché much? Snapping people away is so Thanos-five-years-ago." I'm joking, but my knees are shaking and my heart is beating out of my chest. I know Amira would say we have to stop him from getting the Ring. I can't let him....I won't....But what do I do?

As you look a near-certain death in the face (it has more ears than you thought it would), you realize you have one last trick up your sleeve. Your way: Attack first, maybe disorient the dev with dazzling wordplay, then make a break for it and try to bust your way through the magically sealed doors. Or Amira's way:

Stall for time. Figure out a plan, hoping it involves as little death or dismemberment as possible. Your way is faster, even if it means meeting your doom. Amira's way is safer, but your doom might be dragged out. Which way will it be? Design! Your! Destiny!

I close my eyes. I know what I have to do. Sometimes *Design! Your! Destiny!* decisions aren't life-or-death choices at all, because even if you flip the page and land in a moat with kid-eating crocodiles who've been starved for a century, you can go back to the choice page and decide on a different destiny. But this isn't exactly a turn-back-the-page situation. I curl my hands into fists at my side and bend my knees so they're ready to spring. I probably have only one shot. Amira's face flashes in my mind. Her eyebrow is raised and she's wearing a frown. I can almost hear the lecture she's about to give me: *Ahriman is the one who stole the Peerless Dagger from the emperor and ripped a hole in the universe. You get that he can totally kick our butts, right? Obliterate us with fire? You can't fight if you're ground into tooth powder! Think, Hamz.* I take a deep breath and open my eyes; Ahriman is giving me this quizzical look like he could hear what I was thinking.

"So…where is this Ring and why do you need me to get it?" I whisper.

"I see you have chosen wisely. The precise location of the Ring is hidden. It will be revealed only when three parts of an ancient oculus are brought together and placed in the Star Axis near the great Mountains of Rock—"

"Back up. What's an oculus?"

"Do humans learn nothing in your schools? It is a type of lens, a small, round window without glass. A focuser of energy, if you will. The light of the North Star shines through it to mark the hidden location on a map."

"Wait. You mean *X* marks the spot? That's an actual thing?"

"It is unknown if it is an *X* or…" Ahriman shakes his head. "No more questions. You are the Chosen One; Suleiman left the oculus for you to find. That is all."

"Whoa. Amira is gonna go bananas—in a nerdy way—when she finds out about this."

"Your sister will not touch the oculus. Only the true Chosen One can find it and is worthy. Despise Suleiman as I do, I know he would not allow a mere girl to be recognized as a true heir."

"That's sexist! My sister can do anything. She got her orange belt in karate and she's the one who kicked—"

"I will brook no opposition. You find this or else all whom you love will suffer. I have had ages, trapped in brass and stone, to contemplate tortures I will visit upon my enemies."

Gulp. I think this is what teachers mean when they say you're stuck between a rock and a hard place. Except it's usually about getting caught sneaking an extra Halloween cupcake and then lying about it even though three other kids saw you do it, which is not something I did. And is something I totally made up as a metaphor right now for this particular situation.

I nod at Ahriman and wrap my arms around my middle. He grabs me by my collar; I feel the heat from his fingers. "Hey, easy! Why are you so hot to get this Ring anyway? Haha, get it, because you're a creature of fire?" Amira thinks my puns and wordplay are silly, but it's the only way I'm stopping myself from melting into a puddle of fear.

"Have you not yet understood, small, feeble-minded human? The bearer of the Ring can control jinn and the weather of the entire planet and speak to animals. When I have the Ring, I shall command all jinn who reside on Earth to pledge fealty to me, and when we break through the emperor's enchantments on the Obsidian Wall, every creature in Qaf will do my bidding. All human and jinn kind shall bow down to me. Control the Ring, control the worlds."

CHAPTER 5

You Break It, You Buy It

Amira

WHAT IN THE WEIRD ANIMAL KINGDOM IS A JINN JAY?

Why do these birds have teeth?

I'm falling!

Spiraling.

The ground is so close.

So close.

Five seconds to impact.

At least we missed the glass dome of the library.

Are those rosebushes? I'm going to face-plant in rosebushes!

I'll be scarred for life! I'll be scarred for death!

I'm too young to die!

My mind screams as I plummet toward the ground. My life flashes before my eyes, but I'm only twelve, so instead of a feature-length movie, it's one of those animated shorts, which honestly seems so unfair because I have done a lot of amazing things. Saved the world, for example. And Qaf. Eaten sheep brain cutlets. Gotten my cheeks pinched a million times by aunties at weddings. Put up for ten years with my annoying little brother, who I'm pretty sure snuck into my room to find the birthday gift I was making him. (For the record, it was a Model Magic Zendaya sculpture—the flying horse, not the actress—and it was awesome!)

Hamza. I'm supposed to be saving Hamza and instead I'm going to bite it. Wow. These are a lot of thoughts to have while plunging toward death. Time really does slow down near the end. Wonder if that's physics, because of the speed of the fall and how gravity affects—

Ahhhhhhhhhhh!

I close my eyes so I don't have to face the thorns stabbing them. If only I could've made it to thirteen so I could've experienced real teen life and not been stuck in tween limbo. *Sigh.* Goodbye, world. Goodbye, chance at winning first prize in next year's science fair. Goodbye, space camp. Good—

"Are you done yet? Holy moon craters! Human children are very, very dramatic."

I open one eye at the sound of Aasman Peri's annoyed, hoity-toity tone. Was I talking out loud? I can't believe I have to go through life and death with her getting irritated at me for being human.

"Are we dead? Is this Jannah? Are you going to follow me around for eternity?"

"Open both of your eyes. You're not dead. I saved you. Again."

I twist my neck to look up and see that Aasman Peri has caught me inches before my face plants in the rosebushes. We're hovering above as she beats her wings, her face twisted in a scowl. She flies a few feet over to a patch of grass and drops me with a thud.

✦ ✷ ✦

YOU BREAK IT, YOU BUY IT

"Ow! Was that really necessary?" I groan.

"Sorry." Aasman Peri shrugs. "My delicate wings couldn't take your human weight."

"I know for a fact that you can carry more weight than me. You powered my entire bicycle over here." My bicycle. Oh no. I push myself up and brush off some leaves and twigs and scan the small garden we're in. I look past the rose hedges and see my bike—now a twisted piece of metal on the sidewalk. Ugh. I loved that purple iridescent bike. "How am I supposed to explain this to my parents? It looks like it got run over by a car."

"Getting run over by a car would've been far better than having your flesh torn off by a mob of angry jinn jays."

My jaw drops. "Uhhh, can you please try to be less graphic?"

"Humans just can't handle the truth."

I roll my eyes. "We have to find Hamz. Who knows where that—what's his name—"

"Ahriman. His name is Ahriman. And he's the one who sent the jinn jays after us. They have been his allies since before he was entombed in the moon. He's definitely out for vengeance. Probably more."

I gulp. "More than vengeance? What's more than ven—"

I can't finish my sentence because there's a sudden loud flapping and I'm being lifted by my arms and backpack by an angry mob of jinn jays. "Hellllppppp!" I scream as I squirm and twist, trying to get away as we lift off the ground. Up close, they're even more terrifying. I was totally right about the teeth! All the meanness of jays plus piranha teeth and super bird strength.

"Do something!" I yell at Aasman Peri.

"I am!" she screams back as she flies up and pulls two small daggers from her belt.

"No! No! If you miss, I'll get stabbed!" The jinn jays are tugging at my backpack. Oh no! The jade tablet. Is that what they're after? How do they even know I have it? I wonder if they have X-ray vision. Whoa. A research project on bird vision could be—*ugh. Think, Amira! Focus!* I start writhing even more, hoping it will slow our ascent. But if they work for

Ahriman, they'll take me to Hamza. Maybe I should let them take me. If Hamz and I are together, we can figure out what to do. Then again, that whole getting-my-flesh-torn-off part does not seem appealing. At all.

"Stop moving around so much," Aasman Peri yells at me, annoyed. "I'm not going to be responsible if my dagger goes through your arm!"

The talons of one of the jays dig through my sleeve and I see little pops of red blood seep through my baseball tee. Ugh. I'm going to be sick. I'm getting dizzy.

"Wait! Don't!" I scream at Aasman Peri. I close my eyes and hear loud squawks right by my head, then a flurry of wings flapping; we're swirling around, doing dips and circles in the air. I'm pretty sure Hamza would say these are evasive maneuvers.

One of the jays screams. It sounds almost human. Ow! It bit me! I open my eyes as Aasman Peri's dagger makes contact with the biting jay on my right arm. It squawks and gets dusted in a minitornado swirl. I jerk to that side, my body at an angle as her other dagger misses the shrieking target. With one arm free, I shrug the backpack off my right shoulder so now I'm dangling diagonally in the air. Maybe that wasn't the best idea.

C'mon, Amira. You can do this.

When we're sparring in karate, Sensei Seijo tells us to be creative. When you're in a fight, you need to think on your feet, or, in my case, in midair. Whatever. The advice still applies. I take a deep breath, trying not to look at the ground, and ball my right hand into a fist and deliver a variation of a gedan barai—a kind of block—sweeping my fist along my left shoulder and bonking the biting jinn jay on its surprisingly hard head. I improvised and it did the trick! The jay wails and screeches as it dizzily spins around, then plummets into the thorny rosebushes below and gets obliterated into a swirl of dust. Yes! Two down, two more to go.

My backpack and I are too much weight for the jays tugging at me, though they're flapping madly to try to keep us aloft. I grab the left shoulder strap with my right hand, trying to shake off the last two jays as they try to yank away my backpack. It's a tug-of-war, which I don't think I can win. Aasman Peri is running around below, trying to aim her daggers at them, but we're spinning and moving so much she can't get a clean throw. If more jays show up and try to pull me higher, I'll break something (or worse!) if I fall. I have to jump. Now.

Keep your knees bent, Amira. Drop and roll. Drop and roll.

I shrug off the left shoulder strap, close my eyes, and fall.

I drop right onto my butt, then quickly roll over onto my back. I make eye contact with Aasman Peri, who lofts a dagger toward me. It falls inches away from my face. I grab it and push myself up and we both hurl our daggers at the birds, dusting the last two jinn jays, watching as my backpack plunges to the ground.

I lean back on the grass, trying to catch my breath. My heart is racing. "Aaaaaargh! I think my tailbone is broken," I groan.

"You're welcome. That's the second time I've

saved you from being eaten by jinn jays in the last five minutes."

I sit up, wincing at the blood blooming on my arm and shoulder. "What are you talking about? You could've murdered me with your dagger at least twice in that situation. And I'm the one who dusted that jay onto the thorns. Even you have to admit it was a good move."

Aasman Peri snorts. I take that as a yes.

"Can those birds really eat people?" I ask, pulling off my dented helmet and pressing my hand into my shoulder. The bite's not horrible, but it definitely stings, like when you wipe out on your bike and bang and scrape your knee against the sidewalk.

"Not birds. Jinn jays. And yes, didn't you see their teeth? Ahriman fashioned them into an army long before my time. In the days of the ancient jinn." Aasman Peri hurries over to me, unsnaps a small bag at her waist, and takes out a bronze-colored tube of ointment that she rubs over my jay scratches and bites. I feel better almost instantly.

"What is that?" I ask.

"Zindagi Balm," she says. "The balm of life. It can heal small wounds that are not deadly or poisonous." She recaps the tube and slips it into her bag.

"Is that a fanny pack? Peris wear fanny packs? My mom would love you."

"They are very practical. Besides, we can't wear those ugly, clumsy things on our backs. How would we fly?"

"Backpacks. They're called—oh no. My backpack." I look around and see my backpack twenty feet away, in tatters. "Oh, please, no," I say as I scramble toward it.

"Are these backpacks very valuable? I'm sure you can replace it. Oh, it's not a family heirloom, is it?" Aasman Peri frowns.

I don't even need to unzip my pack, because there's a tear along the top. I stick my hand in, hoping against hope that it's not the worst-case scenario. I pull out the jade tablet and suck in my breath. I show its face to Aasman Peri. She gasps when she sees the million tiny cracks across the surface.

"No. No. No," I say as I sink into the grass, the

broken tablet in my hand. It's weird, but I feel all those cracks in my heart. That tablet was the only connection to what happened in Qaf, and right now, it's my only link to Hamza and the only source for warnings. Now it's busted.

"How could you not protect the tablet?" she screams as she hurries over to me. "That was a gift from Suleiman the Wise—his knowledge contained within. You can't walk into a store and purchase one!" Aasman Peri raises her hand to her mouth and shakes her head. "I thought your brother was the clumsy one!"

"Why are you blaming me? If Suleiman the Wise was so smart, maybe he should've made it unbreakable or given it a case. And maybe instead of offing them, we should've tried to capture those jinn jays and forced them to take us to Ahriman. And Hamza."

"And then what would you have done? Trust me. You don't want to be in Ahriman's clutches. His furor after being entombed for a millennia will be even worse than Ifrit's—you know, his son who you vanquished."

I chew on my lower lip a little. If Ahriman is that angry, my brother might not have much time. "We have to save Hamz," I whisper.

Aasman Peri flies into the air. "I saw Ahriman's twister land near a stone building with a pointy red roof not far from here."

"The Oriental Institute? That's super close. Hurry!" I say as I take off running in the direction of the OI, choking back tears as I picture Hamza in the clutches of that monster. I hope we're not too late.

CHAPTER 6

Occu-Pee, I Mean, Occu-py the OI

Hamza

MY JAW DROPS OPEN. AMIRA WOULD TELL ME TO SHUT MY mouth because I'm catching flies, but honestly, I'm sort of hungry, and flies are at least protein, right? Did scary dev-dude just say, *Control the Ring, control the worlds*? The Ring that controls all fire creatures, can change the weather, and lets you talk to animals? It's very Doctor-Dolittle-meets-Storm-meets-Thanos. That's sort of a cool but also an absolutely, totally terrifying mash-up! A world-ending, scary-type situation.

Dang it. I really need to pee.

"Follow! Small human! Now!" Ahriman bellows, and his voice echoes in the marble entryway of the OI.

Breathe, Hamza. Do not hyperventilate. Do not pee. Make your brain work. I look around; there's scaffolding and buckets of paint and some lumber. I know they're doing upgrades, but I wonder if I could use this stuff to my advantage. Assess the situation. That's what Amira would say. I'm assessing. Assessing. Assessing. Assessing. . . . I'm waiting for my brain to load.

Nope. My brain can't assess right now because it's screaming at me to run. It's that whole fright-or-flight thing. No, that's not it. It's *fight* or flight. I'm definitely not fighting this guy. And I can't fly. Wait, is that a metaphor? Wings would be so handy right now. Also, I wouldn't mind a bucket of wings from Harold's Chicken. Extra hot sauce. There's a fifty-fifty chance I could get sick, but so worth it. If I had wings, I could fly to get wings! Double wings! A wing-a-palooza.

A loud clap snaps me out of my wing drooling. Ahriman claps his red hands again and tiny sparks fly off his pointy fingers. How does he not singe his nails? Or skin? That always bothered me about heroes or, uh, villains with fire powers. How do they not burn themselves? It makes no sense! Is their skin protected from all fire or only theirs? "Hey," I shout at Ahriman. "Watch it, buddy! There's a lot of flammable stuff in here! Not to mention priceless artifacts!" Whoa. An Amira sentence just came out of my mouth. She's been a terrible influence on me.

"I said follow, human. Not speak!"

"Can you at least use my name? It's kind of rude not to, and the way you say *human* sounds like an insult."

"It is an insult. But fine, *Hamza,*" Ahriman says, a smile snaking across his creepy face.

The way he says my name sounds like an insult, too. Maybe that's just his bad-guy voice.

"Where are we going?" I ask as he starts walking down the giant main hall of the OI.

"Do you not listen at all? Pay attention, or I will turn you to ash!"

I was so right about those Thanos vibes.

"I'm sorry," I say. "I told you, I needed to pee. Then I randomly started thinking about wings. The eating kind and the flying kind. Hey, do you have hot wi—"

"Silence! Great fires of Qaf! Do you have no filters? Is this the way of all humans? No wonder you are such lowly creatures. You subsume your energy spouting worthless gibberish about consumable wings." Ahriman rolls his eyes and for a second all I can see are flames in the sockets. I shiver from the extreme haunted Halloween house–level creepiness.

"You wouldn't say that if you'd had hot wings from Harold's before," I mumble. I don't tell him that I talk a lot when I'm nervous. That would give him an advantage, not that he doesn't have every single one already. All I seem to have is the incredible ability to annoy him, which could come in handy, maybe, if it doesn't make him turn me to ash! And as I always say, use the skills you have to meet the moment. Actually... I never say that. My dad probably has, though, and it sounds pretty good to me.

I shut my mouth for a minute as we walk past glass cases filled with old vases and pitchers and jewelry. Ahriman reaches out his hands to his sides and does this flick-of-his-wrist thing. Maybe he's stretching? He was cramped up for a very long time and—

Crash!

A row of pedestals holding the artifacts crumble to the ground, sending bits of glass and pottery everywhere; jewelry scatters across the floor. I may not be a giant museum buff, but this is awful!

"Uh, excuse me, Ahriman? Did you not see the signs that say, DON'T TOUCH? This is a museum, dude. You're wrecking priceless stuff," I mutter. I probably should keep quiet, but my mom thinks it's physically impossible for me because my brain constantly whirs with creative ideas. Pretty sure that's science giving me an excuse to talk nonstop.

He scoffs. "These are all looted and stolen goods.

None of them belongs in this place. Nor do I have use for these human trinkets."

"Okay, I get it, but do you really have to ruin everything?"

"I am ruin. This is but child's play. A lively diversion."

I gulp. *I am ruin* is a very, very evil-y thing to say. It's definitely a villain who is totally bad and can't be redeemed and who doesn't feel sad when he hears the memory of his mom's voice or picks up a kitten and is reminded he was once good. Nope. This dude is pure evil. So I'm definitely not going to win by appealing to his good side. He doesn't have a good side.

"Okaaay. What about the security system? If you don't want to attract attention, then maybe you shouldn't destroy everything in here. There's alarms and stuff." Wait. I shouldn't have said that. The alarms going off would be good. I *want* the alarms to go off, then someone can find me. But I also want him to stop destroying everything. Dilemma!

Ahriman laughs. "The small human, er, you, Hamza, are entertaining, in your own strange way, like a court performer. I have disengaged all alarms, cloaked all visual devices. And none can see me—or any form I take—without the collyrium of Suleiman on their eyelids."

The collyrium. The magic eyeliner Maqbool put on us so we could see him and Abdul Rahman and all the other creatures of Qaf. Wish you were here, Maqbool. Wish you were still alive. You're the only one who truly appreciated my jokes during near-death experiences.

"So you hacked the system? That's pretty impressive for a bajillion-year-old dude. I mean, I still have to explain the three different remote controls to my dad. Did you have a phone when you were buried on the moon or are you just a quick learner?"

"Foolish child. I merely possessed one of your most renowned information technology experts, a so-called hacker, as you say, and ordered him to do my bidding. He seemed particularly inclined to understand commands. This is by far the simplest way to get things done." Ahriman shoots a spark from his fingers, and a giant clay urn bursts into a million pieces.

I shield my face from the flying pottery and stone projectiles. So much for alarms helping me out. Dilemma solved. "Hey, you know, if you need me to help you, maybe you could cut it out before I get murdered by a jagged piece of marble."

Ahriman ignores me and flicks his wrist, and giant stone tablets hanging on the wall—the kind with super-old-timey emojis that tell a story—come crashing down. "This is really, really excessive and unnecessary!" I can barely hear my own voice over the sounds of all the destruction, but this is wrong and I have to say something. My mom would be so proud of me right now.

We turn into a huge gallery—I remember when my class came here last year. This room was everyone's favorite. It's super echoey, which is hilarious if you're making fake fart noises with your armpits. But also at the end is the biggest, giant-est sculpture I've ever seen up close: the *Lamassu*. The guide said it weighed more than twenty SUVs and it's about four times as tall as me. It's a huge, winged bull with the head of a human and the wings of a bird that was built by some great king. I guess he didn't actually build it but probably forced a bunch of people to build it for him, maybe on pain of death. I don't always pay attention in history class, but I don't think kings actually do any work or fight many of their own battles—mostly they order other people to do it. The *Lamassu* reminds me of the simurgh that flew us out of the City of Gold before it collapsed.

Oh no. My mind wandered off again. Amira always says that I need to focus, that I'm a procrastinator. But I think of myself as a procasti-creator. Just because I'm not doing the thing I'm supposed to be doing doesn't mean I'm not thinking of something else that's a lot more interesting to me. But this is one time when focus would be good, because Ahriman has stopped in front of the giant *Lamassu*. He's sliding his bony red fingers across it, and it's leaving burn marks on the stone. And Amira thinks I'm bad at following museum rules because I took the Box of the Moon out of its case. That was one time! She'd go bananas if she saw Ahriman trashing the place.

Another thing I remember our tour guide saying when I was here with my class: The king who built the *Lamassu* put a spell on it. So that anyone who disturbs it would be cursed. Something about your vitality being sucked away, blah blah blah, your dreams withering on burning sands or something. The guide said it was an old myth, but when we had to research more about the *Lamassu* for class, I found out that two guys on the French archaeology team who dug it up died within a few weeks of each other after they got back home. They were both found with their eyes and mouths open wide and their hands reaching for something. Creepy. Technically, these were only rumors because of bad paperwork or no autopsies back then or something, but still...that doesn't sound like a legend to me! It sounds like a death curse.

I wonder if I should say something to Ahriman. Because burn marks definitely seem to count as "disturbing." I don't want the curse unleashed, but technically, I'm only an innocent bystander. I mean, he's the one touching it when there's this giant sign that says DO NOT TOUCH. I'm about to open my mouth and say something in case of guilt by association. Is that how ancient curses work? I don't want to chance it or end up scared to death with my mouth open.

"Ahriman, I think—"

Ahriman pulls back his hands. Phew. I don't have to warn him. We'll avoid the curse. One thing I don't have to worry about.

Then he balls his hands into fists and punches the center of the *Lamassu*.

"Nooooooo!" I yell, but my voice is lost in the huge thunder of a ton of stone collapsing into rubble. I squeeze my eyes shut.

Look, I appreciate a good mess. I mean, my mom refers to my LEGO area as Mess-O-Potamia. But this is tragic. When I open my eyes, Ahriman is standing in front of the crumbled stone, the human head of the *Lamassu* on the ground, gazing up at him. I shiver. The curse is unleashed. Or at least I think so.

That's what the snarly look on the *Lamassu* seems to be saying.

"I disdain the haughtiness in its eyes," Ahriman says as he does a 180-degree head turn to look at me.

Blech. I forgot that some jinn and devs could do that. My blood goes cold. He destroyed that sculpture for looking "haughty," whatever that means. Stuck up, maybe? How can a statue look stuck up? I don't know. But the *Lamassu* did have this look that Amira sometimes gets when all the cousins are playing Mafia and she's the murderer.

Ahriman looks down a small hall to the side as the stone dust settles. "There!" he shouts. He seems to glide to a small marble pedestal. I don't think I ever noticed it before and I've been in the OI a bunch of times. When I catch up with him, I see he's staring at a smooth, smallish object. It's a broken piece of something bigger. I stare at it, my stomach grumbling.

"A donut!" I yell.

Ahriman turns to me, his bushy eyebrows raised.

"What? It looks like part of a chocolate-glazed donut. I told you I was hungry."

"This is one-third of the oculus. Once I have its mates, I shall find the location of the Ring of Power." Ahriman narrows his eyes.

"That thing is going to find you the Ring? No offense, but it seems a little underwhelming. I was kinda expecting more, you know, gems or fancy carvings. It's basically a bite of a smooth, glazy, marbly donut."

Ahriman reaches out for it with both hands. Honestly, not sure why he thinks he needs both hands. This thing isn't even in a glass case. How valuable can it be? It's held up by an iron cradle. That's all. Put together, I bet the whole thing is about the size of a cereal bowl. Ahriman wraps his fingers around it and lifts.

But nothing happens. I wonder if super glue is holding it down. Ahriman keeps his left hand on the oculus portion and his right on the iron stand. His hand becomes all flame-y, but the oculus doesn't singe and the iron stand doesn't seem to heat up at all.

"Oh, well," I say. "Maybe this means it's *not* your

destiny. I'm going to go ahead and step out. Maybe you should fly off somewhere and figure out a Plan B." I slowly inch away. Maybe this time I can make a run for it.

Ahriman reaches out with his right hand and grabs me by the hem of my shirt, pulling me closer to the oculus. "Hey!" I yell. "Don't rip my shirt! It's a vintage Star Wars tee I got at C2E2 last summer. Have you ever considered asking nicely?"

"You are correct."

"I am?" I scrunch my eyebrows together. "I...I am. That's right! Despite what Amira thinks. I know a lot of stuff. Now what was I right about again?"

"It is not *my* destiny to remove the oculus."

I nod. "Good. Good. See, you're one of the reasonable types of villains. We can agree on stuff. This whole afternoon was a big waste of time, but live and learn. I'll be—"

"It is *your* destiny. Now seize it!"

I pause. "Excuse me? If all your dev-y, fiery strength couldn't get it to budge, how am I supposed to get it off the stand?"

"You will do so or I will turn your vintage tee, as you call it, into dust while you are still in it."

I gulp and cross my arms over my shirt to protect it. "Okay! Okay! Geez. No need to play dirty. Let go of me and I'll try."

"Do or do not—"

"Don't you dare finish that sentence! You're no Yoda!" I shake my head. I can imagine Aasman Peri claiming right now that she invented that line and gave it to George Lucas. Ahriman releases my shirt, and I step closer to the pedestal that holds the oculus piece.

My palms are all sweaty, so I wipe them on my jeans. I close my eyes. *Okay, Hamz. You got this.* I reach out and wrap my clammy hand around the oculus piece. It's smooth and cool to the touch. There are flecks of gold and silver in the dark marbly surface. There's no trace of any heat from Ahriman's flame. My shoulders relax. I thought I was about to get burned. I try to lift it off, but I think it's super-super-glued to this cradle thingy.

I turn my head over my shoulder to spy Ahriman's

annoyed face. I grunt and try to yank off the oculus piece. But a small static shock shoots up my hands and arms. I try to pull my hands off the thing, but now they're stuck in place. "Hey, what the...?" Small golden ropes whip out of the bottom of the iron cradle. Where did these come from? They wrap themselves around my arms like snakes. I pull back, but they're holding me, squeezing my wrists.

"What have you done, foolish human?" Ahriman shouts.

"What have I done? What have I done? Obviously nothing, duh! Can't you see with your flaming eyeballs that I'm handcuffed to this thing?" I tug harder, trying to free my hands.

Then the air around us gets all cold. From the look on Ahriman's face, I'm guessing he did not know this—whatever this is—was going to happen. I shiver. I can see my breath when I exhale; like it's winter inside the OI.

A gray smoky mist swirls out of the ends of the broken oculus piece and rises into the air, twisting as it reaches the ground. I blink my eyes as the mist transforms into a person. A see-through, blurry-edged person. He reminds me of this one uncle at the masjid, with a white turban and dark brown beard.

"Are you... are you... a jinn?" I stumble.

"No," Ahriman says, and I swear his voice sounds almost worried. "He's a ghost."

A ghost? I have to deal with a ghost, too? I know I said I was up for battling a ghost earlier today, but that was before a sharp-toothed, four-eared dev threatened my entire existence and basically the world's existence, too! Honestly, this is extra. Too extra.

"I am Ibn Sina," the man, er, ghost, says in a calm voice. "I am a Keeper of The Ring. If you dare enter with false identity or foul purpose, you shall be condemned. Prepare to meet your destiny."

CHAPTER 7

Riddle Me This

Hamza

THE SMOKE SWIRLING IN FRONT OF YOU IS A GHOST. OR *maybe you're seeing things because you're really, really hungry and, as per usual, you didn't pack sufficient snacks or really any snacks. (Insert your sister telling you* I told you so.*) The four-eared dev appears to be in shock but still has very sharp teeth. If you stand still, the ghost could make you do the unspeakable: pee in your pants out of fright. The jinn could also make you pee in your pants... out of fright. You are handcuffed by golden ropes to the pedestal holding the oculus* *piece Ahriman needs. You could scream and hope it attracts someone to your plight. You could try to Houdini your way out of this. But, FYI, you don't really know magic. Design! Your! Destiny!*

What? No. Worst imaginary chapter ending ever. Houdini did have a lot of tricks for getting out of handcuffs, and I read a whole book about him last year. But they didn't spill any of his secrets! And he also didn't have an angry dev and a ghost with a long beard staring at him. No pressure. *Scream.* Screaming is the only option.

"Heeeeeelp!" I squeeze my eyes shut and yell at the top of my lungs, tugging at the golden ropes digging into my wrists.

"The Golden Threads of Suleiman bind you and cannot be undone," the ghost says. My eyes fly open and I take a good look at him. He's wearing ivory robes and a white turban. His face looks approximately a bajillion years old because of all the wrinkles. And I can kind of see through him, which makes me gag a little.

"Listen, uh, can you remind me of your name again, Mr. Ghost. Uh, sir?"

"Ibn Sina," Ahriman says dryly before the ghost can respond. "How are you come to protect the Ring?"

"Ibn who?" I ask. I know Amira would be yelling at me right now because this dead dude seems famous or important. Or was, anyway.

"Ibn Sina, the famed philosopher and astronomer of Islam's golden age of discovery. Centuries ago, in Earth time. His medical encyclopedias were revolutionary and used for over eight hundred years," Ahriman explains, grinding his sharp teeth. "A mere mortal tasked to keep the Ring?" He shakes his head.

The ghost clasps his hands in front of him and nods very slowly. I wonder if ghosts get tired, because this dude definitely looks like he could use a nap. He opens his ghost jaw and I can see all the way through! He doesn't even have tonsils! I wonder if he got to eat a bunch of Popsicles when he got them taken out like I did. I wonder if he wrote about that in his books.

Man, Amira would be asking him a million science nerd questions if she were here. I wish—

"Silence your mind, Chosen One," Ibn Sina says.

Whoa. He can read my mind?

"I can see and hear all," Ibn Sina says. "It is my gift as a Keeper of The Ring."

"Great. Can you see if I'm going to have lunch soon? Or maybe get a bathroom break?"

"Silence!" Ahriman yells.

"Hey, rude much? I was asking Mr. Sina—uh, Dr. Sina?—a question."

"Young hero, I can see within the parameters of my charge, to protect this piece of the oculus from all who may have foul intentions, who may wish to use the Ring of Power for ill and not good."

"Tell me about it," I say, giving Ahriman a little side eye. "But how do you know I'm a Chosen One?"

"You bear the mark upon your face," he says, pointing to my Majid Mark, the round birthmark Amira and I both have by our left temples. "And the glow of collyrium is upon your eyelids." Whoa. Had no idea my magic eyeliner could make me see ghosts, too!

"That guy," I say, pointing to Ahriman, "is the evil one. Not me. I was literally minding my own beeswax biking in the park and he devnado-napped me and was all: *Control the Ring, control the—*"

"Ahem," Ahriman clears his throat. "Need I remind you that this *guy*, as you so inelegantly refer to me, also holds the fate of your sister and your entire family in his hands?"

I gulp. Why can't this ghost do something besides stand here? Maybe throw some ancient pottery around, knock Ahriman out so I can make a run for it? And, oh, maybe untie my hands from these Ropes of Whatchamacallit?

"Golden Threads of Suleiman," Ibn Sina corrects my thoughts.

"Ugh! Stop that! It's brain trespassing!"

"Young hero, my charge and my powers are constrained. I am here to deliver a message and test the Chosen One. I can go no further. Do little else. Would that I could," Ibn Sina says, his eyes cast down. Not sure if ghosts can feel guilty, but he looks bummed.

"Test? Another test? Ugh! What if can't pass the test?"

"Then you shall remain ensnared to the oculus piece for eternity."

"Wait. What? I'll be stuck in this museum my whole life? Chained to this thing? That's really impractical. Or...wait, would I get sucked into it? Fine, ugh, okay, give me the test. Do I need to shoot an arrow into an apple through a bunch of iron rings or something? That seems really popular in old epics." While I talk, I try to relax my arms and hands to see if I can slip out of the golden ropes knotted around my wrists. No luck.

"The test is a riddle."

I groan. Riddles are so not my thing. "What if I take you on in a game of laser tag, instead? Or maybe a water balloon toss?"

Ahriman makes a low, growling sound, which shuts me up pretty quick.

Ibn Sina places his see-through ghost hand on my shoulder. I flinch, even though there's no weight to it. He looks in my eyes. I want to look away, but when he starts to speak, it's like he's got tractor beams trained on my eyeballs.

"From the depths of the black earth up to Saturn's apogee, all the problems of the universe have been solved by me. I have escaped from the coils of snares and deceits, yet even a will as strong as mine humbly succumbed to one from which there are no retreats." Ibn Sina pauses for a second and then raises a ghostly eyebrow. "To what entity did I yield? Solve this riddle, Chosen One, and the oculus piece is yours."

"Depth of what now? And what does humbly succumbing mean? Ugh. Couldn't your riddle be in nowadays English? How am I supposed to figure out the answer to that?" My jaw drops open, my brain is blank. Whiteboard blank. Totally clueless. "I don't even know what an apogee is. Sounds like a typo for *apology*? Are you even sure it's a real word?"

Ahriman shakes his head. "Great lunar craters! Do humans truly learn nothing in school?"

I shrug. "It's debatable, actually. So can I get a lifeline, maybe phone a friend?"

Ibn Sina looks to Ahriman, then back to me. "He may assist you in the definition."

Ahriman wiggles all four of his ears. That will never not be weird. "It is a point in an orbit when the orbiting object is the farthest from Earth or the planet it's orbiting."

Huh? "That doesn't help at all. You said *orbit* so many times it doesn't sound like a real word anymore. I hate when that happens. Is it a weird brain trick or a brain freeze or—"

"You will answer. And answer correctly, or your sister and Aasman Peri will be doomed." Ahriman bares his vampire teeth at me.

Whoa! Aasman Peri is here? That means Amira is coming for me. I don't say anything, but it's the best news I've had since I puked in the Ahriman tornado.

"Okay, okay. I hear you. Way to ease up the pressure." I turn to Ibn Sina, "Could you please repeat it?"

I close my eyes as Ibn Sina repeats the riddle: *From the depths of the black earth up to Saturn's apogee, all the problems of the universe have been solved by me. I have escaped from the coils of snares and deceits, yet even a will as strong as mine humbly succumbed to one from which there are no retreats*... I take a breath and listen to the ghost's deep voice.

My panicky brain wanders to my dad and Amira. I imagine them sitting at the kitchen counter, giving each other little trick questions and logic puzzles to figure out like the riddle of the Sphinx: *What goes on four feet in the morning, two feet in the afternoon and three feet in the evening*? Humans, because babies crawl, then we walk, and get canes when we're old.

I wish my dad were here now. It's really Amira and him who can puzzle these kinds of things out. In my mind, I hear my dad whisper, *You got this, big guy*. But no, I really don't. *Think. Think. Think.* Isn't it weird how, when you tell yourself to think, you can't think of anything?

What would Amira do? Okay, so knowing my sister, she would say break down hard assignments into smaller parts. Ibn Sina is genius-level smart. He was a scientist and philosopher. Got that. So he figured out a bunch of stuff about medicine and the stars, I guess. And maybe the coils and snares were traps—people trying to trap him with their deceits. But also, back then a lot of scientists were put in jail for their theories, so it could be that. And he stood his ground. Fought back. Escaped all of it, I guess. Except for one person he succumbed to, which means, surrender? And he did it humbly? Which means he was sort of cool with it. He accepted it. Why would you give in to an enemy humbly?

The ropes start tightening around my wrists. "Hey! You didn't tell me there was a time limit. You could at least have given me some music or a giant sand hourglass or something!"

"Focus, young champion. In my heart, I know you are close," Ibn Sina says. It's my first pep talk from a ghost! Cool! But I have to focus. Succumb. Succumb. Humbly. He gave in to something and couldn't go back? A war? No. That doesn't make sense. A person? A king? No retreat. Give in. Give in. What is the one thing you can never go back from but you kind of just accept?

Whoa.

Wait.

I. Have. An. Idea! It may be wrong. I may be stuck here forever in a dusty museum. But a bad answer is better than no answer. Maybe it's not a person he succumbed to. Maybe it's not an enemy at all. When Nani was sick, I was really little and I don't remember that much. But I do remember feeling scared and didn't really understand why people had to die. I still kind of don't. But the last time I visited her, she told me she wasn't scared; she felt peaceful. That her path home was lit with our love. I didn't really get what she was saying, but I think maybe now, I kinda do.

So...

I suck in my breath and whip my eyes open. "Death. You found peace, so you could humbly surrender to death. And it's the one thing you can't come back from."

Ibn Sina smiles and bows his head toward me.

"Is that it? Did I get it right? Was I—" The golden ropes tying my wrists loosen and unwrap.

"Indeed, I lived a fortunate life in many ways. No one can run from death, so I strove to meet this mortal end with humility and equanimity. The oculus shard is yours," Ibn Sina says with a small smile. I breathe a sigh of relief.

He continues. "Only the Chosen One may put the oculus together. Make your choices wisely, young hero. The path ahead is never paved until we set foot upon it. May the road you forge be righteous." He pauses and quickly sneaks a look at Ahriman, then bends lower toward me. His lips keep moving, but his voice is in my head, "Remember, the more brilliant the lightning, the quicker it disappears."

Is that supposed to mean something? Another pep talk?

Ibn Sina stands back up to full height. "Peace be with you," he says, and then gestures with his head toward the oculus piece.

I reach for it with shaky fingers. I lift it off the cradle it's resting on. I expect alarms to blare. But it's quiet. Ibn Sina nods at me and then disappears into a swirl of smoke.

I did it? I did it! I do a double fist pump. Then I realize I'm celebrating getting a piece of the oculus for an evil dev who wants to use it to get the Ring of

Power to control the worlds. So, not good. But I'm counting getting the riddle right and not being tied to that pedestal forever as a win, sort of.

"Come, trifling human. We fly to London."

"Uh, you're welcome!" I say to Ahriman. "You know, it wouldn't kill you to show some appreciation. My mom always says you're never too busy to say thank you." Also, holy cow, London? We're going to London? I have to stall. Amira and Aasman Peri have to be looking for me, but they might not know where I am. "FYI, I don't have a passport. And you can't transport a kid beyond a border without parental consent. It's a rule. They're really strict at the airport about this stuff. Not gonna lie, airport security can be pretty racist, and you have four ears, vampire teeth, and a skin color that doesn't even remotely resemble any human on Earth. Pretty sure you're going to get flagged."

"Enough, narrow-minded fool. No others have collyrium on their eyes. Why does this simple logic fail you? Besides, when I say fly, I do not mean on one of your metal bird contraptions. How ridiculous."

"Maybe being thankful is beyond your abilities,

but could you at least stop calling me names? I mean, I just got you a piece of the oculus," I say, holding it up to him. Ahriman swipes at it, but I pull it back. "Only the Chosen One can hold on to it, too. Pretty sure that's what Ibn Sina said." Ahriman twists his lips like he's just eaten a lemon and snatches it from my hand so fast I barely saw him move. Okay, only a Chosen One can get it from the pedestal, but apparently any old jinn or dev can hold it once they've gotten me to do the hard work. Figures.

"Do not try to trick me, Chosen One. I can turn things to ash as well as melt them. I'd be happy to demonstrate for you."

I grimace. Message received. I definitely don't want to end up melted. But he also needs me to finish the tasks and put the oculus together. Ibn Sina was pretty clear that only I could do it. Or Amira. If she could get an oculus piece, she could get rid of it, hide it, so that Ahriman wouldn't be able to get the Ring of Power. Amira needs more time. Lucky for her, I'm really good at wasting it. Might even say it's one of my superpowers.

"Look, I know you're all fiery and powerful and can fly, but are you aware of human bodily needs? Food and toilets, for example? Because I need both, right now," I say.

Ahriman harrumphs but nods and I race to the great hall, where shards of the *Lamassu* are littered all over. I rush into the bathroom.

When I get out, I see Ahriman talking to himself, muttering something as he seems to be counting off on his fingers.

"Toilet break. Check," I say. "Now what about food?" Ahriman turns to me, a look of annoyance on his face. I should say *more* annoyance, because I don't think there was ever a time in his life when this dude was in a good mood. You'd think he'd at least lighten up now that he has the first piece. But no, he looks permanently pissed off. "Look, Ahriman? If you want me to get the other two oculus pieces, I'm going to need to eat. Unless you want me to pass out from hunger. You know, I won't be able to solve any riddles when I'm unconscious!" As I speak, green smoke coming from the broken *Lamassu* in the great hall snakes across the floor toward us. Ahriman doesn't see it yet. It's the curse! It's got to be! Holy crud. The curse is real. I keep talking, going on and on about my favorite snacks and how some fries would be really great right now, maybe some barbecue potato chips. The green smoke curls and swirls across the marble floor and through the shards of the destroyed *Lamassu,* then ghostly whispers fill the great hall: *You shall pay for this desecration, your dreams shriveling by the sand's desiccation.* Those words sound exactly the same to me, but whatever, the voice is eerie as heck. Ahriman looks up, trying to locate the sound. So he doesn't see the green smoke start to wrap itself around his ankles until it's too late.

"AGGGHHHHH!" he shouts, and tries to move but seems stuck in place.

This is my chance! I turn and hightail it down the hall, through the lobby. I reach for the door, so close to escape, as Ahriman's voice echoes behind me, "You won't get faaaaaaar!"

CHAPTER 8

Donut Underestimate My Power

Amira

AASMAN PERI IS FLYING ABOVE ME; SHE'S NEARLY AT THE steps of the Oriental Institute. While I'm nearly out of breath, sprinting to catch up. This all would've been a lot faster if my bike wasn't a mangled mess a few blocks from here. There's no sign of Hamza or the Ahriman tornado. I keep looking to the skies in case of another jinn jay attack. Those sharp teeth are going to give me nightmares. I start to get a stitch in my side and pause for a second, sucking in air.

"Why did you stop? We have to get moving," Aasman Peri demands as she flies down.

"Just...need...to...catch...my...breath," I say, my back bent as I clutch my thighs, slightly lightheaded. This is why I do karate and not track. Roundhouse kicks to the head? Yes. All-out sprint for three blocks? No, thank you. "Okay. Okay. I'm fine. What's the plan?"

"Plan?"

"Yeah, when we meet up with Ahriman, what's the plan? What are his weaknesses? How do we attack?"

"Weaknesses?" Aasman Peri rolls her eyes. "It took Suleiman the Wise and his Ring of Power, not to mention his excellent sword skills, to imprison Ahriman, so I'm pretty sure no one in Qaf has figured out his weaknesses."

"So what do we do? Ask nicely and hope he hands over Hamza?"

"I honestly don't think asking is going—" Aasman Peri starts.

"I was being sarcastic! Give me a weapon." The

small dagger I threw at the jinn jay was lost in the rosebushes, so I was literally defenseless now.

"Excuse me?"

"Please? I don't have the bow and arrow anymore or Suleiman's sword."

"Because you threw them into the Magnetic Sea!"

"That's what the simurgh told me to do! You're wasting time! Please give me another dagger or—"

"Fine!" Aasman Peri slaps a small dagger encased in a leather sheath into my hand. The hilt is a dull iron color, not one of the bejeweled ones she usually favors. I raise an eyebrow at her. "It's my least favorite," she says, "but it can still turn any fire creature to ash, so you better be careful where you point that thing, or else—"

Before Aasman Peri can finish her sentence, Hamza bursts through the huge, ornate wooden doors of the Oriental Institute. He looks behind him and then leaps down the stairs. (He's so dramatic!)

"Hamz!" I yell.

"Amira!" he shouts back, and turns to run toward me.

Aasman Peri flies in his direction. I follow; I'm only two strides in when the doors of the OI fly off their hinges, sailing through the air, landing in a nearby tree. That's going to be a tough one to explain. But before I can figure anything else out, I see a cloud of red smoke, twisting around wisps of green smoke, choking it. The red smoke begins to dissipate at the foot of the steps. As it's evaporating, a scary hiss comes from the green smoke: *You shall suffer for this desecratiooooon.* I wonder what that... Wait. What in the—oh my God! A red hand with very bony fingers reaches out of the red smoke and grabs Hamza by the upper arm. He struggles but can't escape the grip.

"Let me go, Ahriman!" Hamza shouts.

"Not until the task is complete," I hear a gruff voice say. Task? What task? For a second, a face emerges from the mist. It's a deep red color like his hands, but all I can really see are four ears and very, very sharp teeth. It sends chills down my spine. He's so much scarier-looking than Ifrit.

The wind around us picks up, sending sticks and

leaves into the air, bending the branches of trees. I struggle to keep my eyes open. The smoke starts to swirl into a twister, engulfing Hamza. No! No! No! Not again. I push into the wind to try to grab him. I hold on to the branch of the nearest tree with one hand and reach out with the other. As the whirlwind sucks in Hamza, he plants his feet on the ground, stretching a hand out toward mine. He's still getting drawn in and my fingers aren't long enough to grab his. "Find the donut in London!" he yells as the Ahriman tornado pulls him in and lifts off the ground, swooshing into the sky. "The donuuuuuuuut..." His voice trails off as the twister disappears in a blink.

I can't take my eyes off the spot where Ahriman just yanked my brother into a tornado and disappeared. My stomach twists in knots. How can we possibly fight that...thing...dev...evil tornado?

"What is a donut?" Aasman Peri asks as she

pushes herself off the ground. Her wings were pretty much useless against the strength of Ahriman's storm, and there's no way she could fly fast enough to catch up to them.

"Hello? Did you not just see what happened? How are you not freaking out?"

"My father always says panicking doesn't help anyone. And I seriously don't know what a donut is, so I'm gathering data. Isn't that something you are always going on about?"

Aasman Peri has a point. But I'm not going to admit it. "You don't have donuts in Qaf? You're really missing out. They're basically thick loops of cakey-fried dough with different frostings and glazes. About the size of your hand."

"That sounds...delicious, actually. I must try some of these donuts! Donuts in London!"

I shake my head. "I don't get it. What do donuts have to do with London? I don't think they're a British specialty? Is Ahriman hungry? Maybe Hamza is trying to feed him poison donuts. Nah. No way. We must have misheard him. Or maybe it was a code!" I say. "Before we figure out how to get to London, we need to figure out what he really meant. I'm assuming he means London, England, and not London, Wisconsin, which I'm pretty sure has only four buildings and probably zero museums."

Aasman Peri does not seem interested in my geography lesson and is already a couple of steps ahead of me, walking through the wrecked doorway of the OI. When I enter behind her, my jaw drops. The entire museum is a disaster. We follow a trail of broken artifacts from the lobby into the gallery and down the grand hall. I stop in my tracks. The *Lamassu*. The museum's most prized possession is shattered. "What did he do?" I mutter.

"They say he has a bad temper. He really must not have cared for all these looted goods." Aasman Peri picks up a broken piece of a vase.

I shudder. If this is how angry Ahriman gets at museum pieces that aren't in their original homes, then imagine how vengeful he's going to be toward the two kids who buried his son under a pile of fake gold rubble. I walk down the side hall and see a pattern of scorch marks on the ground around a plain-looking pedestal with an empty iron cradle on it. Whatever was in that cradle is missing, not broken. This is the only spot not littered with shards of destroyed relics.

"Check this out," I say to Aasman Peri, who is gathering pieces of a vase and trying to puzzle them back together. I lean in closer to read the placard on the podium and that's when I see it: the donut. "It says here that the OI has one-third of an ancient oculus—it's kind of a circular window made of a marbly substance that has not yet been identified!" My mind flashes back to the Box of the Moon, which was made of unknown alloys. This has to be it. I continue reading the placard. "Supposedly, there's a myth that once the three pieces are reunited, they will indicate the location of a lost city where a treasure is buried! That's it! That's it!" I say, pointing to a photo on the placard that shows a sketch of the completed oculus—it looks exactly like a smooth, marble, galaxy-colored glazed donut with tiny gold and silver sprinkles.

Aasman Peri, who was reading over my shoulder, nudges me.

"Excuse me," I say. "A little personal space, maybe?"

She rolls her eyes and points to a line under the sketch of the completed oculus. "It says the other two pieces are at the British Museum in London and the Louvre in Paris."

"That's why Hamza said London."

"British Museum, here we come!" Aasman Peri says. "I'm so interested in the ways humans display stolen antiquities for all to see! It's a strange thing to be proud of. *Come, look at how good a thief I am.* Truly, I am learning a lot on this trip."

"One problem. You can't fly me all the way across the Atlantic Ocean, can you? Ahriman has a big head start on us. We don't have the money to buy plane tickets. Oh! We could sneak you on, maybe? In the cargo hold, but you couldn't really breathe. Plus, it would be dishonest to not buy you a seat. We need solutions, here. C'mon, Amira. Think. Ugh. Even if we could figure it all out, the plane wouldn't get us there until tomorrow morning, British time...."

A smile creeps across Aasman Peri's face. "I really pity your sad human technology. We don't need a plane," she says as she flies toward the exit. "We need the Gate to the Clouds."

CHAPTER 9

Bean There, Done That

Amira

I CHASE AASMAN PERI AS SHE NEARS THE ENTRANCE OF the OI.

"Will you come down! You have to stop flying. Peris are not exactly normal down here."

Aasman Peri descends, a quizzical look on her face. "There's this strange human English phrase that I never really understood until this moment. I have read about it in your ancient media."

I shrug.

"Don't get your underwear in a bundle!" she says,

a wide, sarcastic grin spreading across her face. "You know only people with the collyrium on their eyes can see me. Also babies. And occasionally small children, who are constantly asking me for money in exchange for their baby teeth. What a strange custom! Dogs often see me as well. But in my experience, no one believes kids anyway. And dogs on this planet can't talk, correct?"

"Not generally, no." I sigh. "Well, can you at least walk so I can keep up? And what do you mean by the Gate to the Clouds? Is there a sky portal that can get us to London or something?" I ask as we step out the front entrance. The area around the OI is empty because of construction scaffolding, but some people are not far away, and one of them is pointing to the doors in the trees. Fantastic. "We need to get out of here," I say, and pull Aasman Peri to the side of the museum, behind a row of hedges where no one can see us. Maybe she's not visible to everyone, but I am, and I don't want to draw attention to myself.

Aasman Peri folds her wings and pulls a burgundy cape out of her bag. Not sure how it fit, because her little fanny pack is so small, but in Qaf I learned they got the Marie Kondo organizing thing down. "There, now babies won't try to tug at my wings. They are so grabby and their hands are so sticky. It's disgusting."

"What, don't peri babies have slobbery hands?"

"Of course not, we're perfect."

I roll my eyes. "Please just explain where we need to go."

She harrumphs. "The Gate to the Clouds. In Chicago, it is the passageway to one of the great earthly jinn cities. The entrance is a very large, shiny silver object at the heart of your metropolis. The jinn architect who built the doorway decided to hide it in plain sight. Very clever if you ask me. Humans see their reflection in it, but creatures of fire can see the grand jinn city of Abr ki Darwaaza."

A shiny object in the heart of the city? What is she… "Oh! You mean *Cloud Gate*! That has to be it!"

"Yes, yes. That's what I said. Have you not been paying attention?"

"Well, actually, you…" I stop myself, because

getting into a debate about *words* is really beside the point.

Whoa.

I made a choice not to get into an argument about something that I know I am 100 percent right about! My counselor at school would describe this as growth mindset. And for the record, Aasman Peri did call it by the wrong name, but I'm not rubbing her face in it. Yay, me!

"Anyway... we call it the Bean!"

"The Bean? That is a highly ridiculous name."

I shrug. "Maybe, but it works. If that's where we need to go to get to London, then c'mon. We can grab the Number Six Jeffery Express bus and it will take us right there," I say as I start running, Aasman Peri in tow.

"How exciting! I've never been on a human bus before!"

"I thought you said this was an express," Aasman Peri groans in my ear as the bus slows down for a bus stop. "This is very, very slow transport."

"Sssshhh. This is actually a very fast bus," I say as an elderly gentleman sitting across from us at the back of the bus looks up at me and nods and then quickly buries his face in a book. Ugh. He can't see Aasman Peri, so he probably thinks I'm one of those awkward weirdos on the bus who randomly talks to people. But whatever, he's the one wearing dress socks with sneakers. *Weird is awesome!* I hear Hamza's voice in my mind. I guess he was kinda right. I really, really hope he's okay. If wishing hard enough can make something come true, that's what I'm doing right now.

The bus stops along Michigan Avenue and I nudge Aasman Peri; the old man looks up at me again because I appear to be elbowing thin air. We hop off as a dude cruising on an electric scooter *while* staring down at his phone comes barreling toward us. "Look out!" I yell as I dive out of the way, headfirst into a flower bed. Aasman Peri whips off her cloak and flaps her wings so a gust of wind hits the guy, not just slowing him down, but pushing him backward. The confused look on his face cracks me up. He puts his feet down to stop the scooter and looks around, unsure what exactly happened.

Aasman Peri walks over and offers me a hand so I can stand up. I brush off some dirt and flower petals from my hair. "Nice move," I say.

"I know." She shrugs, then casts her eyes up at the shiny, silvery Bean sculpture that looks like, well, a giant mirrory kidney bean. It's the coolest sculpture ever. You can see yourself in it, plus the entire skyline. There's tons of tourists, taking selfies and goofing around. I've never seen anyone frown when they're in front of the Bean. It has to be one of the happiest spots in Chicago. Maybe anywhere.

"It's magnificent," Aasman Peri says as we climb up the stairs and step onto the giant, terraced stone courtyard that is the Bean's pedestal.

We start walking toward it. I've never seen Aasman Peri in awe of anything before, and, I mean, we rode a flying horse through a glittering dragon's mouth into a secret tilism and that didn't even impress her, so this is really something. "I've been here a million times," I say, "and it's amazing every time. But I haven't seen any trapdoor or anything."

"Of course you haven't. If humans could see it, they'd all clamor to get into Abr ki Darwaaza. They say there's no place comparable on Earth."

"Wait, you've never been?"

"Not to this particular jinn city, but I've studied it, done a lot of research on the jinnternet, and Abdul Rahman gave me a full rundown of it in case we needed supplies or help," Aasman Peri says as we approach the underside of the Bean.

The Bean is curved, and when you walk underneath and look up into its mirrored surface, you can see a million reflections of yourself. Aasman Peri reaches into her fanny pack and takes out a silver ring with a large green stone in its center and traces the pattern of a door in the metallic surface of the Bean. The outline glows green. She traces a small circle in the center, which I guess is a knob. No one around us notices at all.

"Does that turn into a door or—"

Before I can finish my sentence, Aasman Peri grabs my hand and pushes me through the outline she made and I stumble through liquid metal. It reminds me of the Lake of Illusion except without the giant serpent that can eat you. It feels cool on my skin and a little sticky, like a toddler's hand after lunch.

"You can open your eyes now, scaredy-cat." Aasman Peri shakes my shoulder.

I'm about to make a slightly rude comment, but when I pop my eyes open, my jaw drops. There's a long, bustling market street in front of me and thousands of creatures of fire, all different sizes and colors, winged and horned and striped and sharp-toothed. My eyes take a minute to adjust. I thought we were going to be in some dark, underground place, but the vibrancy of the clothes and awnings, of the trees and gardens, even the fountain bubbling out pink water in the center of a courtyard, is an explosion of color in my eyeballs. It reminds me a little of Choori Bazaar in Hyderabad—the long street lined with tons of bangle sellers with the colorful glass and metal bracelets floor-to-ceiling high in hundreds of stores with one wall open to the street. You can also get all sorts of costume jewelry there, spices, fabrics, antiques. It's my second-favorite market in Hyderabad after the Gudimalkapur flower market. In fact, this place reminds of that too, because of the smell of jasmine and roses wafting around me, and the loops of bright marigold garlands strung along the storefronts intertwined with tiny fairy lights. (Note to self: Do jinn also call them fairy lights? Maybe peri lights? Is that an insult to peris? Good question to ask someone who isn't Aasman Peri, because I can imagine her getting annoyed immediately.)

"Don't stand around with your mouth open. If a jinn-squito flies in there, you know it can take possession of your body, right?" Aasman Peri gives me a smile and sets off.

I snap my mouth shut. "Wait. Are you being serious?"

She smirks, then shrugs. "Keep up. We need to find this old peri scholar that my father told me about. She can give us the whole story behind the oculus."

I follow her as she winds her way around the market, between the creatures shopping and haggling over fruits and vegetables and clothes. I see a short, round-bellied yellow jinn wearing a sort of sari, hitting a young, skinny blue jinn over the head with her shiny black wooden cane. She's holding up a mango-like fruit, but its peel is studded with tiny pink jewels. "You call this ripe? This? How dare you try to fleece me, you upstart so-and-so! Trying to hoodwink your elder! You bring shame upon your clan!" The young blue jinn makes eye contact with me for a second and I give him a strained smile in return and mouth, "good luck." The auntie beatdown is apparently a real thing whether you're human or jinn.

Aasman Peri ducks under a red stone archway and through a smooth, dark wooden door that has wings engraved on it. We enter a huge oval room full of books. It's impossibly huge. The bookshelves are so high I can't see the tops. There's a wooden table in the center of the long hall, and floating lanterns cast a pale yellow light around the room. "Professor Khusrao! Professor Khusrao!" Aasman Peri calls, and her voice echoes up toward the never-ending shelves. A peri wearing a ruby coat pops out from behind a shelf and softly descends toward us, so gracefully—a ballerina with cream and silver wings.

"Ahh, princess, your father sent word that you might need my assistance," the wizened, old peri professor says. She has bronze-colored skin, a small bright blue mole by her mouth that matches her hair, and about one million wrinkles. Her ruby coat is threaded with gold needlework on the borders. As she nears, I get a closer look—the threads are embroidered into the shapes of books and quills, silver vines connecting them. *Cool.* I wouldn't mind a robe like that for myself. Maybe to wear when I'm doing homework, visiting the library, or even for select group activities. Total honor roll student vibes.

"Princess?" I roll my eyes.

"What? That is technically my title. You know my dad is the emperor. Maybe you should call me that, too, consider paying me some respect." Aasman Peri narrows her eyes at me.

"I bow to no one," I say. "I distinctly remember your dad saying that."

"Ahh, and you must be the hero of Qaf. The Chosen One. One of two, anyway." The old peri smiles.

"She is, Professor Khusrao. Even if looks would deceive." Aasman Peri chuckles. "Amira and her brother, Hamza, proved to be quite resourceful."

Whoa. Was that a compliment?

"In large part due to my help and training," Aasman Peri continues.

Maybe not such a compliment after all.

"Uhh, hi, Professor Khusrao. Your, um, Academic Greatness. Ahriman took my brother and has one-third of the oculus, and we have to go to London to get another part, and can you maybe fill us in and tell us how to save Hamza and, maybe, imprison Ahriman again? For good this time?" I rush out my words. Even though this market is cool, I know every second we're here is another moment that Hamza is being dragged farther away.

"Oh, dear me, that is distressing news indeed," Professor Khusrao says as she flies up and grabs a book the size of an old-school dictionary that I saw on a pedestal in the library once. She brings it down to the table in front of us, unbuckles two elaborate silver clasps, and flips it open to a blank page. Uhhh, this is not what I was expecting. The professor looks at me and smiles. Then places the book behind a small glass window that is set up on a stand on the table. I blink as words slide and shimmer into place and an image of the oculus pops off the page. Literally. It 3D-animates itself before my eyes, turning and twisting so we can see all sides of it behind the glass.

"It's a pop-up book," Aasman Peri says. "Don't you have those?"

I nod, distracted. The oculus looks like it's made of a shiny black marbly substance that contains galaxies. Flecks of silver and gold, tiny sprinkles, illuminate as they catch the light.

"Stars, planets, suns," Professor Khusrao says as she smiles. "Truly a gem of engineering that holds one of the world's great secrets."

Aasman Peri and I both turn to the peri professor

and she continues, turning the pages of the book behind the glass and narrating as each one comes to life before my eyes. "Suleiman the Wise buried his Ring of Power—the great ring that could control all creatures of fire, that could manipulate the weather, and that allowed him to speak to animals—so that his heirs could claim it."

My eyebrows shoot up hearing this. Talking to animals would be pretty amazing. Does it apply equally to land *and* sea creatures? Is it mind-to-mind or do animals understand all human languages or... oh... whoa, what if the Ring is a universal animal/human translator? That would be amazing! What material could it be made of? (Note to self: Investigate elements that have transitive properties or enable telepathy. Total winner at the science fair if I can figure this out.)

While I'm imagining the blue ribbon on my trifold science fair poster, Professor Khusrao continues, "It is by the power of this Ring that Suleiman defeated the evil Ahriman, banishing him to a brass vessel that he buried deep beneath the moon's surface."

"I still don't get why Suleiman didn't stab him with his sword or dust him with a dagger or shoot arrows at him and bury him in rubble like we did with Ifrit," I say.

"Ahh, an understandable question, young human. Ahriman is no mere dev. He is one of the most ancient creatures of fire, from an old line of beings, now nearly vanished from all realms, save the Emperor of Qaf and a few wizened, old souls." The professor grins. "It is said that Ahriman cannot be slain by the blade of a mortal. Some doubt whether he can be slain at all, even by celestial steel. According to legend, his ultimate demise would come at the hands of jinn alone—jinn warriors empowered by the Ring of Suleiman. Similarly to the Ring, this army is also lost, buried by time."

I gulp. If we can't destroy Ahriman and the jinn army that can defeat him is maybe a myth, how can we do anything to stop him? "Can the oculus help? That's the key to finding the Ring, right?"

"Indeed, wise hero. The oculus is bound to the Chosen One—the heir of Suleiman. Only by your hands can it be made whole again."

"Or my brother's."

"Or your brother's." Professor Khusrao nods. "Once the oculus is pieced back together, it is said there is a map at Star Axis that appears only when a beam of light from the North Star shines through the oculus, thus illuminating the location where the Ring of Power is buried. But the burden of this Ring is great. And as is true of so many magical objects, legends have grown around it. Some say it has a will of its own. Others say no mortal but the great and gifted Suleiman could ever wield it."

"So we basically have to piece together the oculus, get to this star place, figure out the whole X-marks-the-spot thing, then go dig up an ancient, powerful Ring and somehow keep it out of Ahriman's hands?" I sigh. Sure. Easy peasy. No problem. (Spoiler: It's a big problem.)

The professor twitches her nose. "In essence, yes. This is the task before you. It is a dangerous one, and I warn you that Ahriman takes no quarter. His furor over the death of his son is outmatched only by his greed to control the Ring and so control the worlds."

Aasman Peri bites her lip.

"Dang! That family is a serious bunch of control freaks," I mutter as ice runs through my veins. How am I possibly supposed to do all this? Save my brother? Save the world? *Again.*

"To London!" I shout, but my heart isn't really in it. I'm just trying to psych myself up. Professor Khusrao flies off to a far corner of the long hall and returns with a metallic-looking backpack and hands it to me.

"Once I heard that Ahriman had escaped, I was afraid things would come to this. I prepared these provisions for you and weapons for the battle ahead."

I unzip the pack and find a bow and arrow in there along with a dagger and some snacks, even some hand sanitizer. Definitely could not get this stuff through airport security. I mean, the sanitizer is clearly more than three ounces. I take my busted phone out of my tattered backpack and shove it into the shiny new one. Then remove the broken jade tablet and reluctantly hand it to the professor. "Maybe you can fix this? Or find someone who can?" It feels weird to give it away; it feels wrong that it will be out of my sight.

She smiles at me in this soft way that reminds me a little of my mom. "I know this is precious, and I will do my best to mend it."

"Thank you, Professor." Aasman Peri bows her head and places her hand on her heart. "My father is indebted to you for this kindness."

"There is no debt, princess. This is my duty. I shall stay here and prepare the jinn and peri for battle on the Chicago front, should it come to that. But if Ahriman gets the Ring, he will be able to control us all and command us to do his bidding. Good luck, young friends. Peace be with you on your journey ahead."

I nod and raise my hand to my heart in a gesture of thanks, imitating Aasman Peri. I hope I get to come back here, I think, looking around at the books. I bet I could write the most incredible research project on this place.

"Hurry," Aasman Peri says as we leave the scholar. "We need to get to a broom closet."

I hurry to follow her as she somehow is several

paces ahead of me already. I don't want to lose her in the crowd. "Hold up! You're going too fast! And why do we need brooms? Do they fly?"

Just as I catch up with her, Aasman Peri comes to a sharp halt, and I bump into her. She gives me this very exasperated look, her nostrils flaring. I give her the same look back. "We're here," she says, pointing to a plain, old wooden door that says CUSTODIANS on it. She opens the door into an office that is...a large broom closet. At one end is a desk, with a jinn in army-green overalls scribbling away at something. He raises a finger, gesturing at us to wait.

I take a look around. This place is a bit dank and dusty, but I have a feeling it's no ordinary broom closet. Rows of colorful brooms stand organized in large orange buckets. The bucket of brooms with violet bristles is marked with a label that says GLASS. Other buckets have labels that say: SMOKE, FIRE, ASH, EARTH, CERAMICS, MOLTEN METAL, SOLID METAL, CONCRETE, GOO...goo? The shelves above have various boxes and bins all marked with similar labels. It's all quite impressively organized.

"Now what can I help you with?" The jinn raises his very large bespectacled face. It's a glaring shade of neon green, and it's hard not to stare. "A human!" he suddenly yelps. "Why, who do you think you—"

"I am daughter of the Emperor of Qaf. And *this* human is a Chosen One, savior of Qaf. And we seek your assistance."

"Ahh, excuse me, princess." He jumps out of his chair and adjusts his tiny, round metal glasses. "I think I need a new prescription for these things," he mutters. "Amar Akbar Anthony, president of the JEIU, at your service."

"JEIU?" I ask.

"Jinnator Employees International Union, Miss Chosen One," he says, making me giggle a little. Jinnator.

I think Aasman Peri knows what I'm laughing at because she says, "They clean up messes that humans make."

"That's what human janitors do, too," I say.

Amar Akbar Anthony and Aasman Peri both

start laughing like I've said the most hilarious thing they've ever heard.

"No, miss. The messes we clean up on Earth tend to be of a more supernatural or disastrous type."

"Yeah, that giant mess at the Oriental Institute, for example," Aasman Peri says.

"Indeed. I have my best crew on that already. Every vase, artifact and even that giant *Lamassu* will be glued or soldered to original condition. No one will be any the wiser."

"Whoa. You can do that?" I ask.

"It is one of our two prime responsibilities. Humans, admittedly sometimes because of jinn mischief, can create quite horrifying messes. In fact, the entire reason we were founded 136 years ago is because right before the dedication of the Statue of Liberty, a rowdy group of jinn gave chase to some humans to scare them and the arm and torch of Lady Liberty ended up falling into the harbor. It was quite a disaster. But we had the area cloaked, an illusion put in place for the humans while we fixed the mess. And had the Lady back in order before the ceremony. No muss. No fuss," he says, rubbing his hands together. "You know, I've always liked that statue. And especially the poem on a plaque there about welcoming all to America's shores. Those are nice sentiments. If only your kind could find a way to put them into practice." He gives me a sidelong glance.

I nod. Thinking of all the ways America hasn't lived up to those promises because of racism, because so many elected leaders don't have love and generosity in their hearts. Gen Z is better than that, though. I know we are.

"So what's your second responsibility?" I ask.

"Transport!" Aasman Peri yelps. "This is going to be so fun. And Ahriman won't know about it."

The jinnator hands Aasman Peri a dull brass key on a tarnished chain. She turns it over to me. "It doesn't go with my outfit. At all," she says, looking down at her long, gold-embroidered kurta pajamas. I know the green chemise and tight pants are her traveling clothes, but they're still wedding-guest fancy.

I slip the chain over my head and hold the key

between my fingers as it starts to give off a small yellow light. My eyes look to the jinnator for answers.

"Of course, forgive me. The JEIU runs broom closets in every great city on Earth. Our biggest cities have multiple closets. Each closet is connected—a network of portals across the globe. Ahriman will be unaware of them because the entire network was created during his imprisonment." The jinnator shudders. "May you imprison him again soon, Chosen One. The key around your neck will glow as you near any closet portal. You need only to use the key and enter the closet, and a jinnator will be immediately summoned to your aid."

My eyes light up. "So the travel is instantaneous?"

We did a big weather unit last year and went to this exhibit at the Museum of Science and Industry, where you can sort of simulate a tornado in an enclosed chamber to study its properties. And our guide said that the fastest speed a tornado was recorded traveling at was around seventy miles per hour. So if London is...

"Uh...does anyone know how far London, England, is from here?" I ask.

"About four thousand Earth miles," the jinnator answers. "We have to know distances in multiple systems. Really would be helpful if America could just go metric."

Aasman Peri is giving me a weird look, but I don't care. "At seventy miles per hour, and with London four thousand miles away, it would take Ahriman's tornado about fifty-seven hours to get there. We'll totally beat him!" I do a little fist pump, but then I think about my poor brother, who is going to be whirling around across the Atlantic, potentially non-stop puking his brains out.

"While it is exciting news that some humans can do math in their heads, it hardly matters in this case since Ahriman isn't actually an earthly meteorological event. He's a supernatural creature made of smokeless fire. One of the most ancient. He can travel at incredible speeds. We'll be lucky to get there at the same time as him."

My heart sinks a little. Normally I would be begging to explore this incredible jinn city, right here in Chicago, in the Bean! I'd be asking the jinnator for an explanation of the physics of the jinnator network and how it manipulates space-time. But all I can think about is Hamza and how every new thing I learn about Ahriman only makes things feel a million times worse.

Aasman Peri looks at me, and I'm pretty sure she can guess what I'm thinking. "We need to get to London, now. The British Museum, to be precise."

Amar Akbar Anthony hurries us to a door at the back of the office. A closet in a closet! He gestures for me to unlock the door with the glowing key. I do, and we step into a regular, old, smallish broom closet. There are mops in here. A trash pail. Some garbage bags. And an electrical panel that the jinnator opens. He enters in some numbers with shaky fingers and spins a dial and shuts it. He sees me staring at his jittery hands. "I get a little nervous under pressure! But those JPS coordinates should do the trick. It will get you inside the British Museum. We actually have quite a few closets in London. The jinnator network there is very strong. First-time travelers might experience a slight dizziness, some dehydration. Possible hair loss, and your fingernails may fall off, but that is only in the rarest of cases! By traveling via the network, you agree that the JEIU is not responsible for loss of limb, life, or otherwise normal human functioning. Have fun!"

"Wait! Did you say my fingernails would fall off?" I yell as a loud whirring noise fills the space around us. "And what does 'otherwise normal human functioning' mean?"

Amar Akbar Anthony smiles and begins to shut the door. "You might want to close your eyes so the blue lights don't temporarily blind you. Bon voyage, as you humans say!"

"I don't think—" I can't finish my thought because a gust of wind smacks my face as the room starts to spin. I squeeze my eyes shut and reach out to grab onto something because the floor starts to fall away.

AAAAHHHHHH!!

CHAPTER 10

(A) London Bridge Is Falling Down

Hamza

"GAH! SLOW DOWN! IT'S LIKE I'M IN A BLENDER! I'M NEVER going to look at a smoothie the same way again!"

Ahriman's voice echoes around me. "We must make haste!"

"It's your choice. Get puked on again or slow down. Honestly, it's a no-brainer."

"Fine. If only to get you to stop talking. Do all modern humans speak at this dizzying rate?"

"No. I'm special. It's a gift," I say as the whirlwind

slows down around me. I flatten my hands against the spinning smoke, and I stick to the interior like I have suction cups on my palms. This is better. At least I'm not being battered around inside the tornado. Okay. I'm going to open my eyes. I'm going to be okay. Deep breaths. Deep breaths. I think this is the yoga breathing we learned in gym.

You rode on a flying horse and in a flying throne. You scaled the highest wall at the rock-climbing gym. You also frequently get dizzyingly vomit-y when faced with heights. Do you kick against the devnado, hoping to slow down Ahriman so Amira can get to you, working against the centipede force...no, scratch that, centripetal force...of the twister? Possibly risking injury or death. Or do you continue to cling to the walls pretending you're riding the most evil Gravitron in the world, making it easier for Ahriman to travel and get to the next piece of the oculus. Honestly, both of these are terrible choices. Design! Your! Destiny!

What? No. That was the worst *Design! Your! Destiny!* choice ever. Of course, it was all in my imagination and, oh, holy puke-worthy carnival rides, I really, really wish this were a book so I could cheat and go back a couple of pages. But I can't. I take a deep breath. I hear Amira's voice in my mind: *C'mon, Hamz. You got this.* I flash my eyes open and look down through the small hole at the bottom of this swirling funnel I'm being spun around in. Uhhhh, holy—"Is that the ocean? Ahhhh! I one hundred percent do not got this! I can see the ocean through a hole in a devnado that I am swirling around in! Okaaaay. No big deal. I'm okay. I'm okay. This is fine. This is all fine. So normal."

Ahriman's voice booms from inside the tornado. "I was imprisoned in that brass vessel for millennia, but even I know your strange soliloquy is not normal. Are you unaware of the concept of keeping thoughts to yourself?"

Rude! I get that this guy is super evil and wants to take over the world and make all jinn and humans do his bidding or whatever, but he could at least be polite about it. I'm about to say something, but I decide to shut my mouth and close my eyes. My mouth because it's probably a good idea not to give away everything I'm thinking. And my eyes because even though the Atlantic Ocean is cool as a concept, staring down at the angry blue-gray waves is not helping me keep it together.

The devnado starts to slow, and I see twinkling lights below us over a clear night sky. That must be it! I see London...I see France...I see Ahriman's underpants. Hahaha. But for real, I don't actually want to see dev dude's underwear. Sometimes even I know when I've gone too far. But it's hard to pass up a good line!

We slow even more, and then I feel the tips of my toes touch solid ground, but that's only for a second, because I immediately fall over, biting it on a narrow sidewalk. My first close-up view of London is a bunch of dirty cobblestones with random pieces of gum and other goop sticking to them. *Gross.* It reminds me of when our two-year-old cousin came over and wiped her gloppy toddler hand across my face after eating applesauce. *Blech.* Even I thought it was disgusting, and I have a high tolerance for mess. Wish Amira were here....She would totally have hand sanitizer. I push myself up and turn to see the devnado shrinking. Ahriman spins out of it; for a tiny second even he looks a bit dizzy and grabs his head.

I look beyond him and see a wide river that looks really dirty and a bridge behind us. "Hey! Is that London Bridge? It's more modern than I thought it would be and doesn't seem to be falling down at all."

Ahriman shakes his head and gets this annoyed look on his face. Dang, he must have been the worst parent ever. "That is Waterloo Bridge. There have been many London Bridges, some of which collapsed, hence that human ditty you're referencing."

"Whoa. You actually got a sort of not-ancient reference."

"When I possessed the IT expert, I was able to access a type of program that allows you to see different places on Earth via map coordinates and gives tidbits of historical information."

"Google Maps? Google Earth?"

Ahriman scrunches his bushy eyebrows together. "Uhhh. Yes. I believe so. I was surprised that humans came up with such a clever and useful tool. Normally everything you do is so clunky."

"Listen, if you think Earth is the worst, you can stick yourself back in moon rocks!"

A low growl comes out of Ahriman. I can't say it comes from his mouth, because his lips are shut. He seems to be snarling with his whole body, and it sends electric shocks of fear right into my gut. I look around, trying to turn away from Ahriman's beady-eyed gaze that is the creepiest of creep fests. I see a black oval structure that's twice as tall as me and maybe three times as wide with a sign that says TOILET around the top. It's an oval, UFO-shaped restroom! And it reminds me that I have to pee. "Dude, I really need a pee break, okay?" I say, pointing to the toilet UFO.

He narrows his eyes at me. "Again? Humans are truly inefficient creatures." I make pleading eyes at him, so he nods with his lips turned up in a sneer, like he's grossed out by me. *Whatever.* I cautiously walk up to the funky-looking toilet. I turn to glance over my shoulder at Ahriman and see he's done that 180-degree head-spin trick to watch me. Worst and best trick ever. But when I get to the sliding door, I notice a coin slot.

"I have to pay to pee? That's terrible! Peeing is a human right! Also, I don't have any money," I say to Ahriman. "I swear I'm going to pee in this river if—"

Ahriman harrumphs and sends a pulse of flame toward the coin slot. It heats up and the latch on the sliding door unlocks. Phew. Accident averted. I've never peed in a public toilet UFO thingy. It's kind of cool, actually. I step inside and slide the door closed behind me. A light turns on.

Uhh. That thing I said about it being cool? Totally wrong. The outside looks all metallic sci-fi-ish, but the inside is a regular old public toilet.

When I step out, I see Ahriman bent over, whispering something into the river. Maybe this is my chance. I could push him in and make a run for it. Where would I go? The embassy! Yes, the US Embassy, that's where Americans in trouble are constantly gunning for in movies. There's got to be one here. Somewhere. I bend my knees, clench my hands into fists, and pull them back, ready to take off, when Ahriman stands, raises his palm over the river, and says, "Utao. Utao. Utao."

A bright blue light appears in the dark river, and the water starts angrily sloshing around. A human-shaped wave shoots out of the water and lands on the pavement. Ahriman turns to face it. There's a small circle of flame *inside* the watery figure. How does that even work? I keep staring, my mouth open as the water spins and transforms into a...girl. She has long, shiny blue ombré hair and shimmery, iridescent skin. She looks right at me with brilliant silver eyes and smiles. Wow. "Whoa," I say to her, "I'm not sure what you are. But there should be comic books written about you."

She giggles and cups her hand, raising it slightly toward her forehead—I've seen some people in Hyderabad do this when they say their greetings. It's called an adab. "I am Bijli," she says. Her voice is tinkly, like a high key on a piano. "I am a baharia. One of the last ancient jinn of the Earth seas."

Ahriman steps closer to her and puts his hand around her upper arm. I hear a sizzling sound and steam rises from where he touches her. She winces.

"Stop that!" I say. "You're hurting her."

Ahriman ignores me. "I call upon the baharia now to repay that which you owe. To hold fast to your oath. Do you agree? Or will you suffer my wrath?"

Bijli closes her eyes for a second and wiggles her way out of Ahriman's grasp.

"What's happening?" I ask her. "What do you have to pay? Money? Did you lose a bet?"

She gives me a small smile. "I wish that it were merely money. Many Earth moons ago, we baharia roamed the warm, wide waters of the Pacific Ocean. At peace. At leisure. Coming to the aid of ships that may have strayed off course."

Whoa. I wonder if they're the reason we have mermaid stories!

Bijli continues, "But a kraken ripped the seafloor and pulled many of my sisters into the deepest molten earth. One of my sisters called upon Ahriman for help. He fought the kraken, pushing him back into Earth's mantle. And rehoming us here, to keep us safe, should the kraken emerge again. But it was not a gift freely given. We now owe him a debt."

Ahriman bares his teeth. "Your sisters sought

me out. I gave my aid. I saved those of you who remained. Now you must pay. You know it is impossible to refuse."

I don't know what to say. Bijli looks really sad and Ahriman's anger heats the entire sidewalk around us.

"What form of repayment do you seek?" Bijli asks.

"We must have safe passage to the British Museum. None may follow us. Flood the bridges. Seal it off from all."

Bijli sucks in her breath. "What do you intend to take from the museum?"

"The oculus piece!" I shout. "He's making me piece them back together. He'll hurt my family if I don't."

"Silence, human!" Ahriman roars at me.

"You are the Chosen One?" Bijli whispers.

I nod, a frown on my face. I don't feel much like a Chosen One right now. Unless it means chosen for really bad luck. She nods in return. She knows we're both stuck.

"When we do this, then our debt will be fully repaid. We no longer owe you our allegiance?"

Ahriman narrows his eyes at her and then nods in agreement. "You shall be released from your bond."

Bijli walks over to me and places a hand on my cheek. It's cool and watery. "It was an honor to meet you, Chosen One."

I'm glad it's dark out, because I blush a little when she says that. Embarrassing!

"Suleiman the Wise entrusted you with his secrets. And with his powers. Have faith in yourself as we have faith in you. Peace be with you," she says.

"And also with you," I respond.

Bijli points her hands above her head, her palms meeting, and dives up into the air, arcing into the water and transforming back into the water figure I first saw when she appeared, a circle of flame in her middle. Drops of water are all around me. I want to smile because that is one of the most amazing things I've ever seen. But I can't. My hands are shaking and my eyes sting. I don't want to cry. I can't cry. I don't want to show Ahriman my fear. But who am I kidding, he's got to already know how terrified I am. Scaring people is what he does, but I have to ignore my fear and pretend to be brave, otherwise, I'll freeze in place. *Fake it till you make it,* Amira and I kept saying in Qaf. I guess it's going to have to work here, too.

Ahriman turns his back to me and looks into the river. "It begins," he mutters.

I rush to his side to watch as bright blue lights fill the river. And the level of the water right below us starts to drop. I look to the left and see all the water getting pulled back, like an invisible hand is dragging it. Then it rises into a giant wall.

Oh no. Oh no. "Run!" I yell to the few people on the bridge above us. I see them turn to look at the river and then I hear screams as they rush off the bridge. There's the sound of honking and cars racing away. Then the wall rears up and the bottom starts to move and the top crests into a wave and…uh-oh. TIDAL WAVE!

CHAPTER 11

Donut Stop Me Now

Amira

I CAN'T OPEN MY EYES. I REFUSE TO OPEN MY EYES. IS THERE any mode of fire-creature transport that doesn't give me the sensation of getting sucked into a black hole, losing all sense of space-time?!

The spinning stops. I feel all my organs lift up like when you jump on an elevator while it's moving and then they settle back. I suck in my breath and open my eyes.

"It's still a broom closet," I say.

"Wow. Humans really do have a profound grasp of the obvious," Aasman Peri smirks.

"Let's go! Hamza needs us." I reach for the doorknob.

Aasman Peri puts her hand on mine. "Listen, Ahriman isn't just incredibly dangerous, he's also a trickster and can possess you, and you'll be none the wiser. We probably can't take him on by ourselves, so I've called in reinforcements."

I nod. I'm glad we're getting some help. But to be honest, my one and only priority is to rescue Hamza. If Ahriman needs a Chosen One to help him complete his mission to collect all the oculus pieces, then it makes sense for Hamz and me to get as far away from him as possible. Run. Make sure our parents are safe, too. But since he's pretty much a bajillion years old and nearly impossible to defeat, how long would we have to hide for? Our entire lives? I mean, we'll always be the Chosen Ones, even though I find that a highly debatable term and am still not sure it applies to us since it kind of started with a case of mistaken identity, then maybe became a self-fulfilling prophecy. And, yeah, it's, uh, pretty complicated. But...

"Charge!" While I'm dueling with vocabulary words in my brain, Aasman Peri unsheathes one of her daggers, pushes past me, and rushes out the closet door. Straight into...a small, round table with a red-and-white-checkered tablecloth on it and a small vase of yellow daffodils. The smell of sugar and coffee fills the air.

"This does not look like the British Museum," I say. Despite never having visited, I am pretty confident I'm right as I scan the dark, empty space, taking in the counter, the blackboard menu with all sorts of tea listings on it, and the various cakes and pastries in the glass-fronted display case. I pick up a menu from next to the cash register: BRITISH MUSEUM TERRACE CAFÉ. "We're in the wrong place!"

"Perhaps the coordinates Amar Akbar Anthony entered into the JPS were a little off." Aasman Peri frowns.

"A little off? It's super off. The off-est. That Jinn Positioning System needs a serious update! It's totally glitchy!"

"But look." She points outside the plate glass window. "There's a sign pointing over the bridge that says BRITISH MUSEUM."

I look outside and see that we're on a sidewalk by the Thames. Honestly, I think it should be written *t-e-m-z* because that's the way it's pronounced and having that *th* in there is extra confusing. I never realized how hard and weird the English language sometimes is until one of my cousins visited from Hyderabad and asked why *ph* sometimes has an *f* sound and why *gh* had to exist at all. Good questions. Anyway, there's the Thames and a sign that shows the British Museum across the Waterloo Bridge.

My stomach grumbles so loudly Aasman Peri shoots me a strange look. "Sorry," I say. "I'm starving."

Ugh. There's so much sugary, sweet goodness in here that the healthy snacks Professor Khusrao packed for us don't tempt me at all. I don't think there's any packaging that could make Peri Blue Turnip Cakes seem appetizing. Dang. I sound like Hamz.

Aasman Peri rolls her eyes. "There's food all around us; why don't you take something?"

"Uh, because all I have is twenty dollars. American dollars. So I can't pay for it, and that would be what we call stealing."

"That museum is full of stolen stuff," Aasman Peri harrumphs. "Here." She lifts up the round glass lid of a cake stand and pulls out a blueberry scone and hands it to me. "Just eat it." Then her eyes grow wide as they fall on another stand piled high with... chocolate-glazed donuts.

She looks at me, her mouth in a perfect O.

I nod. "Yes, those are donuts." I expect her to grab a couple, but she's almost frozen in awe. They do look delicious, but who knew donuts could have such a strong effect on anyone... well, besides Hamza. I reach for some waxed paper, grab a bag, and drop a couple in there. I feel so guilty doing it, though. "For the record," I continue, "I think this is totally wrong and I've never stolen anything in my life."

Aasman Peri snaps out of her sugar dream daze and turns to me. "I promise, if we rescue Hamza, *and* save Earth *and* Qaf from complete evil-dev domination, we will figure out a way to pay for this with proper, uh... ounces."

"It's pounds! I thought you said you were Qaf's premier scholar of all things human."

"Ounces! Pounds! Frankly, I don't understand why everything isn't the metric system. Can't this planet be unified about anything?"

"Cat videos, maybe? TikToks of chubby babies laughing? Besides, money and the metric system are totally unrelated things.... I think."

Aasman Peri shakes her head, but before she can give me a sarcastic reply, alarms start blaring all across the city. I shove all the food into my backpack as we race out the front door of the café, just as six peris dressed in matching silver-and-turquoise kurta pajamas and with different lengths and styles of magenta hair descend on the sidewalk. An arc of embroidered letters near the right shoulders of their uniforms reads: *Peri Royal Institute*. But there's no time for introductions.

"Princess, we received your message from Chicago's

lead jinnator. My name is Nayeli and we are all at your service." I'm mesmerized because, when Nayeli talks, their voice sounds like a song.

Aasman Peri says something to them in a language of Qaf. I don't understand her, but she's gesturing a lot with her hands. As she's talking, I step closer to the river's edge, the loud alarm ringing across the city and echoing down the streets. I watch as people scatter, quickly taking shelter in homes and buildings. It's dark, too dark, and I realize all the lights along the bridges and in this entire quarter are out. Birds are squawking in alarm, flying higher and away from the city. Then I hear a muffled roar and I turn to look down the riverbanks. I see a giant wall of water rising up from the Thames, higher than the surrounding buildings, and a blue glow is coming from it. My blood freezes. That's not a natural phenomenon.

"Tidal wave!" I scream. The wave is so huge it could drown half of London.

"It's the baharia! Antivortex!" Aasman Peri yells. And the six British peris fly up into the air, all their actions in unison, and start flying in a circle. It's a fairy merry-go-round but so fast it's a giant blur of funnel, streaks of silver and magenta, spinning faster, rising high into the air, higher, generating more speed. Then, they dive down right into the baharia—whatever that is—tidal wave. I see a flash of blue and sparks of magenta. The peris are sucking the tidal wave back into the river, even as it's straining to race closer to Waterloo Bridge.

Aasman Peri grabs my hand, "Don't stand there gawking, we have to get to the museum, now!" We race up toward the bridge and start to cross. My heart fills with terror that we'll all be drowned. I don't take my eyes off the peri funnel and the tidal wave; it's shrinking, but I can see a battle waging inside the water. I stumble and fall on the bridge, skinning my knee. I can't tell through my jeans, but I'm sure it's bleeding. "Wait!" I yell at Aasman Peri, but she's already flown ahead. I push myself up. Grimace when I take a first step to run toward her, my knee throbbing, but I don't have time to find an ice pack and a bandage. In the distance, I hear my brother's voice, screaming, and then drowned out by the sound of rushing water.

When I make it across the bridge, I see Aasman Peri at the bottom of the steps of the British Museum, her daggers out, hovering near a blue watery creature. My eyes glance up—the museum is huge and has a Greek temple look to it, the kind we learned about when we studied mythology in class. It's white stone with huge columns that rise a few stories high. This museum holds so many antiquities—sculptures, paintings, and even the Elgin Marbles that I read about in class. They also have a huge collection of Mughal art from India that I really wish I could see. I push all of that out of my mind. I'm not here as a tourist. I'm here to save my brother. But I don't think we're going to get into the museum that easily. That watery creature I saw from a distance has put up a wall of water behind her and has taken the shape of a girl. I grab the bow from my pack and string an arrow. Even though it's been a couple of months, my muscles move automatically to nock the arrow precisely, to shift my weight into the proper stance that

Maqbool taught me. Then I move to line up directly below Aasman Peri. I understand why she's straining to fly. A gale force wind is pushing against us. That water-girl-creature-thing stands with palms out and open toward us. Her right hand is pushing out—she's creating this wind. I tilt my head down slightly and take a step forward, holding tightly to my bow and arrow. Aasman Peri descends and joins me on foot.

"You don't need to do this!" I yell. "Ahriman kidnapped my brother. I just want to take him home!"

"It's no use trying to reason with a baharia," Aasman Peri spits. "These ancient water jinn are loyal to Ahriman. They're traitors to my father and all creatures of Qaf."

The baharia gets a pained expression on her face as Aasman Peri speaks. "We are bound," she says. "Not by choice, but by an oath made long, long ago, overseen by the great Bahamut, he who supports the very Earth and can create a quake so great under the sea that we would all be swallowed. Ahriman has returned and forced us to pay our debt. We are incapable of refusing such a pact."

"But if he gets the Ring of Power, you'd be under his control forever. Don't you get it? Please, help us. Join us," I plead, hopelessly, while watching Aasman Peri change the grip on the dagger in her right hand and plant her embroidered jutti shoes in a fighting stance.

The baharia turns to me. "Would that I could. Your brother is safe for now. And will be as long as Ahriman needs him to get the oculus."

"And then what?" I yell, fighting back tears because I'm afraid I know the answer. "What happens to him then? He's annoying and really needs to mind his own business, but he's my little brother and Majids stick together."

The baharia looks down; maybe she realizes she's wrong. But I don't have time to wait. Hamza doesn't have time. All of us—the entire world—is in danger.

I shift my shoulders and give Aasman Peri a little nod. She hurls her dagger and I let my arrow fly at the same time, straight at the baharia.

She looks up, her eyes flashing silver. She pulls her left palm back and then thrusts it toward us.

The wall of water behind her shoots in an arc above her head, blocking the dagger and my arrow. As they clatter to the ground, she unleashes a volley of tiny, twisting typhoons from her hand—the spinning, watery bullets are aimed right at us.

CHAPTER 12

Glazed & Confused

Hamza

MY SHOES ARE SOAKED. *ALSO,* I WAS ALMOST DROWNED BY a giant tidal wave that the baharia made. *In a river.* If Amira were here, she would probably explain how bonker-balls weird that tidal wave was by using math or weather science, but I was there and I don't need equations to tell me it was scary as heck! And 100 million percent absolutely not normal.

Right now, I'm being forced to squelch-stomp around in *another* museum. Two museums in one day is a total record for me. But at least I have chips.

Or crisps. Fries are chips. Chips are crisps. So strange! Not sure why they can't just say chips, it's like their English is all weird in...England. Wait. That doesn't make sense. Whatever. These tomato-basil crisps, which I thought would be disgusting, are actually not half bad. And beggars can't be choosers, which is what the head lunch lady at school always tells us when we complain about the soggy pizza crusts even though we're actually buying our food. Adults really are full of strange and confusing sayings that mostly make no sense.

Ahriman is skulking around all quiet. And deadly. Kind of like when my friend Aidan's dog is gassy. Trust me, you do not want to be trapped in a car with that pup. Though at least Aidan's dog wouldn't threaten to destroy your family if you didn't help him find the one thing he needs to take control of all of Earth and Qaf. Unless Aidan's dog is an evil dev, which might explain a few things.

"Hurry along, small human! I provided you with food; no need to be so slow!" Ahriman's voice bellows down the hall as we pass a bunch of...

"Whoa! Are those cat mummies? They mummified cats?! Cool!"

"You are aware, strange child, that to mummify required removing the brains and organs from the beast and that some of those beasts might have been killed for the express purpose of mummification and entombment with their owners."

That description makes me gag a little. *Blech.* I'm pretty sure you couldn't come back from that even if you had nine lives. "Too much gross information," I say to Ahriman. "Have you ever thought about keeping some thoughts to yourself?"

Ahriman stops and looks at me. "I have been thinking of it quite a lot since we met."

I nod.

Hey! Wait. That was an insult. I think.

Ahriman speeds up again through the enormous gallery. I can barely keep up with him, so I don't get a chance to look at much else. Not that I *want* to look at a bunch of old stuff in a museum. Okay, maybe I do a little bit, because some of this stuff is pretty cool, but I'm not admitting that in public or to Amira.

We turn into a long room marked with a sign that says: THE ALBUKHARY FOUNDATION GALLERY OF THE ISLAMIC WORLD. It's dark and quiet, and there are lit-up cases all along the walls and large glass exhibits lining the center of the gallery. There are vases and pottery and ancient books and intricate prayer rugs. There are old Qurans with Arabic written in gold. There are super-fancy robes and marble statues. My parents and Amira would really love this place. If I weren't on a doomsday mission with a terrifying dev, I'd maybe check some of this stuff out, maybe even read a placard. Ahriman takes another turn into a room with a bunch of instruments and tools. Like ones we saw at the eclipse astronomy exhibit. Amira's nerd brain would be going haywire looking at all these astrology artifacts. No. I think it's astronomy. Some of it kind of seems more astrology-ish, though. Why do they make so many words that sound sort of alike to describe stuff that's also sort of alike? Do language makers not realize how confusing that is? Is language maker a job? If it is, I bet I would be awesome at it.

I'm so busy trying to remember the exact difference between astronomy and astrology that I nearly bump into the case Ahriman is standing in front of. It's the second piece of the oculus, and it's the same as the first, a shiny, glazy giant bite of donut with gold and silver sprinkles inside it. I didn't have time to really study the first shard. I mean, I'm not exactly an archaeologist, but now when I stare into this oculus piece, it's mesmerizing. All those tiny sprinkles look kind of like galaxies and constellations and stuff. I rub my eyes to make sure I'm not hallucinating from hunger, but I still see the universe in that chocolaty, marbly glaze. I don't know if Ahriman notices the same thing, and I don't mention it. See, I can totally keep some things to myself. This time the oculus piece rests on a Lucite stand held up on a dark brown pedestal. Only problem, there's a glass box around it.

"Bummer! Even though I'm a Chosen One, I can't reach through glass. That'd be a seriously awesome trick, but we didn't get any real powers." I'd hoped Amira and Aasman Peri would've maybe figured out a way here by now, but I'm not sure how they'd even get to London. Maybe Aasman Peri could fly them over? Oooh, maybe Zendaya came, too. I really miss that flying horse. Who is 100 percent absolutely not named after my celebrity crush. Totally not, no matter how much Amira teases me about it.

Ahriman raises his hands in front of him, and the red of his skin turns even redder, a deep, deep bloodred, almost purple. He's heating them up. Oh no.

The evil dev is busy preheating his hands as if they were an oven before you make cookies, except without the cookies. Or the oven. Using this moment, while he is focused elsewhere, you could push Ahriman from behind, hoping he falls onto his flaming hands, setting himself on fire, while you make a run for it. Or you could stall, causing a distraction, hoping help arrives in time, because so far he seems immune to his own heat, knowing that sometimes inaction is the best course of action. Design! Your! Destiny!

Geez. Really wish I had powers right now to zap myself someplace. Preferably a restaurant. An ice-cream shop. A taco truck. Any place but here. But

I'm the only one standing between the oculus pieces and Ahriman's world-domination dreams. Who knew being a hero came with so much thinking and so many hunger pangs?

"Hey!" I say. "Uh..." *Think, Hamz.* What's going to distract him? "Oh! Did you hear the terrible news? A cheese factory exploded!" I wait for him to turn away from staring at the flames in his hands, to look at me. Maybe he just needs the punch line. "Da Brie was everywhere!" I snort and start laughing. That's totally a good one. But I don't even get a grunt from Ahriman.

Okay, different angle...

"Ahriman! Yo, Ahriman! If the oculus is so powerful, why didn't Ifrit ever try to get the pieces? I mean, if they're the key to the Ring of Power, why didn't *he* try to kidnap me and Amira, bring us back to Earth, and make us do his bidding? Basically, what you're doing." Was it totally dumb to bring up Ifrit? His son that got smoked under a heap of rubble in the City of Gold tilism? Because of me and Amira. Maybe. But he's rudely immune to my jokes and it doesn't seem like Ahriman is a big comic or Star Wars fanboy, so I don't think I can get his attention with geek talk about, say, who shot first, Han or Greedo (duh, it was Han).

"You dare bring up my son? You who caused his demise?" Ahriman lowers his hands. It's working! I'm outsmarting him! Or at least annoying him enough to distract him!

"Well, actually, to be fair, it was Amira and me, together. Because teamwork makes the dream work." My voice fades to a whisper while Ahriman's eyes bore a hole through me. Not literally. Though, I guess, maybe he could totally burn a hole in me. But, la-la-la, I have a very vivid imagination, so I'm pretending I didn't say that so I won't think about it.

Crud. Now I'm thinking about it.

Ahriman sighs. I think it's a sigh, because small puffs of smoke shoot out of his nostrils. I take a step back in case he's about to get really pissed off. He needs me alive to get the oculus, but he could singe my eyebrows right off if he wanted to.

"Who can say why my son did not think of this?

Perhaps he did not have a true warrior's cunning. Perhaps it was his mother's failure for encouraging him to hide rather than fight. He chose to avenge me using others to bring you down. Rather than confronting Shahpal bin Shahrukh and facing you directly from the start. But in my absence, he was raised to be a coward."

This delay scenario is brilliant! I'm a strategy genius! I'm playing three-dimensional checkers. Or is it chess? Either way, I'm using my brains and not just my foam dart bowcaster to get the upper hand here (wouldn't mind if I had it with me, though). "Not to be all on Ifrit's side or anything, but it's kind of not fair to blame his mother. I mean, she was pretty much a single mom since you were impri—"

Ahriman tightens his jaw, and his hands clench into fists. Ooops.

"I mean, uh..." I stumble for the right words. "Since you were away for most of Ifrit's life, right? Hundreds of human years or whatever? That's gotta be rough. I don't know the child care situation in Qaf, but our neighbor Jake's parents are divorced and his dad lives in California. And once I heard his mom telling my mom about how she sometimes had trouble finding babysitters for him when she had to work late. So once in a while he comes over to our house for dinner when his mom is stuck at her office. My mom always says it takes a village to raise kids and do laundry. Ifrit didn't exactly have a village in his fake-gold tilism."

I swear Ahriman's shoulders droop a little, but the angry look on his face doesn't change. Honestly, I think it's just his resting dev face. He would probably look even more scary if he tried to smile with all his vampire-y teeth. His chest starts to heave up and down, like he's the big bad wolf about to blow down one of the three little pigs' houses. Uh-oh.

"His failures are not my doing!" Ahriman yells. "Though I need you to get the oculus pieces, I will remember your insolence. And you will pay for it! You cannot imagine the suffering I can visit upon you."

I gulp. That extremely vivid imagination I mentioned? Well, it's imagining all sorts of terrible tortures right now!

Ahriman raises his palms and places both on the glass case holding the oculus. But for a second, nothing happens. He gets a slightly confused look on his face, then narrows his eyes and clenches his jaws in focus. Finally, his hands turn that dark red again and I can see and feel waves of heat coming off them. The glass around the oculus ripples, then melts, sliding down like a curtain of crystal clear liquid before hardening into curvy, wavy shapes around the base of the pedestal.

"Now you can take the oculus," he seethes, a little out of breath.

Crud. I tried to stop him. Or at least slow him down. I really did. I need to up my game, though, because nothing I'm doing is working... yet.

"Hang on," I say. "There's scorching-hot steam coming off that melted glass. If I put my hand above it, my skin could burn off. And I can't get your oculus if I have to get rushed to the hospital, now can I?"

Ahriman shakes his head. "Humans really talk too much." He picks up the dirty, ripped hem of his long kurta and begins using it like a fan to cool down the melted glass. His hands move too fast for me to follow. No way that's gonna—dang. The wave of melted glass now has little droplets of ice crystals on it. That trick would really come in handy when I'm trying not to burn my tongue on freshly grilled kebabs that I can't wait to eat. I sigh. My mom makes the best kebabs.

"Now proceed, or face my unbridled wrath!" He yanks on my T-shirt sleeve and pulls me forward.

"Hey! Remember what I said? Vintage tee, okay? Ease up."

I take a few deep breaths, do an ohm, and say a silent little dua because it can't hurt to take extra precautions. Then I reach for the second piece of the oculus. It feels cool against my skin—it's not hot at all. I suck in my breath, preparing for the golden ropes to handcuff my wrists to the pedestal.

But it doesn't happen!

Nope. The ropes are silver this time instead. Great. Perfect. Glad this was an important detail to change in this booby trap. I wonder if there's also a ghost Keeper here—I don't need to finish the thought, because a spiral of smoke rises from the Lucite base and twists into the shape of a person. Fantastic. This ghost is wearing a green silk tunic and a bright red turban. He has a trim white beard, too, like Ibn Sina. How does he keep it so neat? Do ghost beards grow? Beards must have been really big back in the day. And now, a thousand years later, toss in a couple of tattoos on his arms and this dude would fit right in! It's like how my dad still wears his flannel shirts from the nineties. Eventually, he knew they'd be cool again. Or he really couldn't be bothered to go shopping.

The ghost stares at me. He's kind of smoky and see-through. As if he's there but not *there* there. Which seems pretty ghost-ish or Ibn Sina-ish, since he's the only ghost I've really interacted with. This second ghost keeps staring at me and not saying a word. The silence is getting awkward. "Dude, why are you looking at me like you've just seen a ghost?"

The ghost twists and squirms and his jaw opens and this weird creaking noise comes out. Is that...? The creaking noise gets faster and turns into something that sounds like a horse snorting. Wait. The ghost is laughing? The ghost is laughing at my ghost joke! Thank you, ladies and gentlemen and all gentle-people, making a dusty, old ghost laugh? That's gotta be a first in human-ghost history. I'm pretty impressed with myself.

"I wouldn't be too impressed, young hero," the ghost says.

"You ghosts have to stop reading my mind. Total invasion of privacy!"

"Hamza, I wasn't reading your mind, I was reading your face. It has both joy and excessive pride written all over it."

Ahriman is getting this irritated parent-at-a-bouncy-house-ball-pit look on his face. It's one I've seen a lot in my life. A lot. He shakes his head and walks away and starts looking at some of the fancy robes we passed by earlier. He must figure that since I'm handcuffed and essentially trapped here by a ghost, I'm not going to make a getaway. And he would be right.

I groan. "Fine. Maybe that is what I was thinking,"

I say to the ghost, "but it did sound like you haven't laughed for a million years. So give me some cred."

"To be accurate, it's more akin to a thousand years, but I will allow you this victory." The ghost smiles. Smiles! This ghost is way more laid-back than the other one.

"Cool. Before you give me the riddle, do you have a name? Were you a super-smart astronomer, astrologist, scientist, philosopher like the last ghost?"

The ghost rubs his hipster beard, very old, wise professor–style. "I see you have already met my counterpart, Ibn Sina, one of the Keepers of The Ring. That means you have the first piece of the oculus."

I frown but nod yes. I wish we didn't have the first piece of the oculus. I wish I wasn't anywhere near this second one, either. I wish I wasn't here at all.

"I see." The ghost looks over his shoulder at Ahriman, then turns back to me. "I understand, young hero. I am Abu Sa'id Ahmed ibn Mohammed ibn Abd al-Jalil al-Sijzi. In life, I was an astronomer, an astrologer, and a mathematician."

"Whoa. That's a lot of jobs. Even if at least two of them seem like the same thing. Also, you have a lot of names. If you lived now, your name would've been mispronounced on the regular. And someone would force a nickname on you.... The Sij or something. It would be cool but only if you picked it yourself. Like your artist name." I know I'm blathering on, as Amira might say, but I'm trying to stall as long as possible to give Amira a chance to get here, even though these silver ropes are starting to dig a little into my wrists. It's not much of a plan, but it's better than nothing. I'm totally fine trying to use my wits instead of my fists to outsmart Ahriman, but using your brains shouldn't hurt this much!

"While I have been a ghost and attached to this piece of the oculus for a very, very long time, it has given me the opportunity to observe both the brilliance of human advancement and the oddities of behavior over the years. Of course, I am bound to this pedestal, so it is a narrow, though, in some ways, diverse slice of life. And the nickname situation is most assuredly one of the oddities. Though my friend that you may know as al-Biruni would surely have laughed heartily at the eccentricities of human nature over the centuries."

"Hey! I totally know that dude! He made the Box of the Moon. Did you invent stuff, too, or mostly just look at stars?"

"I did both, in a way. And most prominently wrote that Earth moved on its own axis."

"My sister, Amira, is going to be so jealous I met you! She's *super* into science and astronomy, though, not gonna lie, I think she kind of looks down on astrology. To be honest, I'm still not totally sorted on the difference between the two. My sister has explained it a million times, but it feels like when my mom says she's making yams, not sweet potatoes. All I know is, they both taste great mashed up with tons of butter. The food, I mean, not the science."

Al-Sijzi laughs. "Are you not *into* science, as you say? You know, it is not merely the study of how we live but of who we are and how all living things interact and coexist. How the wondrous cosmos simply is. How we are all made of stardust and can shine in our own ways."

"That's cool and all. But I might be more into science *fiction* than plain old science."

"Who is to say that things that were once mere fictions can't become real."

Look, not going to say this out loud, but this conversation is sorta interesting. Thought-provoking, as my fifth-grade science teacher might say. I squirm a bit. I'm not used to being still for so long. The ropes tighten around my wrists, making me wince.

"I believe the time has come for the riddle. There is no use in delaying further," he whispers.

I look over the ghost's shoulder, and Ahriman is busy melting the glass fronts on the cases that contain old-timey fancy clothes and shoes, some jewelry, too. And he's putting it on—it's a museum thief cosplay–type situation.

"Go ahead. Please make it an easy one. I really don't want to be trapped for eternity in this ancient donut."

Al-Sijzi smiles. "It weebles. It wobbles. All its ice could soon melt, most sadly this is the hand that Gen Z has been dealt."

Uhhhh. My mouth opens in shock. I literally can't believe it. "You're a one-thousand-year-old dead guy who knows what Gen Z is?"

The ghost chuckles, but it still comes out a pitchy creak. "Of course. I'm a millennial, after all." He pauses and stares right at me. I give him a pained fake smile. "From the last millennium! See what I did there?"

Heh. I smirk. Then break into a grin. Ghost uncle's got jokes. "Not bad. But maybe a little dusty. Ha! Because ghosts live in cobwebby places that are usually old.... Well, not you, I guess the British Museum has regular cleaners. And...uh..." The ghost raises an eyebrow at me. "Okay. Fine. Your joke was better. I...ow!" The ropes tighten around my wrists again. *Think. Think. Think.* Every time I tell myself to think, I can't think at all! Ice melt. Melting ice. Iced tea. Ice water. Ice in my soda. Ice in my veins. I grimace as the ropes twist into my skin.

"The champion of Qaf should answer with haste, lest he be hurt," the ghost says, and then stares right into my eyes with his foggy, see-through-ish pupils. "I believe in your ability to solve the riddle, champion. *It* is my life's work." He waggles his ghostly eyebrows a little.

Huh? Why did he stress the word *it* like it was his favorite in the whole English language. Weird choice. I mean, not that I'm nerdy enough to have a fave word, but I'd pick an ice-cream flavor or something. Chocolate or caramel. Solid choices. Oh. Oh. Oh. Maybe it was a hint! His life's work was about stuff melting? I hate when the ice in my soda melts and makes it all watery. Maybe he was figuring out a way for ice not to melt in drinks. That would be a seriously important invention. But watered-down drinks aren't really a huge Gen Z issue. We've had a lot of the world's problems dumped on us but not that. What wobbly thing do we have to deal with? The Jell-O in school lunch? Doubt he ever tried Jell-O. Pretty sure it's too recent an invention for an ancient ghost. How is wobbly stuff his work? What wobbles? His work. His wobbly work. Wobble. Melty. Work.

Wait. Has he been giving me hints this whole time! His work was about Earth on its axis. When we were at the lunar exhibit, I was looking at this astro-globe. Astro...something. And as it spun, my dad said it was cool that it showed Earth *wobble* on its axis! Earth is what's melting. The ice caps! Because of climate change! We saw this whole documentary in science class about this girl with a long blond braid talking about climate change at the United Nations and telling adults to get off their duffs and do something about it!

I say his clue again in my mind: *It weebles. It wobbles. All its ice could soon melt, most sadly this is the hand that Gen Z has been dealt.*

"Earth!" I shout. "The answer is Earth!"

The ghost smiles. And nods at me as the area around us heats up. Ahriman is back at my side. I didn't even see him glide over here. He's wearing a dark green robe with golden thread and jewels on it, all of which he just stole.

"Excellent work, Hamza," the ghost says as the silver ropes untie themselves and release me. I rub the sore red marks on my wrists with my fingers.

He continues, "My duty is fulfilled. Now may I offer the young champion some advice before I go to my rest at long last?"

I nod.

"Have faith. Find the courage you know is in you. Keep your wits about you wherever you take aim."

Take aim? Oooh, like with a bow and arrow? Oh man, Amira is the one who's good with that stuff. I totally should've taken bow-and-arrow lessons in Qaf! The ghost is starting to fade away. "Thank you," I say. "You're the fun-est ghost I've ever met."

"I believe the correct English is most fun." Al-Sijzi smiles and bows his head slightly. "Peace be with you," he says, and swirls off into nothing before I can respond.

Ahriman pushes me toward the pedestal. I lift the second piece of the oculus donut off its Lucite stand and stare at it for a minute. Those tiny gold and silver sprinkles that resemble galaxies and constellations inside the black smooth surface of the oculus are spinning.

Ahriman pulls the oculus shard from my hand and raises it above his head like a trophy. He doesn't seem to notice the stars moving at all. "One more piece. One more museum. One step closer to my destiny."

"You really sound villain-y when you talk that way."

Ahriman does not look amused. He grabs my upper arm and pulls me along into the main entrance of the museum. It's so eerie and quiet and dark. Ahriman's entire evil plan is coming together, just like he wanted. *Where are you, Amira? I tried to stall. But I can't do this alone.*

"You are not alone." A voice echoes around me. I look at Ahriman, but it's not him. He's doing this thing where he quickly opens and closes his fists, getting pumped for the devnado transformation. "You and your sister can prevail. Have faith, my friend." It's the voice again. And maybe I really am losing it, because I'm hungry and desperately want to try some fish and chips. My mind must be playing tricks on me because of hunger. I'm having starvation delusions!

"There will still be fish and chips in your future, my champion," the voice says, and this time there's a familiar chuckle. "Truthfully, I don't think you're anywhere near actual starvation."

I know that voice. It's Maqbool, my favorite jinn in the whole world. The one who died saving me in Qaf. I look down because even though I want so much for this to be real, it's only in my mind. "Aww, Maqb—" I start to whisper, but too late, because Ahriman twists and spins and pulls me into a whirlwind, shooting us out of the skylight of the British Museum.

CHAPTER 13

The Key to the Afterlife

Amira

A TEENY TYPHOON IS HURLING RIGHT TOWARD MY HEAD! I grab my dagger and slice through the little water-spout, and it splashes onto the concrete like hard rain. But more are coming, so I duck and dodge a couple, then leap over a small row of hedges before falling onto the grass. I sit up, pulling some leaves out of my hair and wiping away droplets of water from my face.

"Humans are really clumsy," Aasman Peri says, standing over me.

"Go ahead and try to do better... without wings!

Besides, couldn't you have maybe just flown me to safety?" I don't even try to hide my snark.

"I was going to," she says, "but the real danger was pretty much over." Aasman Peri shrugs and offers a hand to help me get up. When I'm standing, we both turn back to the wall of water. But it's not a wall anymore; it's a gentle wave, and it's moving back toward the Thames, the girl with the heart of flame at its center.

As it flows by us, the baharia speaks. "I am truly aggrieved that I was compelled to help Ahriman. He is no friend to the baharia. He is no friend to anyone. But our debt is paid. My tribe is released, and we are now free to befriend and aid those we want to. We are on your side, truly. Take this to heart. And may your courage never fail you, Chosen One." She bows her head toward us and then floats away, back into the river.

Uh-oh. If she's leaving and her only job was to prevent us from getting to Ahriman, that means... A breeze starts to swirl around us, trees bending their boughs as the dust kicks up. Gusts of wind twist from above us. I glance toward the roof of the British Museum and see a gray storm funnel rise from a skylight, the sound of shattering glass punctuating the scene.

"Hamza!" I scream. But I don't think he can hear me. He's somehow inside that tornado. Inside that twister of an evil dev's anger and quest for power.

"We're too late again." I almost cry.

Aasman Peri looks down, her wings drooping. "I know. But we can still gain the upper hand."

"Gain the upper hand?" I lock eyes with her. "How? How exactly can we gain the upper hand on a terrifying ancient dev who not only has kidnapped Hamza but now has two pieces of the oculus, too? He's one piece away from being able to place it at the Star Axis and find the location of the Ring of Power. So, please tell me, how we can turn all our amazing failures so far into a win. Go ahead. I'm waiting." I cross my arms and tap my foot. Rage heats up inside me, sending red-hot flames through my body. Metaphorical ones, obviously, since I'm not a jinn, even if I wish I were right now, because then maybe I wouldn't feel so helpless.

Aasman Peri walks away silently, folding back her wings, and goes to stand on the steps of the British Museum.

Ugh. Now I feel bad. It's not her fault we're in this mess. I'm not sure whose fault it actually is. Ahriman's, I guess? Ifrit's? Stupid destiny? Suleiman? Hamz and I didn't choose any of this. All we did... well, all he did, because technically it was Hamza who set this thing in motion, not that I'm pointing fingers (not exactly). All he did was pick up that dumb Box of the Moon at the lunar exhibit at the start of the summer. He couldn't have known what was going to happen, but trouble always seems to find him. And by extension, me. And now look where we are. All summer long we both were proud of how we defeated Ifrit in Qaf. Even if we showed it in different ways. Even if I hid how amazed at us I was. Maybe I forgot how close we almost came to losing it all in Qaf. Maybe forgetting that was the only thing that helped me "process" it, as the school counselor might say during a social emotional learning chat. I dunno. I never seem to have the right answers. That was one thing I used to be able to count on—having the solutions. Following the facts. Figuring out the math and the physics. But how can I science our way out of a dev kidnapping my brother to steal magical objects from museums all around the world?

I start walking toward Aasman Peri because I need to apologize. I drag my feet. Wishing I could think of a plan. I look up at the columns of the museum. Then almost kick myself because I know what we can do. It's not science, exactly. It's sports. Sort of. Well, gym, anyway. My P.E. teacher's favorite phrase any time we're playing flag football is, "The best defense is a good offense." We've been on defense the whole time; that's why Ahriman is winning. He's one step ahead. Now we have to play offense. Yay! Sports analogies. Oh my God. Who even am I?

I race the rest of the way to Aasman Peri. "Look," I say, a little breathless. "I'm...uh...sorry. But you were right."

"Of course I was." She sniffles. "Right about what? I'm right about so many things."

"About gaining the upper hand! We know they're

going to the Louvre. Even if Ahriman moves super lightning fast, it's not instantaneous, and we have a chance to get to the Louvre with the help of a jinnator. And we're not going in alone," I say, pointing at the six British peris flying toward us now that the Thames is back to a normal river. "We're bringing our own surprise army."

We head inside the museum along with the peris of the Peri Royal Institute—PRI they call it, for short, they told me. Which, weird, because PRI, Public Radio International, was also the name of a radio station my parents used to listen to. Whoa. I wonder if PRI was run by the British peris. The newscasters did have very formal accents.

Now all we need is to find the right closet. I hold up the dull brass key that's hanging on a chain around my neck. Amar Akbar Anthony said it would light up near a portal. And we know there's a jinnator broom closet here in the museum because this is where we were supposed to end up. "This place is huge!" I say. "Are we supposed to walk around endlessly until we find the janitor—I mean, jinnator portal?" I ask out loud to no one in particular. All the peris are flying slightly above my head and they completely ignore me.

"Isn't there a JPS geo-locator for the jinnator closets?" I yell up at Aasman Peri, who is chatting with the British peris. "Hey! Excuse me! Anyone listening? I have a brother to save!"

"We know, impatient human!" Aasman Peri yells down. "We were trying to think of where the closet could be hidden."

"Hidden?" I say. "I thought we just needed the key to open it."

"We do need the key, but the closet doors were created in a camouflaged way—sort of hidden in plain sight. If you know, you know," Aasman Peri says, and the other flying peris nod in agreement.

"But you don't know. So that doesn't really make sense."

"I don't make the rules! Well, not all of them, anyway," Aasman Peri harrumphs.

"Ugh. This place probably has a million doors! How are we supposed to know which is the right one?" Where would you find a hidden door in a museum? Hidden doors are for tricking people, for concealing things, like staircases in haunted houses and evil lairs and superhero caves, a way to enter a place undetected.... Why would a museum want that? Oh. OH. I... A museum might not have a secret door, but some ancient cultures did! Like the Egyptians! When I was little, I used to love visiting the tomb at the *Inside Ancient Egypt* exhibit at the Field Museum. Sure, it's a little creepy to walk inside a place where people were once buried, and it's also not so cool that dead bodies were dug up, but one thing I learned is that Egyptians built false doors into tombs as a way for spirits to open the door to the afterlife. It gave a ghost some options. And it's clever because it's literal, but also a metaphor. "Hey!" I shout. "Are there any ancient tombs in this place? False doors were common back in the pharaoh days of Egypt."

"Oh!" Nayeli, the leader of the British peris, stops in midair and hovers for a second. "I think I know where there's a hidden door! Well, a false door, any-way," they say in an accent that I think is described as posh. "The false door of Ptahshepses! Follow me!"

The peris fly in formation and I sprint after them, entering a huge gallery with artifacts all around us—sculptures of pharaohs and mummies and stone tab-lets and jugs. I want to stop and look at every single one, but obviously I can't. I hope we get back here someday. One day when my brother's life isn't in danger and an angry dev isn't trying to take over the worlds. You know, one day when everything is nor-mal and boring. I miss dull. Boring is underrated.

The peris come to a sharp stop in the air and float down in front of a giant reddish limestone structure with hieroglyphs and figures in profile carved into neat rows. I look down at the key around my neck, and it's glowing bright and warm against my chest.

I approach the door slowly, tracing my fingers over the old, chipped stone to try to find a keyhole. I feel guilty because I'm breaking the big museum DO NOT TOUCH rule, but I don't have a choice. And, secretly, it feels pretty cool to run my hands against the surface of a tomb this ancient, over the same grooves and marks that artisans thousands of years ago made with their hand tools. We still don't even really know exactly how the ancient Egyptians created all the wonders they did with such limited technology. They didn't have cranes to lift things into place. They were a people who definitely scienced their way to solutions.

My finger hits a notch, and the key around my neck glows even brighter, but it's not a keyhole, it's an imprint on the stone. I place my key against it, and the metal of the key morphs into the shape of the imprint.

All the peris, including Aasman Peri, and I gasp. Gotta admit, this is cool as heck. (Note to self: Figure out how the metal morphs. Is it non-Newtonian? Internally heating molecules that engage to change shape? This is potentially Nobel Prize–winning stuff!) The glow of the key dies down and the false door slides open into a stone pocket. The key falls back into my hand and I quickly string it around my neck again. We all enter the small, dark space.

"Fold in your wings!" Aasman Peri yells at one of the peris.

"Pardon me!" a voice responds.

The door slides shut behind us. We're crammed into this tiny, possibly airless space. Maybe this wasn't such a smart idea? Maybe one of us should've checked it out first. I am so glad I'm not claustrophobic!

Torches light up all around us and reveal a small door at the back of the closet. A very, very short jinnator steps out. He's wearing the same uniform as Amar Akbar Anthony. But he looks much, much more annoyed. The back wall is lined with shelves with containers similar to the ones that were in the closet in Chicago's jinn city: SMOKE, FIRE, ASH, EARTH, MARBLE, CERAMICS, MOLTEN METAL, GLASS, GOO, etc.

"Mother of ancient artifacts! Are you all ill-mannered fiends? Cramming yourselves in here in such an improper way? No respect for the space. There are far too many of you! There are weight restrictions! Mind yourselves so you don't topple one of the jinn jars of glue. If it falls on your wings, not even Zam Zam water will melt the goop that would form."

The peris looks horrified and huddle closer, tightening their wings against their bodies.

"Uh, sir, we need to get to the Louvre. Amar Akbar Anthony said you would help us," I squeak. "It's an emergency."

"An emergency? An emergency?" he bellows as he points an index finger up at me. Like I said, very, very short. He'd be almost cute—an extra-wrinkly Yoda, but with smaller ears—if his face wasn't turning purple with anger. "There's no end to today's emergencies! Did you see the disarray at the entrance hall?"

Aasman Peri steps forward. "Good sir, my father, the Emperor of Qaf, commands you to take us to the Louvre at once."

"Fine, fine, princess. Don't get your wings in a flurry." He turns, mumbling as he enters some digits into a panel by the side of the small door. The entire closet starts to spin; I close my eyes as the floor seems to fall away. There are bumps and jolts like we're getting banged around from the outside and then we screech to a halt.

"Out with all of you!" the jinnator shouts at us.

The false door slides open and we tumble out onto a cold marble floor. The door shuts and practically disappears against a white marble wall except for a faint outline underneath a grand staircase.

We cautiously walk out from behind the shadows of the steps and see a sign that says ESCALIER DARU—the Daru Staircase. I suck in my breath and hurry to the front of the immense steps. We're here. Inside the Louvre! And if I'm right, at the top of these stairs is a beautiful sculpture I've only seen in pictures.

Yes! I knew it! Goose bumps pop up all over my skin. Not because I'm facing death (which I could be at any moment) but because I'm standing in front of something truly astounding.

Winged Victory.

I can't believe I get to see this incredible sculpture with my own eyes. Not that there's any silver lining to evil being unleashed upon the earth, but I can't help but stare at this huge sculpture in wonder. I hurry up the stairs, the peris following me. The headless marble statue is beautiful, its wings are out and arched back like it's about to take flight off its stone pedestal. I can't believe someone carved this—the clothes of the statue resemble real cloth, with wrinkles! I glance down at the placard that explains the inspiration of the sculpture and gives its full name: *Winged Victory of Samothrace*. Greek. Second century BCE.

Aasman Peri snorts as she reads the sign. "None of that is right. Look at the wings, now look at ours," she says, motioning to herself and the other peris. "The feather pattern on the wings of that sculpture don't resemble any Earth bird or other Greek sculpture. Know why? This statue is modeled after a peri. The peri sculptor who made this was truly gifted."

I scrunch my eyebrows at her in disbelief, but I don't say anything because we have to get to the oculus piece.

"We need to move, now," I say. "Here's the plan: I'll go find the final oculus piece. Only a Chosen One can take it. Aasman Peri, you and the peris fan out as lookouts. And shout or something if you see Ahriman."

"Shouting is a ridiculous plan." Aasman Peri rolls her eyes. "Here's a better one. Amira, you go to the oculus."

"That's literally my plan!"

"I'm not finished yet. Humans are really so impatient. Nayeli and the other peris will scout the halls for any sign of Ahriman's intrusion and will *peri whistle,* not shout, if they see something, because only other peris can hear them."

"And what will you be doing?" I ask. "Bossing everyone around?"

"I'm not bossy. I'm the boss," Aasman Peri responds with a smile, then shows us a small amber vial that she removed from her fanny pack. "My father entrusted me with these drops of celestial fire. They're going to help me unleash a very big surprise on Ahriman."

"Let's do this!" I say, pumping my fist as all the peris look at me with slightly confused expressions.

The peris fly off, and after checking the museum map, I run to a gallery to my right. There's no trace of

Ahriman. We beat him here! This is going to work. This is working! I hurry down the giant room toward the exhibit holding the oculus piece.

Suddenly, the room shakes. And in the distance, I hear furious, otherworldly roars, their echoes ripping through the museum.

CHAPTER 14

Stay Ghul and Composed

Hamza

I DIDN'T PUKE! THIS FEELS LIKE A MOMENTOUS OCCASION. I was in a whirling devnado, traveling from London to Paris across the English Channel, and I didn't upchuck my guts. Also, did not need a passport and my family didn't get stopped by airport security for a "random" check of our luggage. I may not be the ultimate math whiz, but I'm smart enough to figure out that sometimes when authorities say "random," they really mean "any time we want to because you're brown and that's suspicious." Traveling by twister could really be a bonus for us, except for the part where the tornado is a shape-shifting dev who wants all humans to bow down to him. Yeah, that part... not so good. But I'm working on it.

It's still night when we land in a giant courtyard of what looks like a palace with buildings on three sides making a U shape. In front of us is this totally cool glass pyramid. I've seen the Louvre in pictures and in this one show that has an epic chase scene where this fancy car crashes through the pyramid. This is my third museum in one day, and all these forced-culture, near-death experiences are getting tiring. But I gotta say, this may be the awesome-est museum I've ever seen—from the outside at least.

I hear a groan and grunt behind me; I turn to see Ahriman twisting back into his four-eared, red-faced self. He's on one knee, hand on the ground like he's trying to balance himself. I noticed he was a little dizzy when we arrived in London, but this seems worse. Honestly, I'm usually pretty green-feeling myself when we land, but Ahriman looks more out of it than me. Maybe even weakened? And I swear, as we were about to land, his devnado sputtered a little, slowed down, so I saw Ahriman's red face creepily stretched out for a tiny second. He never faltered like that before.

I wonder if this is my moment; if he's weakened, maybe I could take him, knock him over, maybe, and...

Holy moly! Is that... the Eiffel Tower? Whoa!

My mom loves Paris. I really wish she were with me now. And my dad. And Amira. And I wish it were a real vacation and not this doomsday devnado road trip. And it would be a lot less scary if my family were here.

The Eiffel Tower is all lit up, and a twinkling beam of light from the top of the tower sweeps across the city. My parents came here on an anniversary trip and said it was a magical city because of the culture and the architecture. I kind of get that now. But I'm more interested in the magically delicious part, because they also said Paris has the best pastries in the world. I can't believe I'm not going to be able to try a single one.

"Have faith, young champion, perhaps one day you will."

It's that voice again! Maqbool's voice. Ahriman still doesn't notice it, and I wonder if it's because it's only in my head and I'm hallucinating because of low blood sugar. Or...wait. What if...Maqbool's my Force ghost. Like Luke or Obi-Wan or Yoda. I spin around, trying to spot a lit-up figure. "Maqbool, is that you? Are you the kind of Force ghost that only talks, like when Luke and all the other Jedis give Rey a pep talk? Ooooh, wait. Can you say: 'a thousand generations live in you now'?"

"A thousand generations live in you now," the Maqbool voice says, chuckling.

"Yes!" I whisper-yell, and swivel my head to see if Ahriman heard, but he's talking to himself again. Anyway, Maqbool's voice *could* all be in my head. Amira always says you have to find proof for your hypotenuse. Uh...nope. Wrong word. Hypothesis! I need evidence to know if something is real. I pause. Proof. Proof. Finally, I whisper, "Now make a light saber appear. The green kind. Not red."

Ghost Maqbool or in-my-head Maqbool doesn't respond. My dad always says I have an active imagination. Maybe it's acting out right now. But just because something is in my imagination doesn't mean it's not real, right? You know what, kinda gonna go with it, for now.

"Pssst... was a green light saber too much to ask?" I whisper. "Maybe you could ghost-move something or shout boo in Ahriman's ear and make him jump out of his skin. Maqbool?"

"I have missed these amusements," the Maqbool voice says. "But no time for jokes right now."

"Who said I was joking?"

"You don't need a light saber. Use what you have," ghost Maqbool's voice continues. "Do you remember when Abdul Rahman and I first found you and your sister?"

"How could I possibly forget that? I thought you

were going to poke my eyeballs out when you put the collyrium on my lids. I was scared out of my mind!"

"Yet you still attacked us with foam darts, jumping out from behind that dumpster to take us by surprise with your zombie bowcaster."

"Yes! That was the best!"

"Are you talking to thin air, silly small person? What's the best? Humans are strange—always trying to make something from nothing. Believing in the foolishness of hope when they should despair." Ahriman grabs me by the upper arm and tugs me toward the glass pyramid.

I also hadn't realized I was talking out loud. But that Maqbool voice was right. When we were in Qaf, and Amira and I tossed that spotted ghul out of the flying pot, we used the element of surprise to our advantage, plus a lot of talking as distraction, which is my specialty! Maybe when Ahriman is shifting in and out of devnado, I can use that moment to my advantage—it seems like his moment of weakness, if you could even call that a weakness. Ugh. Where are you, Amira? If you were here, we could figure it out. This is definitely a teamwork-type situation.

I drag my heels as Ahriman pulls me along. Until I come up with a better escape plan, sudden superhero strength, or maybe a way to destroy the oculus, delay is my only hope. I go all limp and noodle-y like I did when I was in nursery school and didn't want to go where my parents were trying to take me. Usually to an Indian wedding where I knew a bunch of aunties were going to pinch my cheeks. I did have really pinchable cheeks—I was a super-cute kid, but being auntie-handled still annoyed me. Upside was they always insisted on my having multiple servings of gulab jamun. Basically, Indian donut holes in sugar syrup. It's so wrong that I'm on a quest for a fake donut, aka the oculus, right now.

"What...what...is wrong with you?" Ahriman pauses while I slump to the ground, trying not to slobber over my donut dreams. "Walk properly!"

"It's the hunger," I say very dramatically. "I don't know if I can go on. Maybe if I got some pastries. A baguette even? A chocolate bar? I hear the chocolate here is very good. A Coke would be cool, but we can't let my parents know, because it's way too late for caffeine. Although, technically, with the time change, it's only the late afternoon back home. Maybe it's more than hunger; it's the jet lag."

Ahriman throws his head back in frustration. Heck, yeah. I still got it. "I will get you food after you deliver the final oculus piece to me. And jet lag does not exist within my tempest."

"No, but queasiness does. It's really not good to travel on an empty stomach. Don't you have motion sickness in Qaf? Don't baby devs and ghuls have that spit-up thing that makes parents walk around with those cloths over their shoulders so their clothes don't get ruined when their kids puke? I had reflux, actually, so my mom says I projectile-vomited, like, three times a day. Whew! Glad I don't have that memory, because it really must've stunk in the house. People always say babies smell sooooo gooood. But they poop in their diapers and spit up all the time, how could that possibly be an odor you want to be around? I guess that's why they say a parent's love is unconditional. If they love that, they'll love any—"

"All the stars in the heavens! Do you never stop talking?"

"Total gift," I say with a smile as Ahriman yanks me through the glass pyramid entrance and down the stairs of the main lobby of the Louvre. If distraction and delay are my only tactics, I'm going to smash it. It's pretty dark inside, except for the lights of the lit-up pyramid above us and some small lights scattered around the museum. The hall is echoey and kind of eerie. Long, dark halls lead away from the main entrance. Definitely a spot where you could imagine a mystery starting.

"Come along. The final piece of the oculus is within my grasp—"

"I think you mean within *my* grasp. Since technically I'm the only one who can get it."

"Silence! At long last I am near to fulfilling my destiny and I will not let the moment be peppered by this odd human compulsion for idle talk. Be silent. You may not be expendable, *yet,* but your family is."

I shut right up. Ahriman zooms over to a large 3D museum map, and he grasps the sides of the clear box it's contained in.

"Hey, up here." I hear a slightly annoyed whisper, but I really don't think it's in my head this time. Besides, why would a Force ghost say that inside my own brain?

Then a small wad of paper hits me in the head. What the . . . ? I look up. A huge smile crosses my face. Inside, at the very tippy top of the glass pyramid, Aasman Peri is fluttering around with a few other fairies. My heart nearly jumps out of my chest, and I put a hand over my mouth so I don't let out a cheer.

Aasman Peri puts a finger to her lips, telling me to be quiet. Like she should tell me to shut up; she's a major talker, too. And brags way more. But I'm so excited to see her I don't even mind (that much). It must mean Amira is near, too.

I pretend to tie my shoe as Ahriman stomps back toward me. He reaches down to grab me when a giant roar fills the lobby and echoes down every hall, so it really sounds like a million roars.

Ahriman leaps up, pulls flames into his palms, and moves closer to one of the dark hallways. He leans forward to listen. There's loud stomping and another gigantic, terrifying howl. I look up at Aasman Peri, who is making some gestures with her hands that I don't understand at all. All I know is, this could be my only chance. With Ahriman distracted by whatever bloodcurdling creature that roar is coming from, I get a running start and leap through the air before landing a two-footed kick right on his butt.

Holy superhero move!

"Oooph!" he yells as he falls forward.

I pretty much land on my backside with a thud, but it was so worth it. I scramble back before he can grab me, because when he turns, he looks extremely pissed! His flaming eyeballs say: *I'll smoke you and all living things*. I push myself up. But I freeze when I glance past Ahriman. Down that dark hall—the one we heard the stomping and the roaring coming from?—there's a ginormous, and I mean humongous, ten-headed, horned bright blue ghul heading right for us.

Move, Hamz. Your feet. Pick them up. This is no time to panic-freeze!

At first, Ahriman scrunches his entire face at me like he's eaten a lemon, but when he turns to look down the hall at what I'm staring at, even he—the most evil being currently on Earth, except maybe for a couple of politicians—lets out a gasp.

Right then, Aasman Peri and two other fairies swoop down, grab me by my arms and shirt collar, and fly off down another hallway.

"Would you mind? This is a vintage shirt," I smirk.

"Perhaps we should drop you, ungrateful Chosen One." Aasman Peri laughs. "That ghul loves devouring small, annoying humans."

"Hey! Who you calling small?"

The other peris chuckle. We hear another roar and a gross kind of gurgling sound, and then thundering shouts and glass breaking from the pyramid lobby. I almost feel bad for Ahriman. *Almost.*

I look back and see the blue ghul stomping toward

Ahriman, who has a sword in one hand and a fireball whirling in another. The ghul's ten heads all have their mouths open and let out gurgly, slobbery shouts like they've just been forced to wake up from the longest nap in the world and aren't happy about it. Each of the heads moves on its own, but right now, twenty eyes look laser-focused on Ahriman. And wow, do all those eyeballs look mad! The ghul spreads its two hands wide and then claps them together, trying to squish Ahriman, who whirlwinds himself out of the way. But before Ahriman can attack, the giant ghul thunders toward him and swats him across the room like a fly. Yes! If I wasn't so desperate to get out of here and help Amira, I'd love to watch this butt-kicking go down!

"Where did that thing come from?" I ask as Aasman Peri flies me out of sight of the fight.

"Suleiman buried it in the Arabian sands in a brass vessel. And there it rested, supposedly for eternity. Until some of your human archaeologists dug it up and put it in this museum."

"It's been here this whole time? That scary, horn-y blue thing? And no one in Qaf was going to do anything about it?"

"Ha! Do you think we have time to go through every bit of looted goods you humans have put in museums because you don't understand that some things that are buried are meant to stay that way? Suleiman the Wise entombed thousands of evil jinn, devs, and ghuls in brass pots and lamps and buried them all over. Besides, humans would need celestial fire to unseal the pots."

"Which you happen to have?"

Aasman Peri nods. "A tiny vial that my father entrusted me with. It's dangerous and volatile. It can melt through virtually all substances on Earth and Qaf. Only the worthy may wield it."

"Pffft. That tiny bottle isn't Mjölnir. And you're not Thor," I say.

"Of course I'm not! He wishes he had my lustrous, dark hair," she smirks.

Behind us, we hear a loud crash; I think the entire glass pyramid might be shattering. Oh no. That's really, really, super, catastrophically bad. I really hope that ten-headed blue ghul is winning, but then what happens? We can't exactly let him loose on the streets of Paris and—

We hear a high-pitched scream snaking through the halls that makes my breath stop.

It's my sister. She's in trouble.

CHAPTER 15

A Riddle, Wrapped in a Mystery, Inside an Enigma. Or Something.

Amira

I HEAR MORE ROARING AND THEN SCREAMS AMID THE sounds of glass shattering. And the way the room is quaking, I swear it's dinosaurs stomping around. Eeeek! I hope there aren't any dinosaurs. It should be impossible, but everything impossible seems real now. And dinosaurs are literally the last thing we need. Though Aasman Peri did say she had a surprise for Ahriman. Dinosaurs would definitely be a surprise. I'll let her deal with it, though. I have to focus. We're running out of time.

I race to the end of the hall and come to an exhibit called *Ingenious Devices of the Banu Musa*. Hey! I know them. They're the brothers who made that automatic flute player we saw at the lunar eclipse exhibit. Cool! The exhibit is lined with glass cases holding books and drawings by the brothers. There are clocks and astrolabes. And...oh, wow. A whole case of objects called "trick vessels." At the end of the row of glass cases is a human-size wooden statue that's maybe a bit taller than my dad. His clothes and turban that must have once been really bright colors are now faded. His hands are held out, palms up, holding a wooden box, and his head is cast down, looking at the object in his hands. It sort of looks like a Rubik's Cube, with each side made up of different colored woods. A placard next to the statue reads: AUTOMATON OF THE OCULUS, CIRCA NINTH CENTURY CE.

Weird. I thought the oculus was donut-shaped.

But whatever. This thing is labeled and is sitting right there. Who am I to argue with something being easy for once? I reach out to grab the cube. I'm going to be gentle, obviously, and I wish I had the kind of gloves I've seen museum curators wear when they're handling rare objects, but it's summer, so why would I have gloves? Even though I feel guilty about stealing from a museum, it's for a good cause. A save-the-world-type scenario. And if we win—no... *when* we win—I can return it. So basically it's like borrowing an old library book. And if we don't win... well, I guess there will be bigger fish to fry, as my dad says. (Note to self: Pretty sure using flimsy excuses are how a life of crime starts? But how do you define flimsy, anyway? Gotta be a bit subjective!)

My hands shake as I reach out for it. *Ugh, Amira. Chill. Stop shaking. You could drop it.* I take a deep breath. I got this. I put the tips of my fingers on the top of the cube. It's strangely cool and smooth to the touch, almost like it was just polished and buffed, which is weird for something that's so old.

I fasten my grip on it, but the second I do, the head of the automaton jerks up. Ack! This thing still functions? (Note to self: If this ancient robot doesn't kill you, determine what its energy source is. Could it possibly be a perpetual battery? That would be revolutionary!) I step backward, pulling my hands away, and as I do, two iron hooks rise out of the floor and white silken scarves wrap around each of my legs. "Hey! What the heck?" I say, looking at the scarves tightening around my ankles and calves. Then a hissing comes from the automaton's mouth as one plume of steam, then another, and a third swirl out of it. (One more note to self: Steam could be the energy source, but where is the water coming from inside the museum? Condensation? This place is supposed to be temperature-controlled!) The plumes twist and turn before me, forming into people. No. Not people. Ghosts? See-through, shimmery spirits.

I scream at the top of my lungs. Ghosts are worse than dinosaurs. At least I could try to hide from a dinosaur. So much worse. I try to turn to run, but the silk wrappings around my ankles tighten. They feel like a million threads cutting into my skin.

"Do not struggle," says a ghost dressed in a long red kurta with gold embroidery along the button placket.

"That's easy for you to say. Try standing in the champion's shoes," says the second ghost, this one dressed in a coordinating blue kurta with silver embroidery.

"Technically, he can't stand in the champion's shoes because we are ghosts and she's human. It could more accurately be described as levitation since we are not bound by gravity," says the third ghost, this one in a green kurta with bronze embroidery.

"Shut it, Hasan," the first two ghosts say in unison to the third one.

"You two are so bossy. You're never willing to admit when I have a point!" Hasan says.

"Why must you be so exacting and literal?" the ghost in the red kurta says. "I was speaking figuratively."

I swing my head from one to the other like I'm at

a tennis match. "Ahem. Excuse me, uh, misters...er, ghost sirs? Friends? Who are you? And could one of you please tell me WHAT THE HECKAMAJIG IS GOING ON?"

There's a ruckus near the entrance of this gallery. "What the heck is going on?" a voice yells.

"I literally just said that!" I yell back as Hamza careens around the corner, sprinting toward me. I've never been happier to see my little brother. Never. Except maybe when he was born and I was two and basically thought he was a doll.

My first instinct is to turn and run to him. But I'm yanked back by the silks. These ribbons are surprisingly strong and painful. "I'm trapped!"

Hamza screeches to a stop next to me as Aasman Peri and three PRI British peris descend to the ground. But before I can say anything else, there's a high-pitched scream; it's not like the roar or the yells I heard before.

"Our sibling!" the British peris say in unison, and immediately fly back in the direction from where they came. Then we hear a thunderous crash.

Aasman Peri looks at me, then my brother, then to the ghosts, then back to me.

"It's okay," I say. "Go help them. We got this." Whatever *this* is. Hamza smiles at me and nods.

Aasman Peri is about to say something, but there's another roar, and she flies off.

"You got three ghosts?" Hamza says as we turn our attention back to the automaton.

"Oh my God, I'm glad you're okay," I say, breathing a sigh of relief. "Also, you are so dead! Mom and Dad are going to kill you. And how did you know there would be ghosts?"

Hamza shrugs, looking a bit too smug, if you ask me. "I had ghosts at the first two museums. They're sort of... um... uhh... Bearers of the Ring."

"Huh? That's like Frodo and Bilbo, dude." I scrunch my eyebrows at Hamz, totally confused.

"No. That's not right.... Oh! They're Keepers of—"

"The Ring," the three ghosts say in unison.

"That's it!" Hamza does finger guns at them. "It's what I said, they're Keepers of The Ring. Like Hobbits."

I shake my head. "That's not even—never mind." There's no time to argue with Hamza about the accuracy—more like inaccuracy—of his Tolkien terminology.

"They're going to give you a riddle. When you solve it, you get untied and get the oculus shard. You'll love it. It's peak nerd questions about astronomy and stuff."

"And you answered right?"

"Hey!" Hamza crosses his arms in front of his chest. "I totally know stuff. And you're welcome, by the way."

"For what?"

"For my stalling so you could get here and we could steal the final piece before Ahriman could get his bony red fingers on it."

"Are you—aaargh. Hamz, we're wasting time!" I turn back to the ghosts. "Okay, hit me with the riddle. These ropes are really starting to hurt."

The third ghost, the know-it-all one in the green tunic, says, "Well, actually, those aren't, in fact, ropes. They're silken threads."

"Whoa, like Spidey!" Hamza shouts, then shakes his head. "Nah. I think, technically, his are made of nylon nanotubes."

"Aaaargh. Who cares? Please give me the riddle; we have to get out of here."

The green tunic ghost ignores me and turns to Hamza. "It is one of my most brilliant inventions, if I do say so myself."

"Would you say it's even in-genie-ous?" Hamz asks, and he and the ghost start laughing.

What is happening? Oh my... "Wait. You three actually *are* the ghosts of the Banu Musa? I know this is an exhibit of your works, but, whoa. You're not just three random siblings who annoy one another and got stuck for eternity with this job?"

"If we're being honest, we're that, too," the one in green says.

"How is this... I mean... I have so many questions. Wow. Wow. You're brilliant. We saw your totally cool flute automaton!" I shout, totally nerding out and fangirling at the same time.

"One of my favorites," the red tunic brother says. "Forgive us for not formally introducing ourselves. I am Muhammad. This"—he points to the blue tunic ghost—"is my brother Ahmad. And that"—he points to the green tunic ghost who is still guffawing a bit with Hamza—"is our baby brother Hasan."

If I wasn't so scared and if my ankles didn't hurt so much, I'd be in awe. I'm in awe anyway, I guess, despite the pain. "I thought there were only two of you?"

"I knew it!" shouts Hasan. "Somehow you two have written me out of the future. I'm the smart one, and you two were jealous."

Ahmad rolls his eyes. "I think you mean the melodramatic one, even a thousand-plus years after our deaths."

"I'm s-s-sorry," I stutter, feeling a bit guilty. "I'm sure I'm misremembering."

"I feel you, Hasan. I'm the smart, forgotten sibling, too." Hamza fist-bumps the ghost, but his hand goes through air.

We hear more roars and crashes, and it's getting louder. I cringe, thinking of the wreckage the jinnators are going to have to clean up. I wonder how many times some of these priceless treasures have been destroyed and put back together with magical jinn glue.

"Hurry!" I squeak.

"There is no riddle, young champion," Ahmad says. "To obtain the last piece of the oculus, you must solve this," he says, pointing to the cube on the automaton's hands.

"How do you solve a box?" Hamza says. "That makes no sense."

The automaton's head swivels toward Hamza and it raises its wooden eyebrows.

"Whaaaaat! No way! Did you see that, sis?"

The automaton raises one creaky leg, then another, and steps toward me. I close my eyes because I'm half-afraid he's going to plow right through me. But he doesn't; he stops in front of me and raises his hands, offering me the cube. I pluck it from his palms. It's oddly light. When I look closer, turning it around, I see grooves on each surface. But they're not even. They're sort of askew. I can't detect any obvious pattern to it.

"I see our champion looks confounded," Muhammad says. "In your hands, you hold perhaps one of our greatest creations."

"Brilliant for its simplicity," Ahmad says.

"And its synchronicity," Hasan adds with a wink. His ghost brothers both swing their heads to look at him, confusion on their faces. "No. That's not the word. I mean, symmetry. Brilliant for its symmetry."

Muhammad shakes his head at his brother. I can relate. "This is a trick box. A puzzle, if you will, that contains the final piece of the oculus."

I groan. A 3D puzzle is not my thing. Why couldn't I get a science question? Physics? Astronomy, maybe? Even chemistry. Not this.

"What's so tricky about it?" Hamza scoffs. "It looks like my Rubik's Cube. I've totally solved that before." He reaches for the box.

"Ow!" I yell. The moment his fingers come in contact with the wooden cube, the silks tighten around my ankles. They're starting to cut off my circulation. "You're triggering the ribbons!"

Hamza snaps his hands back. "You're lucky, I had ropes."

"In fact, these ribbons we devised from silken spider webbing are one hundred times stronger than the material used to build the great tower of Eiffel," Hasan says.

Steel. He means, the ribbons are stronger than steel. *Oh, great.*

"To obtain the oculus, only the champion who removes it from the automaton's hands can solve it. Though, I must say, we only expected there to be one of you," Muhammad says.

"Join the club," I say through gritted teeth.

Ahmad continues, "As you can see, there are grooves in the cube that create four levels. When the grooves are aligned, they can move 360 degrees, left or right. You merely need to rotate each level a certain number of times to unlock the cube, revealing the oculus inside." He smiles. The ghost smiles. He seems proud of himself. I guess I would be, too, if

I'd invented something so cool. But I don't feel much like smiling.

"And I'm supposed to come up with a random series of turns to unlock it?"

"My dearest Amira," Muhammad says, "surely you must know by now, when it comes to the Chosen Ones, there's no such thing as random."

I disagree. Heartily. Because, honestly, ever since the super blue blood moon eclipse earlier this summer, my entire life has felt random. Randomly came across the Box of the Moon. Randomly picked to be the Chosen One. Ones. Randomly lucked out. I've had enough of random. I want order. Uneventful, easy-to-predict order.

Hasan squirms a bit, if a ghost can squirm. "I...I..."

"We can give no further assistance, Hasan," Ahmad chides his little brother.

"The symmetry was created from you, for you two!" Hasan blurts out before putting his ghostly hand over his mouth. He shrugs when his brothers glare at him. "Why are you giving me evil eye looks?"

"Ha! Shade from a shade!" Hamza laughs. Glad someone can be amused right now while my hands are growing sweatier by the second. Hasan winks at my brother.

I start to turn the top level. But stop. "What happens if I don't do the right number of turns?" I ask. "Do I even want to know?"

Ahmad frowns. "Let us not think of such things."

"Yes." Hasan nods. "You still have time before your circulation is cut off!" His brothers glare at him, again. "Sorry," he mouths at me.

I take deep breaths. I'm starting to feel lightheaded. I think I'm getting a sweat mustache. "Symmetry from us. Symmetry from us. For us...," I repeat. I look at Hamza, who gives me a small, fake smile that I think he means to be encouraging. Not working. My eyes flutter to his Majid Mark, the birthmark he and I share, in the exact same spot on our temples. Our relatives all think it's so funny. The same mark on kids who were born about two years apart on...

That's it. That's got to be it. "Hamz! Our birthdays. There's symmetry in our dates."

"Huh? How are August tenth and October eighth symmetric?"

We hear more screams, sounds of fighting. And they're getting closer. No time to explain. No time to debate possibilities. Or probabilities. Or calculate the risks. Sometimes you have to go for it. I turn each level according to our birth months and dates. Eight-ten-ten-eight.

The symmetry that was created from us. From the days we were born.

There's a clicking sound and a whirring of gears, and the box splits open.

"Yesssss!" Hamza whoops.

The ghosts smile and air-clap as a tiny velvet pedestal inside the box slides up and I gently take the third piece of the oculus. It's dark, the deepest black, and speckled with silver streaks and golden stars. Like the whole galaxy is contained in that stone. I put the empty box back in the hands of the automaton. It closes again, and the automaton retreats back to his original spot. The ribbons around my ankles and calves loosen and unfurl; the entire iron hook and silk-spooling device retracts back into the floor.

I look up at the Banu Musa brothers, who all have their hands held over their hearts. Or where their hearts would be if they were alive.

"Our duty is complete," Muhammad says. "It was an honor to wait for you all these years. May you use the oculus in good health."

"Well, Ahriman may have something to say about that," I mutter. My tiny joy at solving the puzzle is completely dampened when I realize what we have to do next.

Ahmad says, "Fear not. Though Ahriman feels like an unbeatable foe, human beings have many, many gifts that jinn and dev do not. You find solutions where many see only problems. You can shine more brilliantly than any mere star whose light shifts and bends with time whereas you stay true to who you are. We bid you peace."

"You might even say you're ingeniously clever." Hasan gives us a small bow. "Peace be with you, champions."

✦ ✷ ✦

A RIDDLE, WRAPPED IN A MYSTERY, INSIDE AN ENIGMA.

The ghosts spin back into vents of steam and twist away, disappearing into the air.

That was a weirdly cryptic but nice goodbye. Hamza and I look at each other. Smiles spreading across our faces. We high-five. We've been through so much and conquered it all. Almost.

"We got this, Hamz," I say.

"All for one, and one for all!" he shouts.

"That's the Three Musketeers, and there's only two—"

"Hamza!" a gruff, terrifying voice bellows from the entrance to the gallery. Hamza and I instinctively take a fighting stance. Me, because of karate training. Him, because of superhero fanboying. Both work.

I tighten my grip on the oculus.

My heart stops. Ahriman is dripping with green goo. And he's got Aasman Peri in his clutches.

CHAPTER 16

Once Bitten, Twice Shy

Amira

"I COMMAND YOU TO RELEASE ME, FOUL FIEND!" AASMAN Peri yells as she writhes in Ahriman's clutches. The evil dev has pinned back her arms and is holding them in his grip. Even from across the room, it looks painful.

He laughs. Laughs. Like he's enjoying hurting her. But I have to hand it to Aasman Peri; rather than acting like she's a captive, she narrows her eyes and gets a very annoyed look on her face.

"How dare you laugh at me. Do you know who I

am? My father will have your thick, ugly red skull for this!" Aasman Peri barks even as she flinches a little when Ahriman tightens his grip on her.

"Your commands mean nothing to me, princess. I do not acknowledge your father's reign in Qaf and dominion over all spirits of fire. And when I unseat him, which I surely will, it is I who will command you," Ahriman snorts.

"Let her go!" I reach for my dagger with one shaky hand, the third piece of the oculus in my other.

Aasman Peri winces as Ahriman pushes her forward into the hall, then turns his eyes to me and my brother.

"Do not dare to raise a dagger to me if you want this peri to live," Ahriman yells. His voice sends a shiver down my spine, but I keep my dagger up. We're not going down without a fight.

"Unhand her, dev breath!" Hamza shouts.

"Hamza!" the dev bellows. "You shall pay for this insolence."

Aasman Peri smiles a little. "Hamza is totally right; you have extremely stale dev breath. You should really consider adding a charcoal powder to your teeth-cleaning routine," she says.

A blob of green goop plops onto Aasman Peri's shoulder. She shimmies her shoulder, and it squelches onto the floor.

"Gross! What is that stuff?" Hamza asks.

Before Ahriman can respond, Aasman Peri rolls her eyes and starts speaking, "The blood of that ten-headed ghul I unleashed. It wasn't as much of a deadly surprise as I was hoping," she says, making eye contact with me. I begin stepping forward while slowly trying to access my backpack. I give an almost imperceptible head nod toward Hamza to step forward as well. He doesn't have a weapon and I don't think I can get him one with Ahriman so close. But he did grab the wooden Rubik's Cube thingy from the automaton's hands when Ahriman came into the room, so that's at least something.

"You know," Aasman Peri continues talking, clearly trying to gain us some time. "That ghul really put up a good fight. He almost had you, didn't he, Ahriman?"

"Do not be ridiculous!"

"Oh, I'm sorry, wasn't it you who was whimpering when he pummeled you, sending you flying across the room into a wall?" Aasman Peri is getting Ahriman irritated. I can tell because little puffs of smoke are coming out of his very red nose.

Hamza and I inch forward so we can flank Ahriman while his attention is locked on Aasman Peri.

"Foolish peri! I felled him with a single slash of my sword!"

"Sheer luck," Aasman Peri says. "That ten-headed ghul was batting you around like a little mouse, and then he inadvertently smacked one of the peris that got too close and got distracted by all the peri screams. You'd think with all those heads he would've seen the sword coming, but nope."

"Silence, peri! Far worse shall befall all of you if I do not get the final oculus piece. Your endless chattering is insufferable. You are nearly as bad as the small human."

"Hey!" Hamza and Aasman Peri both say in unison.

"Jinx!" Hamza says. "You owe me a Coke."

Aasman Peri shakes her head, but I see her lean her body slightly forward. "Are weirdly acidic-tasting human beverages all you can think about, Hamz?"

"Of course not," he says. "I also think a lot about food. I haven't had a real meal in hours! Just these weird chips... crisps... that Ahriman stole...."

While Hamza goes on, I make eye contact with Aasman Peri, trying to send her a message telepathically. I'm making a move. And she needs to be ready to fly—or try to anyway. Aasman Peri tilts forward a bit more and lifts her eyes upward. Ahriman seems to have loosened his grip ever so slightly as he rage-banters with Hamza.

Aasman Peri and I nod at each other at the same time.

She tilts forward even more, then unfurls her wings so they swat Ahriman in the face. He loses his grip on her.

"Now!" I yell. Aasman Peri flies straight up into the air. While I hurl my dagger at Ahriman, and Hamza throws the cube toward his head.

I see everything go down almost like we're in a movie and this is the pivotal slow-mo action scene. The dagger and cube both fly through the air while Ahriman is looking up at Aasman Peri. Yes. Yes. Keep looking up. C'mon, dagger, let your aim be true.

I quickly unzip my bag and drop the oculus piece into it, grab my bow and arrow, and slide another arrow toward Hamza. Even without the bow, it's still a sharp, pointy stick. It's what Sensei Seijo always says: You have to adjust your strategy to the fight at hand.

But Ahriman flashes a sharp-toothed grin at me as Hamza and I race toward him. OH NO. Aasman Peri tries to fly toward us, but he reaches up and grabs her right wing in one hand and then bats away the dagger and then the cube in quick succession with the other. His hand moves so fast I can barely see it. Our weapons fall to the floor like toys. Then he jerks Aasman Peri's wing and throws her to the ground.

"Ow!" she screams, and the sound echoes through the hall.

"Aasman Peri!" Hamza yells as he runs toward her.

But I hold my ground, nock my arrow, and let it fly. It arcs through the air, but Ahriman moves his body just in time so it only grazes his shoulder. He barely flinches. I don't even see blood or goop or whatever.

"I warned you fools! I am not to be trifled with!" Ahriman raises his hands palms up, and small fireballs whir in them. "Hamza! If you want no further harm to come to this so-called royal, this upstart peri, then you will hand over the final piece of the oculus and you will come with me."

"No! Don't be a fool!" Aasman Peri yells.

My heart races in my chest when I see Hamza's shocked expression as he stands to face Ahriman. No. No. No. "Take me," I blurt out. I can't let Hamza go with him.

"What? No, sis." Hamza looks at me.

I ignore my brother and the lump swelling in my throat and keep my eyes fixed on Ahriman. "I got the final piece. I unlocked the puzzle box. You don't need Hamza."

Ahriman laughs again. "You? A girl? A human girl? Were able to obtain the final piece? You must think me a fool to believe such trickery."

"Whoa. Sexist much?" I say. I see Aasman Peri smile a little as she tries to push herself off the floor, her right wing drooping. That's gotta hurt.

"I already told you," Hamza says, "Amira is a total bad—"

"Hamz! Language!" I yell.

"I must admit," Aasman Peri says as she tries to hold herself up. "You have an incredible fixation on not swearing even when facing death."

"I was defending you and your girl power!" Hamza says to me.

"No more talking!" Ahriman yells. "This is not a negotiation. Hamza comes with me now, or I will bring my wrath down upon this peri and all your family."

"I'll do it!" Hamza yells.

"No!" I scream, rushing up to him as he steps toward Ahriman.

"I have to. I can do this, sis." Hamza looks right

into my eyes and nods, even gives me a little smile. I think of our parents and how desperately I wish they were with me, telling me the right thing to do. There don't seem to be any good choices. And we're not exactly winning here. If we fail, it will be up to the emperor and all the armies of the worlds—jinn and human—to try to bring down Ahriman. Aasman Peri told me her dad was putting enchantments in place to prevent Qaf's defenses from falling, but if Ahriman gets the Ring, he'll have power over all fire spirits. If that happens, we're doomed. Right now, Ahriman still needs us, at least one of us. It's counterintuitive, but going with Ahriman now will keep Hamza alive for at least a little longer. Maybe long enough for me to figure something else out.

I nod. "Okay," I say, my voice cracking a bit. I square my shoulders. "I'll give you the piece. But swear you won't hurt my brother, or anyone."

"I have no intention of harming *Hamza*," Ahriman says.

"Amira, you silly human. You can't trust him! He's the most evil of all devs, more evil than Ifrit.

Everything he says is a lie!" Aasman Peri says, limping over to stand against a display case.

I unzip my backpack. I pull out the brown paper bag of donuts I stashed earlier and the oculus piece, and show Ahriman that I'm dropping it into the bag. Then I grab a bottle of water, too, and hold out both toward Hamza. He walks over to me, and I give him a hug. Hugging is not our usual sibling goodbye, but Hamza hugs me back, really tight. "I'll figure out a way to get to you," I whisper.

"I know, sis. We got this," Hamza whispers back, his voice wavering a little.

Ahriman puts his palms down, extinguishing the fireballs in his hands as Hamza approaches him. I run toward Aasman Peri's side. I try to hold her up, but she's started to collapse back onto the ground. We both look up as Ahriman grabs Hamza by the arm.

Hamza looks grim. He didn't even look this bummed in Qaf, when pellets of crystal rain were cutting into his skin and the s'mores in those jinn trees turned out to be hallucinations.

"May the Force be with you, Hamz!" I say.

That makes Hamza burst into a huge smile. "Don't worry, I'm one with the Force!"

Ahriman pulls Hamza out of the room, but before they leave, he reaches into his highly decorated robe and throws down a purple velvet sack in front of us.

"What the . . . ?" I start to say as bright yellow-and-green-striped snakes slither out.

"Nooooo!" Hamza yells as we feel the gale of a whirlwind picking up, twisting Hamza and Ahriman away.

Aasman Peri gasps. "Saw-toothed ghul vipers! Ruuuuuuuun!"

CHAPTER 17

(Star) Axis of Evil

Hamza

"LET GO OF ME!" I SHOVE AHRIMAN AS HE SPINS OUT OF HIS devnado. He teeters a little bit, but I fall completely backward onto hard sand, scraggly bits of grass, and sharp rocks all around me. I push myself back up and run straight at Ahriman, hands clenched in fists, aimed straight at his ugly, evil, vampire-y mouth. But my punch meets nothing but air when Ahriman slips to the side. I spin around, not letting myself fall again. "You said you wouldn't hurt them if I came with you!" I scream at the top of my lungs. There's no one around to hear me. Just me and Ahriman in this desert as the sun is setting.

"I said no such thing. I told your sister it was not my intention to harm *you,* and I have been true to my word." Ahriman sneers and brushes sand off his sleeves.

"If you hurt my family and friends, then you hurt me! You're a liar and a monster. You're worse than nightmares! I hate you. My mom and dad say I shouldn't use the word *hate* that way, but in your case, I know they'd make an exception. And you better hope my sister and Aasman Peri are okay. Or else I'll—"

"You'll what? Talk me to death?" Ahriman doesn't even look at me, just keeps brushing off sand and dirt from his fancy, stolen robe. "You should be thankful that I didn't turn your sister and friend to ash. I've left their fate in their own hands. They'll survive if they're clever. I think I showed quite a bit of restraint despite your impertinent attempts to harm me. It was almost comically entertaining."

I turn my back to him. I don't want Ahriman to

see that my eyes are getting teary. I wipe my runny nose on my T-shirt. I'm using my *vintage* T-shirt as a tissue. That's how desperate I feel. Is this it? Is it all over because we couldn't stop him from getting the oculus pieces? Like, is Ahriman's jinn army going to take over the whole world because of me? How the heck am I supposed to do all this myself? I was excited when I found out I was a Chosen One. It's real superhero stuff. But Amira was right, there are no such things as superheroes. And right now, it feels like the only thing I was chosen for was failure.

"Don't lose hope. Help is not far." The Maqbool voice is talking to me again. Ahriman doesn't hear it. And now I'm 100 percent sure it's only in my head. It's me being desperate not to be alone. My heart squeezes a little.

"I'm not merely in your head," the ghost voice says.

"That's what my head would say, too. And by my head, I guess I mean me?"

"What are you babbling on about, human? We still have work to do," Ahriman barks at me. "Climb!"

I groan. I'm tired and thirsty. I would really, really rather do anything else. Even cleaning my room or organizing my LEGO area or weeding the garden. That's how crummy I feel.

"In case you haven't noticed, we're in a desert. And if you expect me to climb those mountains," I say, pointing to the peaks in the far-off distance, "that you could've easily just landed your devnado onto—" I whirl around to face Ahriman but don't complete my sentence. Behind him is a huge, curved wall with about a million stairs that climb up into a skinny pyramid. Whoa. It's the same color as the rocks and sand around us and looks like it rose out of the desert. But there's a plaque by it, so I'm guessing this was built on purpose.

"Behold: Star Axis. Atop those stairs lies the map that will point the way to the Ring of Power." As Ahriman talks, he slobbers a little bright blue goop on his chin, and dev slobber is as disgusting as it sounds.

"Okay. So fly up there. Grab the map. Easy peasy. Tornado, appear!" I say to him. He just stares at me. "Devnado, engage!" I shout, but still no response.

"You really should consider an activation phrase for your powers," I say. "It gives people a heads-up."

"Of all the dark planets, how is it that you are the Chosen One?" Ahriman shakes his head. I almost open my mouth to correct him, but I don't bother; he'll talk over me, anyway. "I cannot land at the top of the pyramid. The space is too narrow and the oculus crescent holder is too fragile. I cannot risk damaging it. So climb we must. And as I've repeated many times—"

"I know. I know. Only the Chosen One can fuse the oculus pieces and reveal the treasure map. Yeah. Yeah. Okay. Let's go." I'm still holding the bag with the oculus and the water bottle that Amira gave me. I take big gulps and start walking toward the giant, curved wall that looks like a stadium cut in half.

As I arrive, I stop for a second to look at the plaque in front of the stairs and toss the empty water bottle into the trash can next to it. Things may be futile, but no way I'm littering. However, I can't believe that I'm stopping to read a plaque and that I'm actually interested in what's written. Amira is really having a weird effect on me, and not in a good way! The plaque says that Star Axis is a naked-eye observatory. There's something about the stars, geometry, alignment, blah blah blah. And holy...what! There are 147 steps. Ugh. I look up the sandstone staircase that is carved between two long walls that lead you up into the pyramid. It's like walking up to the nosebleed seats in this cut-in-half stadium, but with tall walls on either side of the steps.

"Why do you stop? Climb. My destiny awaits me atop those stairs," Ahriman demands.

"Listen, I'm all for an epic villain line, but yours really need some work. I mean, *destiny awaits*? Talk about a snooze fest. You should really mix it up a bit. Consider, *No. I am your father.* Darth Vader really knew how to pack a punch. My mom told me that she saw *Empire* in the theaters when she was a kid and that people in the audience actually screamed *Noooo!* when Darth said that to Luke. Now that is an epic bad-guy line."

"I am ignoring you." Ahriman shakes his head and looks really irritated.

You, Hamza Majid, are a mere child, kidnapped by one of the most evil creatures ever to set foot on Earth. You have no weapons. Unless you count your constant banter and fast-talking skills as a part of your arsenal. You are being compelled to climb 147 steps in this hot desert at this monument with no snack stand in sight. You wonder if you have any choices left at all. Do you throw yourself to the ground, succumbing to a fate written by Ahriman? Or do you muster your last dregs of courage and remember that Majids never quit (unless ordered to by your parents)? Design! Your! Destiny!

I take a deep breath, narrow my eyes, and get my game face on. Sometimes you need to give yourself your own pep talk. I don't need a book to tell me what my options are. I know. I clench my jaw and take the first step. I'm the one designing my destiny! I raise a fist in the air.

"Is that some sort of strange human ritual along with mumbling to yourself? Is that how all humans ascend steps?" Ahriman shakes his head. "And they say you are the most evolved version of your species."

I gaze up the stairs as they seem to get super narrow at the top. But I think they're actually the same size as where I am now, at the bottom. In art class, we learned about perspective and how it makes things that are far away look extra small. And the top of those stairs looks really, really far away. I can do this. Just can't look down as I'm going up. Here goes nothing. Here goes everything.

I huff and puff and collapse at the top of the stairs. Ahriman steps past me and scans the tiny room. Then I look down. Down. Down. All the way to the bottom of all those steps. *Gulp.* Big mistake. My face gets all sweaty, and I start to feel dizzy. I close my eyes.

"Here it is. At last," Ahriman whispers behind me. His voice is kind of low and has this I'm-in-a-library feel to it. But I don't look at him. I've scooched myself against a wall of the empty room where the stairs led and have my head between my knees, trying to breathe. Trying not to puke. Crud. Every time

I try not to think of puke, it's of course all I can think about. Puke. Vomit. Throw-up. Upchuck. Hurl. Gag. Nooooo. I'm a thesaurus of barf words!

I take a few deep breaths—it's something I've been working on at the climbing gym. I'm getting better with heights, but it's still not easy. The breathing helps calm me down. It "centers me," according to one of the climbing instructors. Of course, it's a lot easier to be calm when an evil dev dude isn't glaring at me all the time with his fiery eyeballs.

My stomach feels a bit more settled, and I push myself up and walk through an archway into a small, square room—the observatory. In there is a pedestal, kind of like the ones we saw in the museums—with a crescent moon–shaped holder that's on a small tripod that seems to be able to tilt. I'm guessing that's what the oculus goes into. It's facing a tall rectangular opening in the sloped wall of the stone pyramid. The sign above says VIEWING WINDOW. The sun has set now, and when I look out the glassless window, I notice it's sort of angled toward the sky. Hey, at least I'm not looking down. Oh, wow. Amira would really love this. It's not even midnight pitch-black dark out, and you can already see little stars popping up in the sky. At the horizon, there's still a tiny stripe of blue.

Ahriman taps my shoulder, and I turn around. He hands me the two pieces of the oculus that he's been holding on to; I still have the third in my sack. "The Chosen One must fuse these together, then place the completed oculus on the stand, tilting it toward the light of the North Star. The location will then be revealed."

"Dude, you do realize there's no map? Right?"

"See beyond your seeing eye."

"Okay, I've had enough riddles for today, thank you. What does that mean?"

"Fix the oculus, first."

"Fine," I say, and then crouch down, placing the two pieces on the ground, my back turned to Ahriman. When I open the bag Amira gave me, I'm confused at first, because I don't see the oculus pieces. It's dark up here and the light is pretty much just from the stars, and I *am* hungry, but I swear...all

I see are chocolate-glazed donuts. What? I reach into the bag, and my fingers brush against the smooth, cool surface of the oculus shard, which is now coated in chocolate glaze. Amira gave me snacks! Awwww.

Oh. Oh. OH! I'm forming the silliest idea ever. But in the absence of a really good idea, a not-so-good idea is the only way to go. I sneak a look at Ahriman, who has stepped toward the viewing window and is muttering things to himself as he points at the stars.

I slip the two oculus pieces into the paper bag with the third and pull out a donut. "Got it!" I yell, partially holding up the shiny, glazed side toward Ahriman, while trying to block him from getting a good look at it.

Ahriman turns to me, the fire dancing in his eyes. "At last. My true destiny, my singular dream of all these many eons within my grasp."

I take a step back. "I'll never let you have it!" I shout, then turn my back toward him and shove the entire donut into my mouth. This plan is ridiculous, but if Ahriman is going to turn me into a carcass of singed, smoked kid, I'm going to have chocolate deliciousness on my tongue as I bite it.

Ahriman grabs me by the shoulder and spins me around; my cheeks are in a chipmunk-storing-about-a-million-nuts-in-its-mouth-type situation. I chew and swallow, chew and swallow. This is an incredibly large donut.

"Nooooo! What have you done, you fool? You ate the oculus? How could such a thing even be possible?" Ahriman raises his fist to the sky. "Of all the ghastly black hole spaghettification, Suleiman! You have created this oculus from a mutable substance? One fit for human consumption? Has this all been your truly bizarre, final trick? To mock me? You always had a human childishness about you. Very well, then, the humans you protected for so long shall suffer endless pain!" Then he turns to me, fire at the tips of his fingers.

I swallow the last bite of donut. And try really hard to keep it down, which is tough because my heart is racing, my adrenaline is shooting through the roof, and I feel faint. Is this a panic attack? I think I'm having a panic attack. Okay. Okay. Run, Hamz.

Ahriman aims his fiery fingers at me and, somehow, miraculously, my feet move and I dash toward the stairs just as a bolt of fire shoots toward me. I dive to my side and it barely misses me, but the paper bag I'm still clutching in my hand goes up in flames. And as I trip and fall, the oculus pieces and one very burnt donut drop to the ground. The bag is turning to ash in my hand. I'm scared I'm going to be next.

"Ha! You impudent creature," Ahriman mutters as he walks toward the oculus pieces, crouching down next to them, placing them so they form a disjointed circle. He looks up at me, his face hard and jaw set. "Make no mistake. Your worth to me is slowly ebbing away; there are but few tasks left." His voice is really low and terrifyingly relaxed as he says this. You know when your parents are super angry at you but their voices get soft? It's the calm before the storm. Ahriman can already devnado himself. I'm freaking out at what his rage storm could be.

He places the three pieces of the oculus in front of me, and I scooch toward them. The broken parts are jagged. It's pretty easy to see which piece goes where to complete the circle—basically a 3D puzzle for toddlers. "Is there some kind of special glue?" I shrug. My heart is thudding so hard against my chest it almost hurts, but I try to shove down my fear. Maybe this donut-eating thing was silly, but it gained me and hopefully Amira some time, at least. Also, I'm a lot less hungry. Bonus! We're not going down without a fight, in this case with food. A food fight! Ha! Even close to death, I still got it.

Ahriman scrunches his entire face at me, then shrugs. "I know of no such glue."

"Great," I say as I bring the pieces together. "Maybe do you have a piece of gum? I've used that as paste before." When I bring the three pieces together, a light flashes from the dark, smooth surface of the oculus shards, like all the star sprinkles in them are actually shining. The pieces draw together, fusing, seamlessly. I stare closer. I can't even tell where it was broken. Whoa. Super Chosen One mind glue is apparently one of my powers now? This is really going to come in handy. I grab the oculus—still sticky with the chocolate glaze—and stand up. I'm almost tempted to lick it, but stop myself.

Ahriman reaches for it, but then pulls his hand back. My grip around the oculus tightens—I *want* to protect this thing, like it's mine. Weird. When I look at it, the stars are moving inside the oculus and forming...are those words? This shiny black donut is talking to me! I quickly glance at Ahriman, who is gazing at the oculus like it's the love of his life or something. He doesn't say anything about the stars moving in it, so I keep my mouth shut. Words form, in letters that I think are Urdu? Maybe Arabic? Or Persian? Even though I sort of know Urdu and a little bit of Arabic, for me, it's sometimes really hard to tell the difference, especially if the letters are written in fancy calligraphy. But then a message flashes in English and quickly disappears: *Water from the sands. Fire from the sky. Uneasy rests the Ring when the claim is a lie.*

Whoa. A secret message. Like the kind the jade

tablet gave us in Qaf. All for me! I have no idea what it means. But maybe I will! At some point! I repeat the phrase in my mind over and over, hopefully memorizing it. I bite my lips to make sure I don't blurt out anything about the message.

"Place it on its cradle. Gently," Ahriman orders me.

I look around. After that donut thing, I'm pretty much out of options up here. I can't exactly jump from this pyramid observatory. Pretty sure I'd end up a Hamza pancake, which I really want to avoid. I put the completed oculus—it's a little sticky from the chocolate glaze—onto the crescent tripod and there's a suction sound. The kind you hear when you stick your palm on the end of a vacuum tube when it's running and your mom isn't looking because you want to see if it's strong enough to suck up your LEGO Venom minifig but your skin gets caught up in the suction. Not that I've ever, ever done that. (P.S. It's totally strong enough.) Anyhoo... there's the sucking sound from the oculus holder and then... awkward silence. My eyes circle the small oculus chamber, and, well, nothing happens.

Ahriman doesn't look upset, though. Kinda the opposite. His eyes get all fiery inside, tiny flames in the place where his pupils should be. This eye effect he has is both gross and cool.

"Tilt the oculus toward the North Star," he says, pointing to the rectangular window opening.

"Uhhh, if you wanted a Chosen One who understood nerdy star stuff, you should've picked my sister."

Ahriman huffs and pulls me over to the window. "There," he says, pointing to the brightest star in the sky. It's so dark and, holy smokes, I've never seen so many stars in my life. I jerk away from him and walk back toward the oculus. I go around so that when I look through the donut hole of the oculus, I can see the stars outside the rectangular window. I tilt the crescent-tripod thingy so that the North Star is right in the center.

"Step away," hisses Ahriman.

"'Thank you' might be a more appropriate response. And are you sure you read the instructions on this right? Because nothing is happening. Zippo. Zilch.

Nada. Are there supposed to be fireworks? Maybe some glowing? Do you need reading glasses? I'm totally familiar with mistakes caused by old people not wearing their reading glasses. And you're the oldest creature by a lot and...oh...uh, not that you don't look good for your age...."

I trail off because as I'm going on, a yellow ray of light beams in through the window, shooting through the center of the oculus and pointing to a spot on the sandy floor. Ahriman gets down on his hands and knees and blows away a layer of sand with a giant huff.

There's a map etched in the stone floor. And the starlight beam focuses on a specific spot. The map isn't marked with names or anything, but from the outlines of the countries, I think it's lighting up a place in the Arabian Desert, maybe?

If this didn't mean the end of the world as we know it, I would actually be impressed, because this is so dang cool. But all I feel is hollow inside because I've failed at everything so far.

Ahriman hoots and whoops and jumps up and

down, wiggling his four ears and doing a wave with his fingers interlaced....Is that supposed to be... dancing? Is he dabbing now? That's so seven years ago. I mean, my mom has a picture of me doing it with my nursery school classes. Embarrassing.

Ahriman's jumping for joy. And that makes me feel so tiny, like I'm sinking into the sands, being swallowed up by this giant observatory. I don't know where Amira is or even if she and Aasman Peri are okay. We haven't stopped Ahriman, and now he knows where the Ring of Power is. He can defeat the armies of Qaf with that ring, control them, then take over all of Earth. I sink to the hard, sandy floor. How is one kid supposed to fight this? I don't think I could even write fan fiction that would get me out of this conundrum.

"Have faith, young hero," Maqbool's Force ghost voice whispers in my ear while Ahriman dances around. "Do not give up. Your efforts thus far have been both valiant and tasty. It is not yet the end."

"I wish the end would hurry up and get here. The waiting for the disaster is the worst part. It reminds me of when we watched this documentary about the *Titanic* in class, and everyone knew it was going to sink, but we were all on the edge of our seats waiting, hoping it wouldn't happen. This one girl, Aria, totally bawled; all she kept saying was there was enough room on that door for both of them. I had no idea what she was talking about till someone said it was about some old-timey movie also called *Titanic*. But even knowing what was going to happen, it was still scary watching the reenactment of it sinking with all those people in the freezing water and the band playing as it sank. Did the musicians really do that? Was that brave? Stupid? A little bit of both? Maqbool, you listening? Any thoughts?"

"What are you going on about? That old fool jinn Maqbool can't help you now." Ahriman has finally stopped his gloat dancing and is paying attention to me again.

I pop up off the ground, clench my hands into fists, march over to Ahriman, and kick him in the shin. I have nothing to lose at this point. Pretty sure a fiery, ashy future awaits me.

Ow.

I think that hurt me more than it hurt him. Still worth it.

Ahriman shakes his head. "You cannot hurt me. Soon my power will lie beyond that of any man, creature, or Chosen One. Now we must away to the hidden Ring and my hidden army." Ahriman wraps his hands around the oculus.

"Hidden army?"

He pulls up on the oculus as he responds. "Did I not tell you? The Ring of Power is buried with an enormous jinn army, waiting to be awakened, waiting for a master to command them. And that master will be me."

I suck in my breath. My blood runs cold. I keep thinking this situation can't get worse. And then it does.

Ahriman groans trying to lift the oculus, but he can't. It's stuck. Sort of glued in place. Super Chosen One mind-glued, perhaps? Then he grabs a sword from his side and tries to hack it off. It doesn't even make a scratch on the oculus or the crescent tripod. He motions for me to try. I can't lift it, either.

I'm waiting for an explosion of anger, but Ahriman just scoffs. "I see Suleiman the Wise has yet more tricks. Well, never mind. I need no souvenirs. The oculus has served its sole and final purpose," he says, and then stares right at me, the flames in his eyes burning bright. "And now you, Chosen One, shall serve your final purpose."

As you hear Ahriman utter those words, you wonder if there is any way to stop his eventual worlds domination. Will you…

Record scratch. In those *Design! Your! Destiny!* books, there's always a choice at the end of every chapter, usually an obvious one. But right now, I don't think there are any choices left for me.

CHAPTER 18

Pole (Star) Position

Amira

"RUN!" AASMAN PERI SCREAMS, AND THEN SHOVES ME toward the entrance and away from the bag of snakes Ahriman unleashed on us. *Vipers,* she called them. Saw-toothed ghul vipers. I trip and stumble as I scramble out of the room toward the Daru Staircase. "Help! Peris! Jinnators! Someoooooooone!"

I watch as Aasman Peri flies up haltingly. Ahriman really hurt her wing and she can't fly right. I see her straining, trying to pull against gravity. I watch in horror as one of the ghul vipers rears up and jumps toward her, biting her on the leg. "Ahhhh-hhhhh!" Her scream makes goose bumps pop up all over my arm. She's never screamed like that before—no matter what we've faced. She half-flies, trying to kick off the floor when her boot touches it, and then falls through the large arched doorway as the army of snakes slithers toward her.

She's writhing in pain, kicking at nothing. "No! No! You can't take me!" she yells. The snake bite has made her delirious! I grab her arms and try to pull her away, but the vipers slide closer and closer, their tongues flickering in and out, taunting us.

"En garde!" a voice yells from behind me. It's a slew of jinnators armed with brooms and mops, with the PRI peris flying behind them. They rush past us, and the jinnator brooms and mops morph into long swords. Whoa. Handy! The vipers rush at them, but they are no match for the *snicker-snack* of their jinn blades.

Three of the peris fly down to us. Nayeli, the leader, takes Aasman Peri's head in their lap and whispers something to her in one of the languages

I heard in Qaf. The other two rip apart her lower pant leg and reveal the viper bite. It's red and bloody and there are two big teeth marks in it. The peris exchange worried glances. "Help her!" I plead.

"We will," one of the peris says, reaching into a small pouch at their waist. They pull out a crystal vial with a clear liquid in it. They pour two drops of the thick liquid into each viper tooth mark. It foams, and Aasman Peri yells out, but the wounds slowly close until all that's left are two small red welts.

"I know what that is," I say, thinking back to our time in Qaf. "Zam Zam water."

The peris nod.

"Her wing!" I add, pointing to the one Ahriman damaged. Aasman Peri moans as the three peris slowly turn her over and get to work on her wing. One adds Zam Zam water to it, while another pulls out a spool of shiny golden thread from her pack. Using a fine silver needle, she begins sewing the tiny tears that have cobwebbed in the membrane of her wing.

I hear a hissing sound; one of the vipers was

hiding behind a small bench. It slithers toward us and rears its head, its tongue flickering at me and the peris. I grab my dagger and cut through its skin as it falls at my feet in a pile of dust.

The jinnators destroy the remaining vipers, and a thick black ash covers the floor.

"Sacré rouge!" one of them says in a French accent, shaking his head. "This will be an enormous endeavor to clean up before the museum opens in the morning."

The British jinnator who brought us to the Louvre rolls his eyes. "I've seen far worse. Were you at the Great Pyramid of Giza?"

"Oui!" says a third jinnator. "When the top fell off? La catastrophe!"

The six jinnators all look at one another and exclaim, "Americans!"

"Hey!" I say. "American in earshot."

"Of course there is. Where there's a mess at a great cultural institution, there's almost always an American involved," the British jinnator says.

I scoff. "Please, I mean, you live in England. Have you seen your rowdy, racist soccer fans? Besides, it was actually a dev who caused this mess! And who hurt Aasman Peri and kidnapped my brother and wants to take over the worlds. Maybe get some perspective!"

"You're both right," a voice croaks from behind me. "Both the Americans and the British tend to cause messes wherever they go—literally and metaphorically." I turn to see Aasman Peri sitting up. She looks pale and tired, like she's been sick with the flu for a week.

I rush over to her. I almost hug her but stop, remembering she's not big on hugs. "I'm so glad you're okay."

"Don't be melodramatic. It was a small ghul-viper bite. I've survived worse." She grins. The three peris surrounding her help her up. She takes a deep breath and then shoots up in the air, flying around and coming to hover above the *Winged Victory at Samothrace* statue. She draws her fixed wings back into the same pose as the statue. "See," she says. "This sculpture was totally based on a peri."

I smile. But my heart's not totally in it. As happy as I am to see Aasman Peri healed, I'm terrified for Hamza. I'm scared of what Ahriman will do when he gets that Ring of Power. At this point, it feels like a done deal.

"We have to get to Ahriman," I whisper. Even if it feels impossible, we can't give up. He has my brother. "We have to stop him."

The curmudgeonly British jinnator looks down at the floor. "He's so far ahead of you. It's better to devise a Plan B."

"There is only one plan. To stop him. To get the Ring of Power first. We may be down, but we're not out." I punch a fist into the air. I only half-believe what I'm saying, but fake-it-till-you-make-it worked for me before, so I might as well try it again. "Trust me, I have a plan."

The jinnators look at one another again and then turn to me, warm, wide smiles on their wrinkly faces. "Americans," they say together.

Okay, so my plan was maybe not the most detailed. But it was better than doing nothing. I asked a jinnator to take us to Star Axis, but there was apparently no closet portal at the giant monument. So he took us to the next closest spot: Anton Chico, New Mexico.

It's absolutely in the middle of nowhere, USA. But before shoving us out of his broom closet, the jinnator did us a favor by calling a Checker Cab—I kinda remember my dad telling me they were the old cabs they had in New York City. (I guess they're in other places, too?) We watched a double feature once about a kid who kept getting left behind by his family when they went on vacation (honestly, who forgets a kid?), and when that kid was in a Checker Cab in New York, my dad actually paused the movie to tell us about the history of cabs, because, as my mom says, he's a lovable nerd. My mom's sort of a nerd, too. Wish those two nerdy parent were with me now.

It's dark out, and I keep pretending that this place is less creepy than it is. Wish that cab would get here already. Aasman Peri and I are waiting outside an empty bus station for the cab to arrive. She looks tired. Weak. I keep asking her if she's okay, but she keeps barking at me that she's fine. I watch her for a second, and I swear I hear her say, "It's my mind and you're not invited!" Weird.

"Hey, are you talking... Look out!" I yell as a yellow cab with stripes of bright red and orange flames painted along the side comes to a screeching halt in front of the curb. The words CHAKKAR CAB are printed along the door. Wait. A *Chakkar* Cab. Not Checker? Chakkar, like the Urdu word for "dizzy"? Uh-oh... not inspiring confidence!

Aasman Peri flies up in time to avoid getting hit with a plume of dust and sand. Me, not so lucky or winged. I pull out a hand wipe from a small packet in my backpack. Sure, the worlds are about to be taken over by an evil dev, but that's no reason to forget good hygiene. I wipe the grime off my face and toss the wipe into a trash can as Aasman Peri flies back down and is chatting with the driver through the open window.

"Let's go," he says, and bangs the outside of the car door with his palm.

Aasman Peri and I slide into the back seat. I try not to stare at the driver, who has two small horns sticking out of his lavender-colored face and thick black plastic glasses pushed up on his nose. "Can you please take us to Star Axis, uh, sir?" I ask.

He snorts. "You can call me George. My full name is George Dutton Aurangzeb Nizamuddin Jahan."

"Uhh, George?"

"All right. Go ahead. I've heard it all before. Yes, George is an unusual name for a jinn-dev. But my mom—she was the jinn—really loved shape-shifting into students and taking classes at the local university. She named me after her favorite professor and some of her royal Mughal friends. Kids in jinn school mocked me a lot, mispronounced my very long name on purpose. I mean, it's hard enough being a do-nasli, a two clan. But I'm pretty sure I'm the only fire spirit with that full name on Earth."

I nodded. "Yeah, people can be pretty harsh sometimes if you're even a tiny bit *different*."

He shrugged. "Being unique is cool."

"Totally agree!" I say as George steps on the gas and I'm pressed back hard into the plasticky seats. The. Cab. Is. Flying! Flying cars exist! I knew it! Hamza would be so excited if he were here. As the cab lifts higher into the air and zooms us through the desert night, Aasman Peri grabs onto me, like she's never flown before. Guess she only trusts her own flying?

"There it is!" George points to a tall, skinny pyramid jutting straight out of the desert high into the sky. At first, it's hard to see in the darkness, but as we get closer, I realize how huge it is. It's sandstone, so it blends with the surroundings, but it's clearly man-made. Whoever designed it was a genius. All the angles are perfect, and from above it, I can see a very long, narrow set of stairs cut into a curved wall that leads up to a small chamber at the top of the open-air pyramid. This is so cool.

I glance at Aasman Peri, and she looks a little

green around the gills. The peris at the Louvre told me that she was okay but that she still might be a bit weak and wobbly as her body recovers fully from the viper bite.

"Can you take us down, please?" I ask.

"Down? It's much faster to jump from here. I'll hover above, no problem."

"Jump? I'm a person. A human person. We break way easier than jinn and dev and have no peri wings." As I say this, Aasman Peri opens the door on her side and flies out. "Thanks for waiting!" I yell down at her.

"Right. Right. Good point. Humans break. . . ." George rubs his stubbly lavender chin.

"Hurry up, slowpoke!" Aasman Peri says. I take a peek and see she's about fifty feet below, standing in the small room at the pyramid's top.

"I've got it!" George says, and then hands me a rope. A rope.

"What am I supposed to do with this?"

"Tie it around your waist. I'll tie the other end to the doorframe and help ease you down. No worries! This is very strong rope. I got it at the Abr ki

Darwaaza market when I was visiting an aunt in Chicago."

"C'mon!" Aasman Peri is getting antsier and bossier by the second and it's really annoying me. "Your brother needs you!"

Knife in the heart. She's right. I'm having a mini panic attack up here while we still have to figure out where the Ring is buried. I loop the rope around my waist while George ties his end to the doorframe and then twists the rope around his very thick and muscly arms.

Okay. Okay. I got this. I've totally done way scarier stuff than jump out of a floating cab onto a pyramid. No problem. I open the car door. My breathing gets shallow and fast. I can't do this. I can't do this. Wait. I have to do this.

"Shove her!" Aasman Peri instructs George.

"What? Wait! Noooooooooooo!"

George listens to Aasman Peri and gives me a nudge. My life flashes before my eyes. Well, my day, anyway. What a day. What a nightmare. Terrible. Horrible. Day. Caused by Hamza biking off when he wasn't supposed to. When I rescue him, I'm totally kicking his butt. If I survive this fall.

AHHHHHHHHHHH!

I close my eyes. This fall is endless. I bet I missed the chamber on top of the pyramid. Oh God. This rope isn't long enough. Why isn't George pulling me back. I'm not going to make it. I'm going to dieeeeeeeee.

"Ow!" I feel a pinch on my arm.

"Open your eyes, silly, and for all the heavens' sake, stop screaming. You landed a while ago."

I flip open my eyelids. Oh. I look up and George is leaning out of the cab, giving me a thumbs-up. I force a grin and a thumbs-up in return. I quickly untie the rope from around my waist, and George pulls it back up into the cab.

"I got another fare! Nice meeting you! And good luck, funny girl!" I wave at George as the cab swooshes away.

When I turn back to Aasman Peri, she's muttering to herself again, leaning against one of the smooth walls of the pyramid. "You okay?" I ask. "Maybe sit down? Do you need a swig of water?"

Her eyes flash in anger at me. "I'm fine," she almost snarls. I wonder if mood swings are part of the viper bite. I mean, I guess I would be pretty pissed off if I were in her boots, too. Then she points to a smaller inner chamber I hadn't noticed, through an archway. "It's in there, the oculus observatory chamber."

I step toward the oculus—it's totally whole now. And there's streaks of donut glaze on it. Hamza, I hope that you at least got to eat one and that you used hand sanitizer before you did. I can't even tell that the oculus was ever broken. It's cradled in a crescent holder that's on a small tripod on top of a stone pedestal. It's tilted toward a rectangular window. I've seen a lot of pretty fantastical things this summer, but I'm not sure if I've seen anything as beautiful as this: A perfect ray of pale golden starlight is shining through the window and through the narrow hole in the oculus onto a map etched on the floor.

I get closer to the map and see a pinpoint of starlight marking a spot in the Arabian Desert. That's where it is. The Ring. Ahriman. Hamza.

"It's the light of Earth's North Star," Aasman Peri

says. She's limped up to the entrance of the oculus chamber. Her face looks a bit brighter now, though, so that's good. "The story goes that the Chosen One would find the location of the Ring of Power by piecing together the oculus and pointing it in the direction of the star—the one humans used for millennia to guide them."

I stare at the star point at the map and then back through the oculus, then look at Aasman Peri. Not sure why she's repeating all this info. Does she not remember I was there when the professor told us all this?

Something doesn't feel right.

"*Earth's North Star. Earth's North Star,*" I whisper to myself.

I step over to the rectangular window and gaze out at a small slice of the sky. The builder must have created this as a way for humans to observe the movement of the stars and moon and sun in relationship to Earth. When I was really little, I thought it was funny to think about how Earth was both spinning like a top and moving around the sun at the same time as the moon orbited around us. It must have been so strange for ancient people to see how the stars moved. Wouldn't that have totally freaked them out? Some scientists and astronomers were jailed or even murdered because people thought they were heretics for claiming the sun is the center of our universe and Earth revolves around it, that Earth spins on an imaginary axis that kind of wobbles. I guess that's why the architect of this place called it Star Axis, because you can observe the movement of Earth by seeing how the stars move in the window over the course of a night. It's a naked-eye telescope that wants you to take your time and realize how the night sky changes. How we can actually observe it the way our ancestors might have thousands of years ago.

Oh. Oh. OH.

Wait a minute.

Hold on.

Idea forming...

Adler Planetarium Astronomy Camp knowledge gears spinning.

The sky...

The stars...

Our ancestors.

That wobble. That weird Earth-spinning-like-a-top axis wobble means that our planet leans a tiny bit. The wobble is a kind of tilt. The astronomy camp counselor showed us by spinning a giant globe in the classroom. A toy globe spins smoothly; it doesn't tilt or move at all except going around and around in a perfect rotation on its imaginary axis. But that's not how it works for the actual Earth. Earth is more like a spinning top. While the top is spinning around, it also tilts a bit in one direction or another, eventually falling on one side. Earth isn't going to fall over (hopefully), but it does tilt a tiny bit, first in one direction, then back toward the other direction. It's a super-tiny amount. Humans can't notice it in our lifetime. But it makes a difference for when scientists think about GPS, programming satellites, or observing the stars because, over hundreds and thousands of years, what humans see in the night sky shifts a little bit. If I stood in this exact spot, at this exact same time, every night for a thousand years, looking at the exact same place in the sky, the stars I would see would be different, slowly shifting a tiny, itsy bit each night.

Oh my God...I think I know what's wrong. Science will save us! We did a "stars of the ancient peoples" unit in camp—and for us, now, the North Star is Polaris. But, but, but, but, a long, long time ago, it wasn't. The North Star is a position, NOT a specific star. So for Suleiman or even for the Keepers of The Ring, it was a different star. I scan the slice of sky that I can see through the rectangular observatory window. "There it is!" I scream, pointing to a star that isn't Polaris, the star that we *now* call the North Star.

"What are you mumbling about?" Aasman Peri asks, looking really bored.

"We had a whole project on this at camp! When the oculus was made...when the Ring was buried... the North Star wasn't Polaris. It was Thuban. Look!" I point to the brightest star in the Draco constellation. "Ahriman pointed the oculus toward the wrong star! He's digging in the wrong place!"

✦ ✷ ✦

POLE (STAR) POSITION

Oh my God! This is it. Our chance. Science, if you were a person, I would kiss you! We can still beat him to the Ring. Rescue Hamz. And make everything right. Aasman Peri is muttering something again, but I've totally tuned her out. My brain is all science now. I carefully tilt the tripod crescent that the oculus is resting on so that it lines up with Thuban. The light fades from the map, from the place where Ahriman must be digging. C'mon. C'mon. I know I'm right. Earlier this summer I said I didn't believe in making wishes on stars anymore. But right now, I do. Please, starshine. Wish I may, wish I might, harness the power of science tonight!

I step back from the oculus as a bright beam bursts through the narrow window, bathing the whole pyramid in a warm light, as a bright golden ray shoots through the oculus and sparks a spot on the map. It's still the Arabian Desert but a totally different location. I bend down and touch the spot on the map, watching a bit of starshine dance on my fingers. When the tip of my finger meets the light, a name etches itself in illuminated gold script: UBAR.

"The lost city of Ubar?" Aasman Peri gasps. I hadn't even heard her step up to me. "The fabled ancient city of Suleiman. There are no real records of that place. Some of the old Qaf scholars say it was merely a myth that Suleiman himself created to throw people off the scent of the Ring of Power."

I jump in the air, my fists raised. I turn to Aasman Peri. "Don't you see what this means? The Arabian Desert is huge and the place Ahriman is searching is probably hundreds of miles away. We can still get the Ring before him! How do we get there? Call the cab again? Use the broom closet portals? Is there some other fast flying method that can get us there in a blink?"

Aasman Peri is pacing, whispering to herself, her back turned toward me.

"Hey! Are you listening? We finally have the upper hand. We have to—"

She whips her head around and hisses at me, sticking out a slithery green serpent tongue. Her eyes have gone totally white. My blood goes cold.

"Thisssss issss working out even better than we thought it would." A hoarse voice comes out of Aasman Peri's mouth as one of the ghul vipers slithers out of her bag and wraps itself around her arm.

I scramble backward. "Aasman Peri?"

A voice like sandpaper laughs. "Sssshe's gone. She tried to fight it. But peris far sssssstronger than her have sssssssuccumbed to possession by viper bite." The words are coming out of Aasman Peri's mouth, but the snake is her ventriloquist! I shudder as tingles shoot up my spine.

Possession. She's possessed.

I take a deep breath, ball my hands into fists at my side, and try to stand firm. "Aasman Peri, can you hear me? Fight it. You can fight it."

"Humans truly are foolssssss. It's hard to believe that either you or your brother were Chosen for anything. But I will ssssssay this for you, you played right into my hands. Ahriman only wanted me to watch over you, but now you've delivered him the Ring."

"What? No!" I reach for my dagger and look at

Aasman Peri, my friend. It's her body, but it's not her mind. I don't want to attack her. But I have to. I suck in my breath and then let out a roar as I charge her.

She flies up and back, then hesitates. For a brief second, her eyes are brown again. It's the real her.

"Aasman Peri!" I stop abruptly, not wanting to hurt her.

But her eyes roll back in her head, once more turning a foggy white. A snarl crosses her face. She flies toward me, feetfirst, like she's sliding into home plate in midair, and thrusts her boots straight into my chest.

"Ahhhhhhhh!" I scream as I'm thrown back, hitting the wall before sliding to the ground.

She laughs. "Thank you for your sssssservice, Chosen One. Ahriman will be mossssst pleased to receive this information," she says before flying off at a speed I've never seen her wings take before.

I let my body go limp on the floor as tears flow down my face. She's going to tell Ahriman everything.

What have I done?

CHAPTER 19

My Life Is in Ruins

Hamza

"WE'VE BEEN DIGGING FOREVER," I GROAN AS I WATCH THE sun rising, making the sand hotter every second. "And by digging I mean you getting all devnado-y and making sand fly everywhere," I shout to Ahriman.

He ignores me and stalks up a sand dune. When we got here, I thought Ahriman was going to whirlwind this sand away, but we sort of sputtered when we landed. Even now he's pretty much walking or stomping around, even digging with his hands a little, which seems like a weird choice to me.

Dunes are all around us. If life as I know it wasn't about to end, I'd find a way to hack something into a snowboard so I could surf down these hills. That would be wicked awesome! We're surrounded by dunes and then long stretches of sand for miles around. So far the Arabian Desert is similar to the Michigan Dunes except there's no Great Lake and this desert is way bigger and hotter and there's an evil red dev stomping around like a hangry little kid who just got told he couldn't have a second scoop of ice cream. Not that *I've* ever acted that way. I swear, I haven't (that much).

"I do not understand," Ahriman says. "This is the place on the map. A city should rise upon summoning. The Ring should already be upon my hand!" Ahriman raises a fist to the sky very, very dramatically. I guess all that time imprisoned in a brass lamp stuck in the moon really gave him the opportunity to perfect his evil bad-guy routine. "This is your subterfuge!" He points at me.

I throw my hands in the air. "Are you serious? I'm not the subterfuger...subterfugitive, or, umm, subterfugitor, or whatever! You've literally been in my face whole time, and, in case you need reminding, it was you who told me where to point the oculus. Do you actually think I could find the North Star on my own? If you think about it, this whole sweaty, sunburn-y situation"—I gesture around me at the open desert—"is on you."

"You dare accuse me of sabotaging myself? Typical human illogic! That makes no sense!"

"Or does it?" I raise an eyebrow at him and cross my arms over my chest like I've made a really good point. Because I have. Our SEL counselor once talked to us about how sometimes people are afraid of their own success. They're afraid of failing, so they give up rather than try. *Say yes to yourself,* she told us. I really took her words to heart and kept saying yes to myself every time I wanted a snack between meals. My mom wasn't too happy about that. When I told her I was the boss of me and was saying yes to my dreams, she told me that maybe my dreams should be bigger than snacks, which, I dunno, I can dream of very big snacks.

While I'm fantasizing about an ice-cream scoop the size of my head with bits of chocolate-covered pretzels in it, I notice Ahriman bending down, whispering into the sands. That dude is losing it. When I look up, I see a fast-moving bird heading right for us. Dang, it's super fast. And huge! Weird. I look away but quickly turn back.

That's no bird.

It's Aasman Peri! She's coming to rescue me! Yes! Finally, the element of surprise I was looking for! Sneak attack. I bet a whole battalion is behind her. I can't let Ahriman see her. "Hey! Have you checked down here?" I call to him.

"Of course, I have!" Ahriman responds without looking at me. "You saw me do so."

"No, I mean this exact spot, right where I'm standing. My secret Chosen One tingle is telling me this might be it."

Ahriman stands up. "What is this Chosen One tingle to which you refer?"

"Oh, uh, you know, like a Spidey, er, I mean, a

very special sense only I get.... The hair on my arms stands up, sometimes there's goose bumps. It's an indicator that something is wrong, er, I mean, right! It's an indicator that there's a Chosen One–type scenario about to go down. I really started feeling it when I put the oculus in the holder at Star Axis, maybe it gave me this power."

Aasman Peri is coming in hot. I've never seen her fly so fast. *Pull out your daggers,* I want to shout, but I can't give her away! C'mon, c'mon. I plant my feet in the sand, which is much, much harder than it sounds. It's very shifty. She's almost here. Almost. I make my hands into fists, getting ready to fight.

Ahriman raises an eyebrow, then sighs. "Fine. This so-called tingle of yours better be right. We will search the sand flats again. The Ring must be here. Perhaps it is buried deeper than I thought."

Aasman Peri hovers right behind him. She looks weird. Her eyes are all white. Man this sun glare is bad. "Think again," Aasman Peri says.

Oh, this is going to be good. But where's that

battalion? Amira? Aasman Peri lands right next to Ahriman. What in the name of strange peri logic is she doing? Why aren't her daggers out? Why isn't Ahriman attacking her?

"You're digging in the wrong place, masssssster." Aasman Peri smiles at Ahriman and then whispers something to him as he nods.

Wait. What? Master? "Nooooo!" I yell. "What are you doing? Why are you hissing? And is that... why...why do you have a forked tongue!" That's when I see it: one of the snakes from the museum, slithering up from her boot. She lowers her hand and it wraps itself around her arm like a pet.

Ahriman and Aasman Peri slide down the dune toward me. I reel backward, trying not to stumble. I can't take my eyes off her. It looks like Aasman Peri, but her eyes are white and she has a snake tongue and...oh oh oh, this is bad bad super super bad.

"I can tell from the look of shock in your eyes that you have figured it out," Ahriman says to me. "Bravo. You have proved yourself not as dumb as I thought you'd be. Yes, my ghul vipers are no mere serpents. A single bite means possession." Ahriman grins, showing all his sharp teeth.

"What about Amira?" I want to sound angry, like I'll get revenge if they've hurt my sister, but I can barely say her name without my voice cracking.

Possessed Peri sneers at me. "She's fine. For now. Stranded on top of the Star Axis. I'm sure *someone* will find her before her water runsssss out."

I fall to my knees and close my eyes. *Maqbool? You out there? I'm reaching out with my mind in case you really are a ghost and it's not just my imagination hoping you're here and are real. Well, as real as a ghost could be. I need help, but Amira needs it mo—*

I don't get a chance to finish my ghost begging because Ahriman grabs me, and we whisk away across the desert.

The spot we land in is... exactly like the spot we left. Nothing but dunes and sand everywhere, including up my nose and in my ears, and I don't want to know where else. Possessed Peri—I'm going with this as her villain alter-ego name—lands next to us. I can barely look at her. I mean, it's not *her* her. It's a Venom-type scenario. And I'm really hoping she's going to be more like Spidey, who fights off the alien, er, ghul viper thingy, instead of Eddie Brock, who's all, *Hey, cool, I'll be host to this evil black ooze.*

Possessed Peri steps in front of me and narrows her creepy white eyes, like she can read my mind. Fine. I stare back. *C'mon, Aasman Peri. I know you're in there,* I say to myself, hoping my brain waves will get through her thick viper-infested skull. *Be the hero. Or at least the good kind of antihero, kinda Loki-style. You know, a powered person who loves snarky quips and is a bit too into excessive violence, but mainly against bad guys who really deserve it, like you-know-who.* Possessed Peri blinks, and for a second, her eyes go back to Aasman Peri's brown ones that always look bossy. Only this time, they look scared. *Fight it, Aasman Peri.*

While I'm trying to communicate telepathically

with the real Aasman Peri as opposed to Possessed Peri, who's evil dev's right-hand fairy now, I see Ahriman pacing around, almost like he's measuring something. He has his eyes closed and is talking to himself. Glad I'm not the only one. Of course, if Amira were here, she'd say that maybe it wasn't good to share a habit with the guy who's trying to take over the whole worlds.

Amira, I don't know how to help you. Maybe ghost Maqbool will find you. You figured out how to walk through an oobleck wall and you're a nerd who always gets A's. Please, please, science your way out of being stranded alone in a desert a million miles away from here.

I feel like a balloon that's just been deflated and is flying around the room, about to shrink into nothing but a wrinkly blob of plastic.

"Ubar," Ahriman bellows, and his voice bounces off the dunes. "Even the most ancient of fire spirits thought this place a myth. Suleiman!" he yells to an invisible audience. "You thought you were so clever. Yet here I stand, free and about to defile your legacy.

Destroying the *Lamassu* was merely the beginning of the desecration this foul planet will suffer at my hands."

"What's Ubar?" I ask, interrupting another one of his villain speeches. Ugh. Even I've had enough of them, and I write fanfic that's pretty much 50 percent bad guys talking about how awesome they are right before the hero kicks their butts. A butt-kicking hero would come in real handy right now.

"The lost city of Ubar, city of myth, was said to have been a lush oasis, its riches renowned across the inhabited worlds. It was once a bustling marketplace, a center of the frankincense trade. The fragrance of this city was once so intoxicating it could be smelled oceans away."

"I'm guessing people can smell *us* an ocean away, too, because it's hot and I'm feeling prettttty darn stinky. And your dev sweat is dripping off your nose. Even your four ears are glistening. Which, gross."

"You mock me? Even now? So close to the end of all things as you know them? So close to my ascension? I shall show you the power of my four ears." Ahriman kneels and places his two left ears to the ground. He closes his eyes, like he's meditating.

I start moving away. I don't think there's anywhere I can run to, but I have to try. What else do I have left? But I barely take two steps before Possessed Peri gets in my face. "Uhh, have ghul viper spirits not heard of personal space?" I ask.

She laughs. "Sssssspace? Ahriman sahib can drop you in sssspace if you demand more of it. Perhaps your sister can join you. She must be exquisitely parched by now."

"Shut up!" I yell. "You better—"

"This is it!" Ahriman shouts. "Here. Right here. I can hear the resonance of a thousand jinn warriors longing to be unburied. You"—Ahriman points at me—"come."

Possessed Peri shoves me toward Ahriman, who grabs my hand and holds it down to the sand. He's right. There is some kind of...energy. I get a creepy-crawly feeling all over my skin. I can't believe it—I

DO have Chosen One tingle! And it's not just that I can sniff a bakery from a mile away. This is real. I feel fire spirits. Ahriman holds my hand to the ground and starts whispering words in a language I can't understand, except for one phrase that pops out at me. I know it. I used it. I dreamt about it. *Iftah ya Simsim. Open Sesame.* Words we said to call up a box from the sea around the Island of Confusion. It's not just in stories, it's a summoning enchantment, for real, but in a jokey way. Even at the end of the world—maybe especially—I appreciate the humor.

The ground starts to shake. I jump up. The tops of the dunes around us start to collapse. Oh no! It's going to be an avalanche of sand. A sandvalanche. Where do I go? There's nowhere to run to in the middle of the desert when there's an earthquake.

Ahriman stands and starts laughing or crying, I can't quite tell which. He pulls me back, and then Possessed Peri grabs both of us, flies us maybe ten feet in the air right before the ground starts to crack and open, and a stone column starts to rise up.

CHAPTER 20

Supahi Ex Machina

Amira

I PUSH MYSELF UP OFF THE FLOOR OF THE OCULUS CHAMber and sit with my back against the wall, my feet splayed out toward the map. It's still lit up from the beam of starshine that illuminates the word UBAR, but the ray is starting to soften and fade because of how Earth is moving. That's the whole point of this observatory, to watch the night sky through the rectangular window and see Earth's rotation and wobble and orbit. I turn my head to stare out that window—it's so quiet and dark outside and the night is bursting with stars. And it makes me feel like the loneliest girl in the universe.

But I can't give up.

Majids don't give up. (Unless our parents tell us to cut it out, but that's usually when we're begging for boba tea or mango ice-cream shakes.) My brother is still out there. Maybe Aasman Peri has been possessed and maybe Ahriman is about to get the Ring, but my whole life is outside that window. My family. My friends. My school. This whole planet. And I'm not ready to throw in the flag. Hang on. Nope. That's not the right metaphor. They don't throw flags. Towels. Towels! They throw in towels when they give up. I can't remember if that's for car racing or boxing. Or maybe shopping on the day after Thanksgiving, when you want to be the first one hundred people in line at Target but don't make it. It's one of those. Maqbool once told us that small humans are capable of great things. And I'm that small human! No. Wait. Wrong again. I might be quoting J. R. R. Tolkien talking about Hobbits. Whatever. The point is, I'm not totally beaten yet. Only very, very lost.

I stand up. Pretty sure my face is streaked with tears and dirt, so I wipe it off with the hem of my T-shirt. I reach into the backpack the professor gave me, shove past my broken phone, dwindling snacks, and empty water bottle, and grab the hand sanitizer. I squirt it onto my palms, rubbing them vigorously. They're probably crawling with germs from that cab. I pull my hair out of my messy braid and finger-comb it into a ponytail. I take a deep breath.

Let's do this, Amira.

Okay, I'm talking to myself, but sometimes you're the only one around to give yourself a pep talk. So, in a difficult, catastrophic, world-altering, highly dangerous situation, what do you do? First, assess the scene: stranded, alone in the desert, miles away from the nearest town with only a few drops of water left and a busted phone. My shoulders sink. No. No. C'mon, Amira. A good place to start is maybe to stop thinking about all the terrible things that have happened or all the horrible things that might happen. And I definitely should not think about how I can possibly explain this to my parents. *Sorry, Ummi and Papa, Hamza wandered off by himself under my watch and got kidnapped by an evil dev who wants to control all the fire creatures in all the worlds, destroy the Emperor of Qaf, take over Earth, and oppress us all by digging up a very old Ring of Power.* It's what Sauron wanted to do with his ring, sort of. There's really a lot of tales of evil rings out there. (Note to self: This would be an interesting essay topic. Could I possibly get extra credit for this?)

"Our historians are certain that Tolkien took that one-ring-to-rule-them-all idea from Suleiman—a far more ancient history." A voice comes from behind me. A familiar voice. A voice of a dead jinn who I miss more than anything. Goose bumps pop up all over my skin.

I whip around.

"Maqbool!" I scream with joy. I run toward him to hug him, but he's like a flickering hologram. He smiles at me and pushes up his glasses. "Are you . . . a ghost?" I ask. "Ooh. Is that the right term? I don't want to offend you if—"

"Ghost is fine, thank you for asking. And yes, yes,

I am. I'm sorry I'm incorporeal; otherwise, I would most certainly and warmly return your embrace."

My voice falters because I get choked up. "I...I can't believe it's you. I thought...I thought...Thank you. For saving Hamza, I mean. In Qaf. For sacrificing yourself for my brother."

Maqbool reaches out and sort of tries to pat my head, but I don't feel anything but a tiny shiver of cold. "I was a very old jinn who had seen many, many adventures. And it was time for my journey in life to come to a close. But it wasn't an end. I've been watching all this time. And it is I who should be thanking you, for your bravery. For saving Qaf. And all humankind."

I look down at my dirty, scuffed sneakers. "But it doesn't matter because Ahriman's back. He has Hamza, and Aasman Peri's been possessed by one of his viper ghuls. I don't want to give up, but I don't know how to win, how to beat him. And even if I could figure it out, how am I supposed to get to the Arabian Desert from here? You can't ghost-transport me, can you?" I sniffle, and my eyes start to sting with tears.

"Alas, no. But all is not lost, dear Chosen One. Not yet. Not while you and Hamza are still able to work together," ghost Maqbool whispers.

"But how can we—" I glance up and see that Maqbool is not alone.

"How we often achieve hard, difficult things—with some help from our friends," he says, and gestures behind him.

Standing there, in a giant black pot, is Razia, leader of the Khawla ki Supahi, the women warrior jinn army of Qaf. She steps forward, her silver braid resting over her shoulder, a dagger sheathed at the waist of her colorful pishwaaz; her arms wide open to me. I rush into them and give her a hug.

"You're here? You're not just a hallucination brought on by dehydration? Where are the rest of the Supahi?"

Razia smiles. "Indeed, I am real. My sisters are organizing defenses in Qaf and preparing certain enchantments that might temporarily work against the power of the Ring. Others in Qaf's defense council are in contact with Earth's governments to warn them of what might come and share our knowledge. So they can all be ready if Ahriman gets the Ring and control of all the jinn armies of the worlds."

I gulp. The governments of Earth know about jinn? And Qaf? I guess it's like the UFOs—they kept those secret, too! "But wouldn't that mean he could control you, as well?" I ask Razia. "Make you do whatever he wants?"

"Yes," she says solemnly. "But let's ensure that such a future will never come to pass." She steps back inside her flying pot and holds out her hand to me.

I look up at her and then to ghost Maqbool, who nods.

I wipe my nose with my sleeve. I'm going to pretty much have to burn this shirt; it's way past saving in the wash. "Okay," I say, trying to steady my voice. I take her hand and step into the pot. "Let's go save Aasman Peri and my annoying little brother. And the whole world, too."

Razia's pot lifts up into the night sky, racing toward Ubar in the Arabian Desert. I clench my hands in fists at my sides and ready myself for battle.

CHAPTER 21

Jarmygeddon Is Nigh!

Hamza

"LET GO OF ME!" I SHOUT AT POSSESSED PERI AS I SQUIRM around in her hands in midair, as huge stone columns bust out of the sand below us.

"If you inssssssssist." She flicks her forked tongue at me.

"No," Ahriman commands. Even though Possessed Peri grabbed us both right before we got pummeled by an ancient city rising up from the ground, Ahriman is now hovering in the air by himself, held up by a tiny tornado under each of his feet. He looks a bit off balance. Still, I'm so mad at myself for thinking this, but it's actually kind of cool—wish I could get those in a pair of sneakers. "We cannot let the human be swallowed by the sands."

"Aww, see, I've grown on you! You like me; you really, really like me," I say. It's true; I win everyone over. Eventually.

"I might still have use for him before I discard him."

"Hey! I'm right here. Can you please stop talking about me like I'm leftover fast-food wrappers." Dang it. Now I'm thinking about french fries.

Possessed Peri flies us up higher because these columns are really tall. And now buildings and fountains and pathways are all pushing through, throwing up geysers of sand. I spit some gritty grains out of my mouth and close my eyes to avoid a full-on sand assault.

I open my eyes again, squinting, because, whew, this sun is hot. I don't have sunblock, and I can hear my mom's voice in my head giving me a lecture about how brown people can get skin cancer, too. I wish she were lecturing me right now, because at least it would mean I wasn't alone and scared and about to get baked by the sun. Did I say scared? I meant can't-feel-my-body terrified. I'm trying really hard not to show it. Fake it till you make it! But it would be so much easier to fake it if I had some real Chosen One powers—invisibility, invincibility, Invisalign-ity! No. Wait. That last one's not a thing unless it's about retainers. Sometimes I get on a roll and my brain gets ahead of my mouth and—HOLY ATLANTIS OF THE SANDS . . . I blink, blink again. No. This is beyond even my hyped-up imagination. The entire super-gigantic ancient city is being lifted out of the sands by thousands of jinn?!

It's a jinn army. A jarmy. And they're rising out of the desert, holding the city on their hands. On their hands! They're the ultimate movers. They're dressed in colorful outfits, like kurta pajamas, and their skin is all different colors. I think my mom would call it jewel tones? They have super-pointy ears. Their pointy-ness would make Vulcans jealous. And their faces are like . . . well, basically regular human faces if we had ruby, emerald, and bright blue skin and sharp elf ears.

"Who the heck are they?" I blurt out.

"The Warriors of The Ring," Ahriman says. "They follow the rule of he who raises the city and wears the Ring of Power. They were the army Suleiman commanded; they built his great cities. Soon, they will build mine."

I gulp.

In unison, they slide this entire city forward and place it on the ground as easy as slipping off their school backpacks—not that they go to school. I mean, they're a kajillion years old. They step to the side as the city settles, taking up formation on the pathways that connect the empty sandstone buildings, their hands behind their backs, their faces forward at attention.

Ahriman flies down, and Possessed Peri follows him, dropping me onto the ground from a few feet in the air. "Hey! Was that really necessary?" I yell, rubbing my backside as I stand up. Who knew a quest would involve so much time falling on my butt?

"Necessity is not fun," Possessed Peri says, and sticks her forked tongue out at me. I wonder if a bit of Aasman Peri isn't in there after all.

I watch as Ahriman walks into the center of the city. Is he limping a little? There's a low, round structure there; it's like the base of Buckingham Fountain in Chicago, except with no water shooting out of the tiers above it because it's just an empty basin.

"Wait. Is this giant fountain the Ring of Power? I thought it was more a *ring* ring, not a circular base of a fountain. I mean, good luck wearing that on your hand. Ring of Power, you're not what I was expecting," I say into the empty fountain, and as I speak, the ground starts rumbling again. Oh no. Please don't tell me there's more stuff buried down there.

A pedestal shoots up out of the fountain. It's not in the center. It's right by me. I called and it responded. Weird. On top of the pedestal is a big vase—big enough for a kid to hide in. A kid my size who is not sure where he's going to run to when this thing ends, whatever *this* is. Whatever *end* means. The vase is a plain old brown pitcher–looking thing that's made of dirt. This is really underwhelming. I bet if some museum got their hands on this, though, they'd call it an "earthenware urn" because it makes it sound more important than "dirt vase."

"At last," Ahriman says, eyeing the vase like it's his celebrity crush. Not that I would know what it's like to have a celebrity crush, definitely not one I named a flying horse in Qaf after. I totally picked the name Zendaya at random. I mean, *boom*, it just popped into my head. I wasn't even thinking about her. Anyway, he's staring at that vase. So I stare at it, too. I notice an emblem stamped into the middle of the, uh, urn. It's round, has a star on it, some letters. I've totally seen it before. I'm sure I have. If Amira were here, she'd know right away. I'd give anything to hear her sound all shocked that I don't recognize this seal.

That's it! It's a seal. The Seal of Suleiman! Like the wax stamp on the back of the letter in that levitating iron chest in the Arena of Suleiman. The letter we ripped by mistake and that burned up before we finished reading the secret message that was just for us. Maybe it had a secret code or something, some words that would help me right now. Because my heart is beating so fast it's going to pound out of my chest, and not in a "Look, is that Zendaya walking into the coffee shop" kind of way. It's more of a "Oh my God, I'm going to die or be forced to do manual labor like clean the toilets in Ahriman's Earth palace" heart-thumping.

Ahriman uses the little-tornadoes-under-his-feet trick to fly up to the pedestal to bring down the vase. It must be super heavy, because he's definitely straining to hold it.

C'mon, Hamz. Think. Because I'm pretty sure Ahriman is about to reach into that million-year-old, crusty dirt vase and find the Ring. Then he's going to control this whole jarmy, march them through the oobleck wall, take command of all the jinn and peris and devs in Qaf, probably imprison the emperor, and then he'll start on Earth.

Ahriman lands and raises the vase over his head and turns around, showing it off like he's won a trophy at a tennis tournament. Power trip. "My dear jinn. Most courageous and brave of heart. Most stalwart.

You who have obeyed and remained loyal to your master, Suleiman, even as he bid you to stay buried for centuries to guard the Ring, will soon be free of this yoke. For I, Ahriman, mightiest of devs past and future, one of the remaining of the great ancient fire spirits, am your kin and your commander...."

Oh brother. Ahriman really loves a long speech. I tune him out so most of what he's saying sounds like *blah blah blah*, Ring of Power, *blah blah blah*, destroy Suleiman's legacy *blah blah blah*, take the thrones of Qaf and Earth.... I'm mostly looking around, panicking, wishing I could think of a plan and wondering if maybe I could sneak behind one of those columns to pee. I know it's gross and I 100 percent do not think peeing in public is okay, but I'm very, very nervous and we're in the middle of a desert and this entire trip has been ping-ponging between countries and time zones and it's messed up my sleep and pee cycles. And did I mention I am terrified that the whole world is going to end because I couldn't figure out a way to stop Ahriman?

"...together we shall know a glory never before

seen on Qaf or Earth!" Ahriman is still going on. This whole time, not one jinn moved. Not one of them twitched their noses, sneezed, raised a hand to tell Ahriman he was getting pretty repetitive, nothing. They're like the terracotta warriors we saw at a Field Museum exhibit. The ones buried with the first Emperor of China. But instead of being made of clay, they're made of smokeless fire. Maybe they're as still as statues, but I'm afraid that will all change once Ahriman puts on the Ring.

He puts the vase down in front of him and it rises almost to his shoulders. That's when I notice a small lid on the top. Ahriman reaches for it, super dramatically, waving his hand and stuff. But when he tugs at the lid, nothing happens. He tries again. Whew, that thing is stuck in there.

"Sealed with celestial fire," Ahriman howls. "You think that would stop me, Suleiman?"

I guess I'm not the only one talking to dead people.

Ahriman then raises the vase above his head and grunts really loudly, enough so that some smoke puffs fly out of his four ears and nose. Oh no! He's going to throw that thing onto the ground and shatter a bajillion-year-old *urn*. There are going to be some really angry museum people in the world if word gets out about this.

The vase lands on the pathway between the fountain and the columns around the city. And, it bounces. No, really—a vase made of clay just bounced like a basketball. Ahriman screams out in frustration. It's honestly kind of funny in a very terrifying way. The vase bounces a couple of more times and rolls a bit until it comes to a stop. Ahriman walks over, stomping, muttering stuff under his breath. Ahriman strokes his throat. I get it; I'm thirsty, too.

"Peri!" he yells. "Raise a spring, for my thirst must be quenched." Aasman Peri kneels down in the sand, and the snake that's been crawling all over her dives into the grains, headfirst, and a minute later, it leaps back out, and a stream of water bursts out of the ground. What the heck? There's water under the desert? I could really use a drink! Apparently, Ahriman can, too, because he leans over and gulps from it like his life depends on it. Weird, because he hasn't really complained about hunger or thirst this whole time.

Wait. What am I sticking around for? He's not paying attention to me at all, and Possessed Peri is following his every move.

I make a run for it, zigzagging through the columns and down a path, running behind a building so I can get a better look around. There's nothing but sand and dunes and emptiness. Maybe if I make it over that dune in front of me, there will be an oasis or a road. There's got to be roads in the desert, right? I mean, people do drive through the Arabian Desert. How huge can it be?

An angry yell bounces off the walls of the city and fills all the space around me like Ahriman's shout has sucked up all the oxygen and blown it out again with a scream. "Find him!" he hollers.

Uh-oh.

I make a dash for the doorway of one of the buildings that might have been an old house, but before I can make it into the home, Possessed Peri grabs me by the collar and flies me back over to Ahriman while her controlling viper curls itself around her boot, flicking its tongue at me. "You don't have to do this," I plead to her. "Aasman Peri, I know you're in there. C'mon, fight it. It's me, Hamza, your friend. Please. I need your help."

She looks down at me, shakes her head, blinks. Her eyes flash back to her brown ones again. "The snake," she croaks. "It has control. You have to—" She blinks again and her eyes turn back to white.

No. No. No.

Possessed Peri throws me down at Ahriman's feet. His sword is raised above his head, and he brings it down against the vase with both hands. All I hear is a clink. His face is ten times redder than usual, and there is a crusty outline of salt around his lips. Gross. He yells again and tries again. But same thing. Clink. There's not a scratch on that vase. That's got to be the strongest dirt vase I've ever seen. The only dirt vase I've ever seen. Ooops. Sorry, I mean, urn.

Ahriman swipes his arm across his lips and turns to me, "You must do it. The vase will only shatter under your hand, I fear. Suleiman tied your fate to the Ring's." This would be a good place for a Hobbit joke, but Ahriman clearly doesn't understand the concept of humor.

As I stand, I grab two fistfuls of sand and throw them in Ahriman's face and make another run for it. He roars in anger and shoots a blast of fire at me that almost singes the hair around my ears. I sprint but don't get far. Possessed Peri grabs me and drags me back to Ahriman.

There's so much rage in his face—he's a bottomless pit of anger. He points his sword at me. I close my eyes. Guess this is it—where I bite it and turn to ash. Then I hear a loud hiss. I open my eyes and see Ahriman holding Possessed Peri by the throat. "If you try any foolishness, I will end your friend," he says, squeezing her throat. "And then I will fly to your home and set it on fire while your parents are inside." I suck in my breath. Aasman Peri's eyes flash from white back to her nonpossessed brown eyes and I can see the fear in them. It's the same fear I'm feeling, too. Then Ahriman hands me his sword. Finally,

I have a weapon. But when will I ever have the chance to use it? We're running out of time.

I nod at Ahriman. I raise the sword above my head. I don't know what other choice I have. Ahriman won. Or at least he's winning. Maybe I can find a way to keep my family alive. And my friends, like Aasman Peri. Amira would tell me not to trust Ahriman, and she would be right. I bring the sword crashing down on the vase. But I didn't even need half my strength. The sword goes through the hard dirt vase like it's made of soft butter. I slice it in half. There, amid the crumbly bits of broken vase, I see a glint against the sand. Ahriman sees it, too.

"Yes! Long last!" he yells. Ahriman lets go of Possessed Peri, who drops to the ground coughing, and then he grabs the Ring, raising it up to the sun and rubbing some of the dirt off it. It's a plain old ring. It's maybe brass or iron? It has a band with one flat side, no stones, and the Seal of Suleiman is embossed on it. A star, with Arabic letters in each of the points.

That's the Ring that will rule all creatures of fire? That can help you talk to animals? And control the weather? I could make that in shop class. If I took shop class.

And Ahriman is talking to it, again. "I have waited so long for this moment, a dream fulfilled, at long last, a chance to relish my revenge. How I planned this, night after night in that small, cramped brass prison. And now the power shall be mine."

He turns to face the jarmy and places the Ring on his left ring finger, then removes it and puts it on his middle finger, and then again on his index; guess the fit isn't quite right. Storm clouds roll in, lightning flashes in the sky as Ahriman raises his left fist into the air. He's laughing and stomping around, making another speech. Dude is really on a power trip.

He doesn't see me. He's not paying attention to me at all. This may be the only chance I get.

I sneak up behind him, his own sword still in my hand. This is my chance. My only chance. I'm Earth's last hope. It sounds cool to say that, but I am so scared I taste metal in the back of my throat. I don't know if I've bitten my tongue or am about to puke, maybe both. I try to force my hands not to shake.

I hear a hissing sound from behind me, but I don't stop. I can't stop. The hissing sound gets louder. Sweat is pouring down my face and getting into my eyes. I'm still not close enough to strike Ahriman. Move dumb, slow legs!

"Hamza! Look out!" a voice screams from the sky as the hissing sounds are at my heels.

CHAPTER 22

Off with Their Tails! Or Heads! (Or Really Any Body Part You Can Get To!)

Amira

A GHUL VIPER IS RIGHT ON MY BROTHER'S HEELS. I SCREAM his name as I descend with Razia in her flying pot, but I'm afraid my voice is lost in the wind.

Razia whips out a bow and arrow but shakes her head. "Too far. If I miss, I'll hit your brother."

I panic, clutching the edges of the black metal cauldron. We're not going to get there in time. Hamza is going to get possessed, like Aasman Peri. "Kill it, Hamz!" I scream like his life depends on it. Because it might.

Hamza turns, looks up for a second, a smile crossing his face.

"Slice and dice that viper!" I yell at the top of my lungs.

The viper raises its head, ready to strike, but Hamza slashes at it. The snake shrieks, then falls; green goop oozes out of it as the ghul viper sinks into the sand. I hear Hamza hoot and as we get closer, I see Aasman Peri. She's fallen to her knees. Oh no. What if killing the snake that possessed her means she gets hurt? What if it means she gets sucked into the sand, too? What if the viper is a mind-controlling, murderous parasite? Like an emerald cockroach wasp! It's one of the scariest real-life things I've ever read about. A tiny wasp with a metallic body that glows bright green. Those wasps inject cockroaches with poison that allow them to take over the roaches' brains and turn them into literal zombies! And then they feast on their blood! Supposedly, cockroaches can survive nuclear radiation, but they can't survive the wasp's zombification. Now all I can picture is zombie Aasman Peri, and that's horrifying! We can't let that happen to her!

Hamza runs to her side. Razia lands and jumps out of her pot, sword in hand. I rush over to Aasman Peri. I watch as Razia advances on Ahriman, who is shouting things at a jinn army that is as still as statues. I know I should help Razia, but I'm barely paying attention. I can't lose a friend. Not again. Not like Maqbool, even if his spirit is still with us.

Aasman Peri is lying on the ground. Hamza's turned her over. My brother and I look at each other and exchange small smiles. This isn't the reunion we wanted. Not over a hurt friend. "He got the Ring, sis. I couldn't stop him," Hamza whispers, his eyes looking at Aasman Peri's still face.

"It's okay, Hamz. You did your best," I say, while checking Aasman Peri's pulse. She's still breathing, thank goodness. I grab a bottle that Razia gave me and lift Aasman Peri's head and tip a little water onto her lips and into her mouth.

"C'mon, Aasman Peri," Hamza says, taking her hand. "We still have some evil dev butt to kick, and we need you. We're getting to the best part."

Hamza looks up at me and nods. "Yeah," I say. "We need your help. Where would we be without your sarcastic quips?"

Her lips start to move. I give her a little more water; this time she drinks it up and tilts her head back asking for more. "You...," she croaks, licking her chapped lips. "You'd be totally lost without me." Her eyes flutter open. I let out the breath I was holding. Hamza falls back on his butt and starts laughing. Aasman Peri pushes herself up to a seated position and gulps the rest of the bottle.

She looks from me to Hamza. "Took you long enough." She coughs. Then a smile spreads across her face. She wipes her hands across her lips. "Ugh. That was the worst. The ghul viper consciousness was in my brain, and now I have a craving to eat mice. Disgusting!"

Hamza stands and reaches a hand down to Aasman Peri as I scramble up off my knees. She takes his hand. As he helps her up, she spreads her wings wide and flies up to take in the scene. Razia has created a kind of fire shield that she's advancing behind, but Ahriman is barely paying attention. He's clutching his throat and blathering on and on to about a thousand jinn who are standing at attention.

"Glad my dad could spare Razia to help us," Aasman Peri says. "Now, as you humans say: Let's do this thing!"

Aasman Peri and I pull out our daggers. Hamza raises his sword, and we shout, together, "Let's goooooo!"

We race forward, joining Razia behind her fire shield, but keeping some distance so we don't get burned. Ahead, Ahriman turns to face us. The jinn army is still standing perfectly still. Are they ignoring him? Maybe the Ring isn't working right because it's a bit rusty? Could it all have been a myth? A trick? Ahriman bends down and starts whispering into the sand, but his hands are clawing at his neck like he's dying of thirst. I catch Hamza's eye as we are charging along, and he shrugs. Aasman Peri is flying right above us.

"What's he doing?" I ask her, hoping she's getting a better view.

"Maybe praying to evil demons that I don't swat him to death with my wings for unleashing a possessive ghul viper on me. I keep wanting to dart my tongue out. He will pay!"

Aasman Peri has a very scary scowl on her face, and that's saying something.

As we're running forward, a glob of sand about the size of a snowball shoots out of the ground by Ahriman's feet, then another, and another, then hundreds. They're sand softballs that fly a couple of feet into the air and fall back, disintegrating into grains of sand again. Well, that's not a very effective defense maneuver.

"Deathstalkers!" I hear Razia scream.

Death—what?

Aasman Peri halts in midair, grabbing me and Hamza by our collars. "Fall back, fall back," she screams. Then I see hundreds, no, thousands of scorpions crawling up out of the sand and rushing toward us. Their pale yellow bodies are the size of a can of tennis balls, their legs (arms?) are neon green, and large stinger tails curve up over them, like they're ready to strike. The scorpions are clearly on a mission. That mission is us.

"Is 'deathstalker' just a scary name or—"

"No, silly human! It's literally what they do, and they're under Ahriman's command. They will stalk you till you're dead. A single sting is extraordinarily painful, but the death is a long, slow allergic reaction to the venom and—"

"Razia can't fight them alone," I say. "So our best option is..."

"Off with their tails! Or heads! Either works!" Aasman Peri shouts.

Razia is slashing at the scorpions with one hand and blasting fire with the other; one after another falls. We move forward, weapons drawn. I raise my dagger, suck in my breath, forcing myself to keep my eyes open and slash at the first scorpion's tail that crosses my path. It screeches like nails on a chalkboard before falling to the ground and getting dragged back into the sands with a small suction sound.

"Yes! Nice aim, sis!" Hamza shouts as he disposes of another scorpion.

Aasman Peri flies ahead, landing by Razia and going back-to-back, spinning in a circle together. All I can see are swords rising in the air, glinting in the sun, and then striking down scorpions that get sucked back into the sand. Hamza and I slash our way forward to join them, but every time we kill one scorpion, two more seem to rise up. We hear pops of sands all around us as deathstalkers burst forth. I catch a quick glance at Hamza as we swipe and cut our way forward. Neither of us lets up, but I can tell he knows what I know—we're losing. We're so close to losing everything.

Then we hear a whoosh, and the entire space around us heats up like we're under two suns. Razia has turned to full flame and is trying to push the deathstalkers away from us.

I pause, catch a breath. Close my eyes for the briefest second.

"It's raining?" Hamza says, wiping a drop of water from under his chin. "In the desert?"

I look up at the cloudless blue sky. "Nah. Dude, that might be spit. Gross." Then I feel a drop on my elbow. Weird, because the rain is falling up? How is that possible? But when I turn my sword hand palm up, I see droplets of moisture. This isn't rain. Could be flying beads of sweat?

A geyser bursts out of the sand in front of us, shooting water high above us.

"Look out!" I yell as I shield my face from the falling water, afraid it's going to be burning hot. But it's not. It's cool and pleasant when it hits my skin, especially under the blazing sun. And when I glance up, I see figures forming in the plume. Figures with a circle of flame at their core.

"The baharia," I whisper.

Hamza raises a fist in the air. "Wonder water power, activate," he yells. And one of the baharia, the one who was blocking my path at the British Museum, raises a fist back.

Each of the baharia shoots streams of water out of their hands, trapping the deathstalkers in bubbles of water, drowning them. As the bubbles burst, the earth swallows the scorpions. Razia is back in human form and joins us in attacking any deathstalkers that get past the baharia.

"You dare defy me, Clan of Baharia! You were once under my protection.... Now you've made me your enemy," Ahriman bellows.

The baharia from the museum takes her human shape in front of Ahriman as the other baharia finish off the deathstalkers with Razia's help. "Her name's Bijli," Hamza whispers to me. "She's so cool."

"As the rules of Bahamut dictate, we are released from our bond to you, Ahriman. We choose to fight for humanity and for ourselves," Bijli says, her watery fists planted at her hips.

"Total superhero pose," Hamza whispers to me, grinning.

Ahriman looks at all of us. At the baharia and Razia. At Aasman Peri and my brother. And me. He scoffs, holding up his red fist, showing us Suleiman's Ring of Power. "It no longer matters. Soon, all of you will fall. All of Qaf, then Earth. And I shall take my rightful place on the throne of all the worlds."

"This dude is seriously into villain speeches," I say.

Hamza nods. "Tell me about it. It's been nonstop. He loves listening to himself talk, I guess." I laugh at the irony of Hamza making that observation but don't say anything to him. It's just so good to have him by my side. No matter what happens next.

Then, I swear, we hear whispers across the sand.

Ahriman claws at his throat and then throws off his robe. We hear more whispers: *You shall suffer for your desecration.*

"The curse of the *Lamassu*!" Hamza cries out. I think back to the broken shards of the statue we saw at the Oriental Institute, at the green smoke that spoke before Ahriman's red hand emerged out of it. It's weakening him.

Ahriman roars, standing straight and squaring his shoulders. He raises his hands in the air and bellows at the statue-like jinn, "Strike them down!" And then he points at us with his ringed finger, very dramatically.

But nothing happens.

"The curse said it was going to decapitate his dreams!" Hamza says.

"What? Like literally chop the head off his dream?"

"No. That's not it. Desiccate it!"

"Dry up? That makes more sense as a metaphor! It's sucking away the life of his dream. Draining him of his power!"

"Yeah, that's what I meant! And ever since, his devnado has been wobblier and he's gotten dizzy, too! Good old *Lamassu* curse! Look, the jarmy isn't listening to him," Hamza says.

"The who, now?"

"The jarmy. Jinn army. Duh."

"Oh, so sorry I couldn't figure that one out." I roll my eyes the tiniest bit.

Ahriman turns his back to us to face the... uh... jarmy and yells the command again, waving his hands around and pointing in our direction. He even stomps a couple of times as if that's going to benefit the situation.

"They're like the terracotta warriors," Hamza says.

My mouth drops open. "Wow. I can't believe you remember that exhibit. Especially since you complained so much about it."

"I know," Hamza says. "This whole experience has changed me. I mean, I've been to three museums in one day."

Ahriman screams and fire shoots out of his hands, but it's not as strong as it was before. The jarmy still doesn't move.

"This is our chance," I say to Hamza. "He's weakened. The best defense is a good offense," I yell, and before anyone can stop me, before I even realize what I'm doing, I'm charging ahead, full speed.

I deliver a mai geri kick straight into Ahriman's back, which pushes him forward onto the ground. I step back into a fighting stance, a dagger in my hand. Razia rushes toward me, her bow and arrow drawn. Hamza reaches me, stepping to my right. Aasman Peri hovers above us.

Ahriman turns to face us, fire in his eyes, flames leaping from his fingertips, and lets out a growl that makes the dunes around us rumble. He increases his size, but I see the strain on his face. Still, he's rising high into the air, twisting into a whirlwind. Razia lets one arrow fly, then another, as a sandstorm engulfs us.

CHAPTER 23

Uneasy Lies the Hand that Wears the Ring

Hamza

AHRIMAN STARTS WHIRLING AROUND IN HIS STUPID devnado, kicking sand up everywhere. Ugh! I'm so sick of sand. If we survive this, I never want to see another sandbox, sandpit, beach, or dune for the rest of my life. There's sand up my nose, in my hair, crusted into my eyelashes. There's probably sand in areas that I don't even want to mention. I'm probably going to have to run naked through a car wash to get it all out.

Razia grabs me and my sister and pulls off her scarf and covers us with it. Abdul Rahman did the same thing with his cloak to protect us from the heat of jinn fire. We can see through the fabric, but the swirling sands can't get to us. I think of how Razia and the Supahi caught me when I fell from the high walls of Suleiman's Arena by interlocking their arms into a kind of net. They really have maneuvers for everything. Totally deserve their own comic book.

Amira pulls me down into a low crouch. Aasman Peri joins us. "Any ideas for how to defeat the evil-est dev in history who now has the Ring of Power?" Amira asks as we hear winds swoosh above us.

"It is very strange that the jinn army—" Aasman Peri starts.

"Jarmy," I correct.

She groans. "Strange that the *jarmy* didn't listen to his command."

"The *Lamassu* curse is weakening him...at least a little," Amira says. I was totally about to say that, but she stole my thunder.

"Maaaaybe," Aasman Peri says, "the Ring *is*

supposed to come to life for the wearer, and that's the signal that the power is engaged."

"Come to life?" Amira asks. "How?"

"What if it talks," I suggest. "Gives some sort of signal? Lights up? Oooh, maybe you get a mind meld with all the jinn you're trying to control." Amira and Aasman Peri both give me these weird looks.

"Talk? Really?" Aasman Peri says.

"What? Why is that so hard to believe? I mean, there's literally a dev making a sand tornado around us while we're being protected by the leader of a battalion of silver-haired jinn who fly around in pots," I say.

"Guys, cut it out. We have to—" Amira begins.

The winds get even more intense. Ahriman's wind power seems pretty much full tilt right now. C'mon, *Lamassu*, let's get this curse up to a hundred or a thousand or whatever way you count. I don't know how long Razia's scarf shield can hold! Through the scarf, I hear a loud sucking sound coming from the sand. Oh, please, please, don't let it be a giant mother deathstalker scorpion coming back to avenge her medium-size scorpion kids.

But it's not scorpions.

It's the baharia. Shooting out of the sand and engulfing Ahriman in a… "It's a water tornado!" I shout.

"It's more accurate to call them waterspouts!" Amira calls above the wind and blowing sand and water spewing everywhere. "The baharia must be drawing on water that's deep underneath the desert. Like that megalake that was recently found under the Sahara."

One thing about my big sis, I can always count on her to give me a lecture about science no matter how close we are to death and destruction. I sort of zone out because I think I'm starting to form a brilliant plan. Those words that flashed on the oculus when I put it together, the ones only I saw that switched from a language I couldn't read to one I could: *Water from the sands. Fire from the sky. Uneasy rests the Ring when the claim is a lie.* The baharia—water—came from the sands to help us. Razia—a jinn made of fire—descended from the skies. So what about that next part. It's got be a clue. I think.

Uneasy rests the Ring when the claim is a lie.

How is the Ring resting? It's not like it's on vacation, lounging around by a pool. Dang. A pool would be nice right now because the sun is brutal and I'm sweating buckets. Focus, Hamz! It's probably not literal, because none of the rest of the message was. Of course it isn't; that would make it too easy. I mean, why help the kid trying to save the worlds' butts, again.

The winds start to die down, and the sand stops swirling. The baharia have brought down Ahriman's devnado, but he's still wearing the Ring, twisting it round and round his finger because it's too loose, I guess. Razia removes her scarf shield and rewraps it around her body in a flash, unsheathing her sword again so she can advance on Ahriman. I see him on the ground, lifting himself up; he's so angry, there's a huge ring of flame surrounding his body. He turns to the jarmy, raises his hand with the loose Ring on it, and starts yelling at them.

Whoa. The Ring of Power doesn't fit him right. His claim to it is a lie. It isn't his to command. It's that thing Ibn Sina said about fowl purpose! No, that fowl means birds. Foul purpose! Ahriman is so foul! I have to get that Ring.

I look down at my hand clutching Ahriman's own sword. A smile breaks across my face. I know what I have to do. Those Banu Musa brothers were right—I'm ingenious!

This is my chance. This may be the worst, grossest idea ever and it's probably going to fail and I'll be a barbecued kid at the end of it. Don't panic, Hamz. Don't panic.

"Use the Force, Hamza. Trust your instincts." It's the voice. Maqbool's voice, again. I whip my head around but don't see anything in the chaos of sand and flames. Maybe it really is in my head. Maybe it doesn't matter. I know what I have to do. "Thanks for the Star Wars reference!" I shout into the air as I draw out my sword.

"Huh?" Amira and Aasman Peri say at the same time.

I smile. "The Force is with me. Follow my lead!" I yell. Time for this kid to design his own destiny!

"AHHHHHHHHHHHHHHH!" I scream all the

way, past Razia and the watery baharia. My body feels jittery but also like I have super strength. Maybe I do. I don't know if Amira is behind me. I don't see anything except my target—the wavering border of flame surrounding Ahriman's body. He's pacing and chanting something. Oh God. Even if he's a little weaker, even if his dream is getting decapitated, desecrated, desiccated (whatever!), he could chargrill me. Roast me. Scorch my amazingly cool hair.

Stay on target, Hamz.

I know that's me encouraging myself, but I 100 percent hear it in Gold Leader's voice from *A New Hope*. I charge forward. I'm only feet from Ahriman. I hear shouts from Razia, Amira, Aasman Peri, and the baharia; they're cheering me on. I got this.

I scream as I leap, rising into the air. Whoa! I'm flying? I'm flying! Yes! I have superpowers! Finally! I've passed all the tests. Earned the gifts of the Chosen Ones. This might be the greatest moment of my life!

Ooops.

Nope.

Gravity is real. And it's pulling me doooooooow-wwwn.

Probably should've used an activation phrase.

(This is definitely not the greatest moment of my life! Maybe top ten; we'll see how it goes.)

I land on my feet. (Phew. Because wiping out during my hero moment would be embarrassing.)

Ahriman turns to face me, a scowl on his face, sneering at me, his sharp teeth ready to rip me apart. He points his left hand at me, palm open, trying to raise a ball of fire, but it's not working. The Ring on his index finger catches the light, showing me my target.

I raise my sword and everything slows down. My body feels like a wet noodle. Ahriman's mouth is stuck half in shock, half in sneer.

"I won't let you turn Suleiman's Ring of Power into your fancy bad-guy jewelry!" I scream.

The air goes all still. There's no wind. I don't see anyone or anything else.

Only my sword, cutting through Ahriman's finger.

CHAPTER 24

Give Me the Finger! No, Not that One, the Other One.

Amira

MY BROTHER RAGES FORWARD WITH A YELL THROUGH the lines of Supahi like a kid possessed. Oh my God. What if he is possessed? Jinn-possessed, bitten-by-a-ghul-viper-possessed?

I race after him. Why isn't Razia trying to stop him? The baharia? He'll get smoked—literally. Even if the curse of the *Lamassu* is weakening Ahriman, Hamza can't take him alone. How am I going to explain this to my parents if I bring him home covered in third-degree burns? But since Ahriman is a fire creature, it's probably exponentially worse! Ninth-degree burns! Twenty-eighth-degree burns! Eighty-first-degree burns!

Hamza's raising his sword as Ahriman turns, his hands out, ready to shoot flames at Hamza.

Oh. OH! Yes! Heck yeah! Hamza *is* possessed. Possessed with an awesome but gross and rather violent idea! I push past the baharia and Razia, cheering him on, just as Hamza brings his sword down across Ahriman's hand, cutting off the index finger that wears the Ring.

Ahriman shrieks. Hamza screams. I yell, too, because everyone is shouting and there's disgusting green goop pouring out of Ahriman's cut-off finger. Ahriman grabs his hand and turns away. Ahriman manages to shoot spurts of flames out of one hand at himself. He's burning himself? No. That's not it. He's sealing his cut-off finger so the goop stops dripping out. That's gotta hurt, but it's actually pretty handy battlefield medicine.

Ahriman whips around and unleashes his flames

at us. His right hand is like a blowtorch, but his other hand has shorted out. Bijli pulls Hamza back, and some of the baharia surround him with a curtain of water. I duck as flames shoot above my head; I crawl on sand. I have to get...the finger. In the chaos of flames and swords and screams, Ahriman kicked his own finger across the sands. Yuck! I hurry on all fours to reach it while trying not to gag. Razia is right next to me and starts to pull me up. But I shake my head. "Distract him," I say to her.

She nods and heads toward Ahriman's right side, drawing his attention so I can get to his left, where the goopy finger is. She raises her sword, deflecting some of the flame back toward Ahriman. Some of the baharia dive back down into the sand, refueling on water and reemerging to volley typhoon bullets at Ahriman.

I stretch out, reaching for Ahriman's cut-off finger, the Ring of Power covered in icky green goo with sand stuck to it. Ahriman sees me out of the corner of his eye and turns toward me, sending a flame shooting in my direction. I'm aaaaalmost there. I reach out, grab the finger. Disgusting! I'm holding a severed finger in my hand. *Pretend it's not real. Pretend it's not real. It's a prop from a haunted house! Halloween costume accessory, not a real severed finger at all. La la. Denial isn't just a river in Egypt!*

Ahriman throws another flame in my direction, but I roll away just in time.

Holding the severed finger in my palm, I expect the Ring of Power to be hot, but it's cool to the touch. I tug it off Ahriman's finger. Blech! This is so beyond gross! I throw the finger in the sand and push the Ring onto my right index finger. It's too big. It's going to slip off. I saw Ahriman twisting it around because it was too large for him, too. Suleiman must have had really giant fingers.

"Yes! Sis!" Hamza shouts as Aasman Peri grabs him, pulling him farther away from Ahriman's flaming wrath.

Then the Ring moves; the metal softens against my finger and shapes itself to my size—a perfect fit. Maybe this Ring was meant for me? Like the sword I chose in Qaf, the one Suleiman left for me. Only me.

I look down at it. A plain old iron ring with a star and some Arabic letters on it, Suleiman's Seal. I scrub off some of the sand. Trying to figure out how to use this thing. Ask it nicely? Beg? Where's an instruction manual when you need one?!

Then it starts to glow.

"I told you!" Hamza shouts at me. "I told you it would light up or something."

I move forward automatically. I don't know why, but I'm being pulled toward the jarmy. Razia is still drawing Ahriman's fire as the baharia whirl up into waterspouts. Ahriman's now-flickering flames meet the water with a hiss as the baharia extinguish them.

Aasman Peri grabs me and Hamza by our collars; she's straining to carry us but deposits us in front of the jinn army. Beams of light shoot out from my Ring, going through the heart of each jinn soldier. They raise their eyes and turn to look at me.

"Sis, it's working! It's working!"

The world seems to fall away for a second as I close my eyes and take a deep breath in, picturing what I want to have happen. Words are on the tip of my tongue. A command that flashes across my mind. My determination rising. "Ahriman ko qatam karna!" I shout as my eyes flash open. *Finish him.*

"Noooooo!" Ahriman yells. He's turned away from battling the Supahi and has come up next to me when he sees the jinn army step forward, stomping toward him. "How is this possible? How could you, a mere girl, have the strength to command them when I could not?" he cries, his voice raspy as he bends over, clutching his knees.

"The Ring was never meant for you," I say, delivering a mawashi geri straight to Ahriman's head, making him fall backward to the ground.

"Yeah!" Hamza shouts. "You're too weak in your head, and your mind, and your brain!"

I shoot Hamza a look because even though he's not quite making sense, I still get it.

Wearing the Ring, commanding the jinn, I understood it. "Your heart and intent were never pure and—"

"The Ring didn't fit, so you weren't legit!" Hamza interrupts.

Ahriman raises his hands to his face as the jinn army stomps toward him, swords and daggers out, a whirlwind of flame behind them.

Hamza hoots and raises his fist. "Yeah, Ahriman! I told you my sister could do anything. She's a total bad—"

"Hey!" I nudge Hamza, trying to imitate my mom's raised eyebrow. "I can't believe what you were about to say." I shake my head. That's twice I've busted him for almost swearing!

A trademark mischievous smile spreads across his face.

The jinn army encircles Ahriman, and all we hear are his screams. When they step away, coming to stand at attention in front of me, we see sticky, blackened scorch marks on the desert sands.

CHAPTER 25

With Great Power Comes Great Response Ability

Hamza

HOLY SCORCHED EARTH! MY SISTER DID IT. WE DID IT! ALL that's left of Ahriman are black sticky marks on the sand, like gum that gets spit out on the sidewalk and becomes a gunky dot over time and one day you step over it to avoid it getting stuck to your sneaker and the adult you're walking with points at it and says that's why you shouldn't swallow gum because you'll get that black gunk stuck in your gut. Forever! Then you get so scared you stop chewing gum for six months and you feel like there's a hole in your life until you buy a pack of Big League Chew. And you still think about that sometimes when you're chewing gum and about how sometimes adults make up weird stories to teach you lessons. Adulthood is a very dark place.

"Sis! You commanded the jarmy! You did it!" I high-five her. Amira looks kind of stunned and woozy; she's shifting her weight from one foot to the other. "Are you okay?" I ask.

"Uh...I think so? I mean, I'm not hurt, but I feel kinda drained?"

"It must be the adrenaline letdown," Aasman Peri says. "I read that humans can sometimes crash after very exciting moments."

"Or your energy is sapped from the incredible power you just wielded! You could be the boss of every fire spirit in the world now! You can control the weather!"

"And talk to animals," a familiar voice speaks from behind us. I turn. My jaw drops. I rub my eyes, but he's still there. A shimmery figure in the desert. It's him!

"Maqbool? You're here? Are you real? Really real?"

He laughs. And it sounds like the laugh I remember. "It all depends on your understanding of what *real* is," he says.

Amira steps up right next to me, and Aasman Peri joins us. I want to hug Maqbool, high-five him, or something, but I can see through the shimmer, so I don't think hugs are possible.

I look at Amira. "Are you seeing this? Wait. Are you about to give me a science-y lecture about the impossibility of ghosts or tell me that apparitions are really due to indigestion or..."

Amira smiles at me and puts her arm around my shoulders, the Ring on her left hand shining in the sun. "Hamz, one thing I've learned this summer is that there are a lot of things science doesn't have an explanation for...*yet.* But that doesn't mean I can't believe in them while I'm trying to figure out how it all works."

"Wait. Don't tell me—that's going to be the theme of your next science fair project."

Then, turning to Maqbool, I say, "I thought your

voice was totally in my head because I was dehydrated and delusional—dehylusional, if you will." We all laugh.

"I have most certainly missed you children." Maqbool grins. "And my voice was in your head, as yours was in my heart."

As Maqbool talks, Razia and the baharia approach him, placing their hands over their hearts when they see him. He nods at them while talking.

"I hate to break up all these feelings going on. But we have to figure out what to do with that Ring," Aasman Peri says.

Everyone nods except me. "What do you mean, 'figure out'? Amira can control the weather now; do you know how many snow days she could make? We'd never have to take a test during winter quarter again!"

Amira frowns at me. "Listen, Indian Spidey, you of all people should know that with great power comes—"

"Yeah. Yeah. I got it. We can't keep the Ring because it's too much power and it could corrupt us and make us all evil-y. And we have to use the power we have now to get rid of it."

Everyone looks at me, their eyes wide with surprise.

"What?" I shrug. "I'm smart. And responsible. Also, I read a ton of comics, so I know how this has to go down."

Maqbool chuckles again. "You are most wise, young hero. Once again you both have shown courage beyond what anyone could expect of you. You have saved us all." When Maqbool says that, Razia and the baharia take a knee, their hands on their hearts. It's cool when they do that but also awkward. I don't get why kings and queens would ever want people to bow down to them. Major power trip, if you ask me.

"So..." Amira taps her lips with her index finger, the one that the Ring is on.

"We have to bury it again?" I ask.

"I think we have to do more than bury it," Amira says. "Even if our intentions are good, who knows what the future holds. And that's really way too much power for anyone—even a Chosen One—to wield." Maqbool's ghost nods.

I sigh. I know what we have to do next. We all do. But it would be so cool to have the Ring's power. We could talk to animals! There's a whole family of trash pandas that lives in a tree in our backyard, and I always wanted to ask them if they get offended when humans make cartoons of them dressed up as thieves. I mean, it's not their fault they have natural burglar masks. And maybe Amira could convince mosquitoes to stop biting me. I get eaten alive every summer. Those little bloodsuckers love me.

While I'm lost in daydreaming about what animals I could ask for rides—I mean, a giraffe would be cool, maybe a dolphin or whale, if I had scuba gear—Amira and Aasman Peri are chatting with Maqbool's ghost, Razia, and Bijli.

Bijli comes up to me. She's in her mostly human form, but her hair is like a tiny waterfall cascading down her back. "It was an honor to meet you, Chosen One," she says, and her smile is so bright and her eyes twinkle a little and…hold up, am I blushing?

No. I'm not at all. It's definitely sunburn because I'm not wearing SPF. Totally why my cheeks feel all hot.

"Meet to honor you, too," I say. Ooops. That's not right. My words are backward. *Awkward.*

Bijli giggles, then gets serious. "I am truly sorry we ever aided Ahriman."

"It's okay," I say. "I get that he forced you to and that you couldn't break the oath, but you really came through in the end."

"Perhaps our paths will cross again." She smiles and waves as she walks away. I smile and wave back. She and the other baharia dive deep into the desert again, the sand quickly filling in the holes they made.

I think about all the things Ahriman forced me to do because he threatened my family. About all the other people and creatures he would've controlled, about everything he could've annihilated if his evil plan would've succeeded. But it didn't work. Because of two regular, geeky kids from Chicago (well, Amira is technically a nerd, but not going to split hairs).

"Hey!" I say to the group. "Does someone have a plan for getting rid of that Ring yet? I'm starving!"

CHAPTER 26

Not All Heroes Wear Capes

Amira

I LAUGH OUT LOUD. HAMZA IS ALWAYS, ALWAYS HUNGRY. Not even evil devs and Rings of Power can get in the way of that. I consulted with Maqbool and Razia; Aasman Peri put in her two cents, too. I know what I have to do.

"So I'm going to command the jinn army to—"

"Jarmy. They prefer jarmy," Hamza says.

"How do you know their preference? I'm the one wearing the Ring of... You know what, never mind. Let's do this and go home," I say.

I walk toward the incredible fossil of a city. Ubar must have been so amazing in its time. Maqbool told me it was once a great oasis. There must have been water flowing from those fountains and flowers and greenery in those giant pots. Kids were probably running around being chased by their parents. Looking at the paths and the courtyard, I can imagine the bustling market—the food and cloth and perfumes being sold. I sigh. Close my eyes for a second. Taking it all in. I swear the smell of perfume wafts over me. I blink. All of Ubar seems to shift right for a second, and that market I imagined appears. There's the sound of water flowing in the fountains. Green palm trees rising high into the sky. I hear a little kid calling for their mother. I shake my head and blink once more. The city shifts back, barren again with the jarmy standing at the ready. What the heck? I'm either dehydrated, seriously low on blood sugar, or need some sleep. Probably all three.

"Take a hero stance," Hamza whispers to me.

I turn to him and shrug. He responds by putting his fists at his hips, puffing up his chest, tilting his chin to pretend he's looking off at something very important in the distance, and getting his serious game face on.

Aasman Peri and I totally crack up.

"Well, you get the idea!" Hamza says, then retreats next to Razia and ghost Maqbool shaking his head. "Hero moments call for hero poses," I hear him mutter.

I take a deep breath, then widen my stance, looking over my shoulder at Hamza, who gives me a thumbs-up. I raise my fist into the air, imagine what I want to have happen, imagine the jinn raising the city on their hands and shoulders, then slowly sinking back into the sands with it. Lost to time, again. *Hope you guys are going to be okay down there*, I say in my mind. And the weird thing is, I get a response. Well, kind of one, where they say, collectively, it's their solemn duty and their honor.

"Ubar zameen mey utarna!" I shout, and rays from the Ring reach out in beams touching the hearts of each jinn. I can't explain how I know the exact command to give; it's always been there in my brain, waiting.

The jarmy stomp their feet, then raise the city—this entire, ginormous, stunning lost place—and then slowly sink into the sand, a whirlpool swallowing them. We watch as the last column descends.

But it's not over yet.

Hamza, Aasman Peri, and I approach the center of where the disappeared city was. I take off the Ring and place it in the sand.

"You're definitely sure about this?" Hamza asks.

"Definitely."

"I guess it's probably what Suleiman should've done in the first place."

"But maybe it was our job to destroy it. And maybe it was Suleiman's duty to bury it for us to find."

"I thought you weren't so keen on that destiny, Chosen One stuff," my brother smirks.

I shrug. "I guess I'm trying to keep an open mind."

Aasman Peri shakes her head. "Go ahead, take all day. Let's have a long, boring discussion about the limitations of human thinking and understanding of time as linear. Not as if the rest of us need to get back to Qaf or anything. I'd like to see my father. Maybe eat some actual good food. Hey, whatever happened to those donuts I was supposed to try?"

Hamza and I look at each other and giggle.

"You should consider Flamin' Hot Cheetos," ghost Maqbool shouts. "They're perfect for your fiery disposition!"

Hamza laughs. "You still got it, Maqbool!"

"Go ahead, do it," I say to Aasman Peri. "We're ready."

Aasman Peri pulls out the same small silver vial she used at the Louvre to "surprise" Ahriman by unsealing the ten-headed ghul. "Only a few drops left. But that's more than enough celestial fire to do the trick," she says. Then she looks to Hamza, "And don't touch it, unless you want your face burned off!"

"Why would my face burn off if I touch it with my hands? That makes no sense." Hamza shakes his head.

Aasman Peri groans. I try to hide my smile.

She opens the vial and pours out one thick golden drop and then another. The liquid looks like lava, and when the first drop touches the Ring of Power, it sighs. Like the whole earth is taking a deep breath. Another drop and the Ring starts to soften, loses shape, until it's nothing but a dark silvery blob on the sand. There's still a tiny light in it, reaching out to me. "Khudafis," I whisper. *Goodbye.* A small, swirling funnel starts to form in the desert and the Ring gets drawn into it; we see it sink deeper and deeper until the sand closes in on itself.

I feel kind of sad about it. Not that I think I should have the power of the Ring, but it would've been amazing to chat with the hummingbirds that visit the feeder in our backyard and ask them questions. For example, how do you fly backward? Does it hurt to flap your wings so hard? Now that would be a cool science project idea. Though would that be cheating? My mom always says we shouldn't be embarrassed to use our gifts. Of course, our dad reminds us that we shouldn't brag and show off. It's honestly a tough call. But I guess I won't need to make it.

"Now what?" Hamza asks.

"This is where I bid you farewell. Know that I will be there for you if you ever really need me," Maqbool says with a hand on his heart, or the shimmery place where his heart would be. "Razia and Aasman Peri will accompany you home."

"Any chance you have a memory eraser that could make our parents forget we were, oh, say, randomly missing for the last...has it been twenty-four hours? My internal clock is all messed up because of time changes," I say.

Hamza scoffs. "Hey, at least you weren't traveling by devnado. The combo of motion sickness and jet lag is killer!"

We all laugh.

Razia steps up. "Two jinnators from the Gate to the Clouds have been dispatched to administer your parents a dream potion from the Neend Peri and leave them a note, in your stead."

Wow. They really can clean up all sorts of messes.

"Oooh, the sleep fairy who made everyone take a nap when the moon broke?" Hamza asks.

"Exactly," Maqbool responds. "They will think the last day has been a dream, and when you return, it will be morning."

"Just in time for them to kill us because of our busted bikes," I say.

Razia smiles. "I have a feeling the jinnators have taken care of that, too."

Suddenly, there's the sound of wings flapping behind us. Then a gust of air sends grains of sands flying. I suck in my breath and close my eyes. Please, I can't handle any more terrifying, murderous creatures.

"Zendaya!" Hamza yells. I open my eyes and whip around and start laughing. Zendaya, the winged, three-eyed horse that Hamz named after his celebrity crush is here. On Earth. Hamz has his arms around her neck and is whispering something to her. Everyone is smiling.

"I guess my dad wanted you to travel home in style," Aasman Peri says.

"I love it when a plan I don't know about comes together!" Hamza grins wide.

We say goodbye to Maqbool. But it doesn't feel sad, not like last time, when he was stabbed with a poison dagger. Now we know he'll be with us, in some way, always. Then Hamza and I climb onto Zendaya's back. With Razia in her flying pot and Aasman Peri at our side, we head off toward home.

We see our bikes leaning against a tree as we land in a small park near our house. Hamza runs over and hugs his bike. Literally hugs it. Zendaya saunters over and nudges him as he starts explaining how bikes work to a flying horse.

"Humans are so weird," Aasman Peri says.

"I told you before," Hamza responds, "weird is awesome!"

There's a small tablet-shaped package on my seat—the jade tablet, fixed, with a small note from Professor Khusrao: *The gifts of a champion are always in your heart (but sometimes souvenirs are nice).* I smile and clutch the tablet to my chest. I may not need it anymore, but it's nice to have a reminder of this summer's adventures in case one day I grow old and have a hard time believing in the weird and wondrous and unexplainable. (Even though I'm going to try really hard to explain it. Science for the win!)

"So I'm guessing there's no way you can stay here, huh?" Hamza asks.

"Me? Why would I want to stay here when everything human is so odd and inconvenient?" Aasman Peri scoffs.

"I was talking to Zendaya!" Hamza giggles.

Aasman Peri raises an eyebrow and we all laugh. Zendaya neighs. I think she's in on the joke, too.

We say our goodbyes. I think we all have a feeling it might not be forever. Then Hamza and I hop on our bikes and race home.

We rush up the stairs, throwing the door open, kicking off our dusty shoes before heading straight into the kitchen. The smell of my mom's parathas fills the air. My dad is sitting at the counter with a cup of chai reading some Urdu poetry out loud to my mom.

"Gross. Is that love poetry?" Hamza asks. "You guys are embarrassing!"

My dad tousles Hamza's hair. "Embarrassing our children is one of the great joys of parenthood," he deadpans, and my mom turns from the stove, nodding and laughing.

"I loved that you two went on an early-morning bike ride! What a wonderful way to start your very last weekend of summer vacation," she says.

Hamza and I exchange looks. It has been an, uh, eventful summer. We saved the world from falling into the clutches of evil. *Twice.* We rode in flying pots, got devnadoed to London and Paris, saw a tidal wave rise in the Thames, discovered an ancient lost city, and watched as it descended back into the Arabian Desert in the hands of a jinn army. Sorry, I mean, jarmy.

Oh no. I forgot to pay for scones and donuts in London! I know we were in a real pinch, but two wrongs don't make a right. Though I think it's fair to say that wrongs can have different weights. It's a real ethical conundrum. Maybe I can Venmo the bakery money. That should work. I know we've encountered terrible jinn and evil devs, but being an accidental thief is the kind of thing that could haunt me forever.

"These parathas are amazing!" Hamza literally whoops while he's eating and then high-fives my mom.

"Dude, can you chew with your mouth closed?"

Hamza shrugs. "I'm starving. That was a very, very long and totally, completely uneventful, um... bike ride to end the summer on."

My parents laugh.

"So what do you think you'll write about for your annual *What I Did on My Summer Vacation* essays?" my mom asks. "Maybe our trip to the Michigan Dunes? Or the lunar eclipse party? That could be a good one for you, Amira."

My eyes meet Hamza's. There is so much to say. So much that happened. So much that changed. So many ways this summer made me rethink how I look at the whole world—and the world beyond this one. About science and magic. About what it means to be a hero, and how you can be heroic in big ways and small, and about the friends and family who help you along the way.

I smile as I grab a paratha hot off the pan. "I'm sure I'll think of something to write about," I say, smirking at Hamza when our parents aren't looking. "There's still a whole weekend of summer vacation left. Anything can happen."

Author's Note

Hi, friends!

I see you're back for more adventures with Amira and Hamza! Or maybe you're encountering these two goofy, bickering siblings for the very first time. Either way, you're the reason I wrote this book, and I'm so glad you're a part of this magical journey!

When I was a kid, I believed in magic. (A part of me still does.) And I also believed in the awesomeness of science (which I do still, even more!). That's how I approached *Amira & Hamza: The Quest for the Ring of Power*—blending the fantastical and the factual to create a new adventure inspired by tales in an ancient epic, the *Hamzanama*, or *Dastan-e-Amir Hamza*. In English, the title is often translated as *The Adventures of Amir Hamza*.

The *Hamzanama* is a collection of stories, originally told through oral tradition, that centered around the great warrior Amir Hamza. And the history of how these stories began and were collected is almost as legendary as the tales within the book. There is no single origin story of the *Hamzanama*, no "first" author. Even though we can't pinpoint the exact inspiration for Amir Hamza, we do know that the story first appeared in Persia and passed through the Arabian peninsula to South Asia and beyond. That's how it eventually came to me—through tales handed down from the courts of India's Mughal Empire through generations, eventually landing with my great-grandmother, who told my grandmother and mother stories about mischievous shape-shifting jinn and peris that could lull you to sleep and warriors battling terrible devs.

For *Amira & Hamza: The Quest for the Ring of Power*, I plucked elements from epic and legend, like Suleiman's Ring of Power and Ahriman's treachery, and blended them with historical figures, like the Banu Musa brothers and Ibn Sina, and situated them in real places you could visit today, like the Oriental Institute in Chicago or the Star Axis monument in New Mexico. I also made a lot of stuff up (this is the super-fun part!), like the oculus and the jinn jays. In many ways, I modeled writing this book after what the ancient storytellers did, the ones who first related the stories of the *Hamzanama*, hundreds and hundreds of years ago, in royal courts and in humble homes. I took seeds from an old tale, incorporated elements of my culture, and put my own spin on things. That's the magic of storytelling—a magic that you are now a part of.

Notes on Fantastical Creatures and Historical Figures

The characteristics of many of the mystical beings in Amira & Hamza are rooted in religious beliefs and influenced by a variety of cultural traditions and legends from across the globe. Stories of these creatures traveled across time and continents and became a part of my own family's lore. But to be clear, the way I portray these creatures is not the only way they are written about or understood—the variations across cultures are huge and interesting, and I hope you can explore some of the amazing stories of these fire spirits for yourself.

A quick note on spelling: Many of the names below are transliterated from Persian, Urdu, and Arabic. These languages are not written with the letter characters we use in English. We take the sound of the letters and "translate" them into English letters, so sometimes you'll see the words written differently because there is not one exact way to transliterate them, as it depends on how the speaker pronounces them.

Fantastical Creatures

Jinn: (You might also see this word written as *djinn.*) According to Islamic tradition, God created humans from clay, angels from holy light, and jinn from smokeless fire. Some jinn are thought to be shape-shifters—they can take human or animal form. They have free will and can be good or evil. They are invisible to humans but can choose to make themselves visible. Characteristics of jinn vary from culture to culture. For example, some cultures say there are different types of jinn—associated with air, water, earth. Some scholars point out pre-Islamic origins of fire spirits that are similar to jinn.

Peri: (Also written as *pari.*) Beautiful, winged spirits with an origin in Persian mythology that spread across the Islamic world. Some believe that peri are a benevolent, if somewhat mischievous, form of jinn. In Urdu, my first language and the language of the Mughal court, the word *peri* is translated as "fairy."

Dev: (Also written as *div.*) A monstrous creature, often depicted with claws and long teeth and horns and sometimes with human bodies but animal heads and hooves. They are frequently at war with peris. The origin of the dev, an evil spirit, is said to have come from Zoroastrianism. Like peris, some cultural traditions say that devs are a category of jinn, a malicious fire spirit.

Ghul: This is a word you might recognize—it's the source of the English word *ghoul.* In fact, the idea of a ghoul was introduced in Europe with the publication of *One Thousand and One Nights.* With an origin in Middle Eastern folklore, ghuls are said by some to be able to shape-shift, and love to live in desserts. They are demonlike, evil creatures that—yup, you guessed it—are sometimes considered to be another category of jinn.

Ahriman: Our big bad guy! Ahriman is the father of Ifrit, the dev that Amira and Hamza battled in Qaf. Even though he is a dev in the *Hamzanama,* the figure of Ahriman predates the *Hamzanama* by over a thousand years and can be traced back to ancient Persian religious tradition (around 1500 BCE), where he was thought to be the source of evil, the demon of demons.

Ifrit: (Also written as *afarit, efreet, afrit.*) Ifrit, the son of Ahriman, is the enemy that Amira and Hamza defeated in *Amira & Hamza: The War to Save the Worlds.* In the Mughal version of the *Hamzanama*, the hero Amir Hamza also battles a terrible demon named Ifrit. But, in reality, the term *ifrit* is often considered a category of demon—one that is very powerful, cunning, and wicked.

Aasman Peri: This snarky, tough friend of Amira and Hamza is the daughter of the Emperor of Qaf in both my books and in the *Hamzanama*, but that is where the similarities end. In the ancient epic, she is a cruel adult fairy who ensnares and marries Amir Hamza in Qaf.

Baharia: The baharia in the book, and notably, Bijli, are water jinn that I based on the jnoun-el-bahar, or jinn of the sea, that come from Tunisian tradition. Jinn tales from Tunisia are unique in many ways, particularly because they incorporate sea jinn, which do not exist in most other Muslim jinn traditions. This might come from the fact that Tunisia has a fishing industry and was also a place where seafaring Carthaginians lived. (I always think it's so cool to consider how history and geography influence legends!) The jinn of the sea were thought to resemble what we call mermaids, and you can see a lot of crossover when you consider the Tunisian traditions with European mermaid folklore.

Bahamut: A creature that lives in the deep seas and appears in both Arabic and Hebrew legend, with a number of variations. According to Arabic lore, Bahamut is an impossibly large fish-like entity that supports the structure that holds up the entire Earth! He's so huge that all the waters of the oceans could fit into a single nostril. Some legends say he is monstrous sea serpent. Others say he is a fish with the head of a hippo. Whatever he looks like, most stories agree that he is a Marid—one of the most powerful and invincible types of jinn—and he also makes an appearance in *One Thousand and One Nights*. His name is the root of the word *behemoth*.

Khawla ki Supahi: The Khawla warriors are a jinn battalion that I made up for book 1 in the Amira & Hamza series, but that was inspired by a real Muslim woman warrior, Khawla bint al-Azwar, who lived in Arabia during the seventh century CE. Said to be incredibly courageous, she disguised herself in knight armor to fight side by side with her brother, not revealing herself until after the battle was over. A skilled horsewoman and weapons master, she became a great general, eventually leading a group of Muslim women warriors into battle with the Byzantine Army.

Razia: The leader of the Khawla ki Supahi in the book is also named after a famous Muslim woman, Razia Sultana, who ruled the Delhi Sultanate, an Islamic empire based out of Delhi, India, from 1236 to 1240 CE. She was the first female Muslim ruler of South Asia. Originally appointed by her father, who believed she was more capable than all of his sons, she was later overthrown by the region's nobles, who opposed a woman sitting on the throne, even though Razia was supported by the general population.

Simurgh: This is one of my favorite creatures! Kind, powerful mythical birds from Persian mythology, simurghs were originally defined as bird-dogs, having the face of a dog and the feathers of a peacock. Their feathers are usually colored bronze or copper, and they sometimes have the paws of a lion. Over time, the idea of a simurgh became linked with other mythical birds such as the Arabic rukh or, in English, the roc, giant eagle-like birds.

Amazing Actual Historical Figures

Suleiman the Wise and the Ring of Power: The prophet and king Suleiman, known in the West as Solomon, was the son of David and is an important figure in Christianity and Judaism as well as Islam. In Islam he is referred to as Suleiman the Wise for his intellectual prowess. His other gifts included the ability to speak with animals and to control jinn. According to legend, his Ring of Power, also called the Seal of Solomon, was made of iron or brass engraved with a five-pointed star. It allowed Suleiman to command jinn and also imprison them in vessels such as oil lamps! (Sound familiar?) But the jinn he put in lamps were probably not the kind that gave you three wishes when you freed them. There are many legends about this ring and what happened to it after Suleiman's death. Some say it was thrown into the sea by a demon and swallowed by a fish. Others say it was buried in the desert along with Suleiman's many treasures, and that legend is partly what inspired this story. Note: Suleiman the Wise is not the same as Suleiman the Magnificent, who was a sixteenth-century Ottoman ruler, who is a super interesting and legendary historical figure in his own right.

Ibn Sina: (Sometimes called Avicenna in the West.) An incredible Muslim polymath (someone with knowledge and skills in multiple areas) from Persia, Ibn Sina lived from around 980 to 1037 CE. He is considered one of the most influential scholars and philosophers both in his time and beyond. The medical encyclopedia he wrote, *The Canon of Medicine*, was widely used for hundreds of years. In that book, published around 1025, he argued for the importance of quarantine to slow and weaken the spread of illness (which, as we well know, still holds very true). He is considered the first to explain that germs cause diseases. It is thought that he wrote 450 books and treatises on a variety of topics, including medicine, astronomy, philosophy, theology, physics, chemistry, and poetry. There is a crater on the moon named after him as well as many existing foundations, prizes, universities, and hospitals.

Abu Sa'id Ahmed ibn Mohammed ibn Abd al-Jalil al-Sijzi: As the ghost of al-Sijzi explained to Hamza, he was a Persian astronomer, astrologer, and mathematician who lived from 945 to 1020 CE. His creations included an astrolabe that showed Earth as rotating on its own axis so that the movement humans saw was based on the rotation of Earth, not the heavens (a revolutionary idea at the time). He was also a pen pal of al-Biruni.

The Banu Musa brothers and the *Book of Ingenious Devices*: These three Persian brothers who lived and worked in ninth-century Baghdad were, well, geniuses! They were astronomers, mathematicians, and scholars who studied and worked at the Bayt al-Hiqma, or House of Wisdom, in Baghdad, Iraq. And the *Book of Ingenious Devices* is a real thing! It was written and illustrated by the Banu Musa brothers around 850 CE. The book has illustrations and descriptions of about one hundred different devices, including automatic machines, called automata. Some of the inventions were inspired by other works, while some were totally original ideas, such as automatic fountains, mechanical trick devices (like 3D puzzles), water dispensers, tools like a clamshell-shaped grabbing device, and mechanical musical machines!

Al-Biruni: Abu Rayhan al-Biruni was an Iranian academic and brilliant polymath who lived from around 973 to 1050 CE. He is considered a legendary inventor, mathematician, historian, scientist, philosopher, astronomer, astrologer, and author (of 150 books!) who could speak multiple languages. There is a crater on the moon named after him, and an asteroid, too. He's thought to be the first person who divided the hour into minutes and seconds on a base 60 system.

Further Reading

To learn more about the *Hamzanama,* some of the creatures I write about, and the real places that Amira and Hamza visit on their adventure, the following books and links are a good start, and I highly encourage googling to learn more about the amazing histories and legends I tapped into for *Amira & Hamza: The Quest for the Ring of Power.*

Books and Writings

The Adventures of Amir Hamza. Translated by Musharraf Ali Farooqi. Modern Library, 2012.

Google Arts & Culture. "The Hamzanama." https://artsandculture.google.com/exhibit/rwKSxX7YjiTZJg.

The Kidnapping of Amir Hamza (illustrated). Retold by Mamta Dalal Mangaldas and Saker Mistri. Mapin Publishing, 2010.

Legends of the Fire Spirits: Jinn and Genies from Arabia to Zanzibar. Robert Lebling. Counterpoint Publishing, 2011.

Victoria & Albert Museum. "Hamzanama." http://www.vam.ac.uk/content/articles/h/hamzanama.

Artworks

The Daru staircase and *The Winged Victory of Samothrace* at the Louvre. https://www.louvre.fr/en/explore/the-palace/a-stairway-to-victory.

The false door of Ptahshepses at the British Museum. https://www.britishmuseum.org/collection/object/Y_EA682.

The *Lamassu* sculpture at the Oriental Institute. https://oi.uchicago.edu/museum-exhibits/khorsabad-court-gallery.

Star Axis, the earth-star sculpture and observatory: https://www.staraxis.org.

Acknowledgments

Writing this Amira & Hamza sequel was an absolute joy. I feel so privileged to continue on this journey with these two fun, loving, brave, bickering siblings, and that's all because of you, dear reader. And I am oh so grateful for you.

Do you believe in superheroes? Ones with incredible vision, kind hearts, and astonishing tenacity? Well, if you ever met my agent, Joanna Volpe, you would, because she has all those things and so much more. I am deeply grateful to have her in my life and honored to work with her. Big love to Jordan Hill for her cheerleading, her belief in this story, and her incredible patience. Thanks also to the wonderful Jenniea Carter and Abbie Donoghue, and to Kate Sullivan for all the keen insight and lovely conversations. Merci beaucoup to Pouya Shahbazian for believing in this story inspired by Persian epic and supporting the hell out of it. Huge cheers and virtual high fives to the entire team at New Leaf Literary & Media for being the best in the business.

Alvina Ling is a dream editor to work with. I feel so lucky that this ongoing adventure of two goofy siblings has been in her oh-so-able hands. Alvina is gracious, supportive, and honest, and I can't tell you how much I value that. A great editor-writer relationship is based on trust, and I trust her to do right by my story, my characters, and me, completely. Working with Ruqayyah Daud is a delight but also so much more—she sees and understands things about the heart of my stories, and I am so grateful for that. My deepest appreciation to the entire, wonderful team at Little, Brown Books for Young Readers—they've brought four of my books to the shelves and made every experience a winning one. Thank you, Emilie Polster, Bill Grace, Cheryl Lew, Mara Brashem, Savannah Kennelly, Victoria Stapleton, Christie Michel, Jen Graham, Nyamekye Waliyaya, Shawn Foster, and Danielle Cantarella. A million thank-yous to Karina Granda for the stunning cover design; Kim Ekdahl, whose gorgeous illustrations brought Amira and Hamza to life; and Kathleen Jennings, whose maps are truly gems. Jackie Engel and Megan Tingley, it's truly my honor be a part of the Little, Brown Books for Young Readers family. Thank you for believing in my words and my work.

I'm eternally grateful for my family, friends, early readers, and advisors who have supported me and cheered me on. Shukria and merci beaucoup to Pierre and Marie France Jonas, Sayantani DasGupta, Patrice Caldwell, Dhonielle Clayton, Stephanie Garber, Karen McManus, Sabaa Tahir, Aisha Saeed, S. K. Ali, Amy Adams, Rena Barron, Ronni Davis, Gloria Chao, Lizzie Cooke, Kat Cho, Anna Waggener, Siena Koncsol. Thank you to the Razvi family aunties and uncles who terrified and regaled the cousins with family jinn stories. Special shout-out to the Imazaki Dojo family for all the inspiration! Osu!

Heartfelt thanks and love to my parents, Hamid and Mazher, and to my sisters, Asra and Sara, who heard story after story over the years and did a great job of pretending they were always listening to me.

Lena and Noah, you are the brightest rays of sunshine in my life, and I am forever in awe of you. You are the ones who made me realize that a human heart is infinitely bigger on the inside than the outside.

To Thomas, my love, truly, this book and all the others only exist because you believed in me and shined a light on a path in the dark wood when I was certain I was lost.